The Colonel stared at Graham for a moment and then went on quietly. "A little more than a week ago, while you were still in Gallipoli, we discovered—that is, my agents discovered—a plot to murder you there. The whole thing was very clumsy and amateurish. You were to be kidnapped and knifed. Fortunately, we are not fools. . . . I have no doubt that he will try a third time if we give him a chance." He leaned back in his chair. "Do you understand now, Mr. Graham? Has your excellent brain grasped what I have been trying to say? It is perfectly simple! Someone is trying to kill you."

JOURNEY INTO FEAR

"MR. AMBLER IS A PHENOMENON!"
—Alfred Hitchcock

Berkley books by Eric Ambler

THE CARE OF TIME
JOURNEY INTO FEAR

ERIC AMBLER
JOURNEY INTO FEAR

BERKLEY BOOKS, NEW YORK

JOURNEY INTO FEAR

A Berkley Book / published by arrangement with
Alfred A. Knopf, Inc.

PRINTING HISTORY
Alfred A. Knopf edition published 1943
Ballantine Books edition / October 1977
Berkley edition / September 1983

ISBN: 0-425-06391-7

A BERKLEY BOOK ® TM 757,375
Berkley Books are published by The Berkley Publishing Group,
200 Madison Avenue, New York, New York 10016.
The name "BERKLEY" and the stylized "B" with design
are trademarks belonging to Berkley Publishing Corporation.
PRINTED IN THE UNITED STATES OF AMERICA

For LOUISE

Verily I have seene divers become mad and senseless for feare: yea and in him, who is most settled and best resolved, it is certaine that whilest his fit continueth, it begetteth many strange dazelings, and terrible amazements in him.

MONTAIGNE

CHAPTER I

THE STEAMER, *Sestri Levante*, stood high above the dock side, and the watery sleet, carried on the wind blustering down from the Black Sea, had drenched even the small shelter deck. In the after well the Turkish stevedores, with sacking tied round their shoulders, were still loading cargo.

Graham saw the steward carry his suitcase through a door marked PASSEGGIERI, and turned aside to see if the two men who had shaken hands with him at the foot of the gangway were still there. They had not come aboard lest the uniform of one of them should draw attention to him. Now they were walking away across the crane lines towards the warehouses and the dock gates beyond. As they reached the shelter of the first shed they looked back. He raised his left arm and saw an answering wave. They walked on out of sight.

For a moment he stood there shivering and staring out of the mist that shrouded the domes and spires of Stambul. Behind the rumble and clatter of the winches, the Turkish foreman was shouting plaintively in bad Italian to one of the ship's officers. Graham remembered that he had been told to go to his cabin and stay there until the ship sailed. He followed the steward through the door.

The man was waiting for him at the head of a short flight of stairs. There was no sign of any of the nine other passengers.

"*Cinque, signore?*"

"Yes."

"*Da queste parte.*"

Graham followed him below.

Number five was a small cabin with a single bunk, a combined wardrobe and washing cabinet, and only just enough floor space left over to take him and his suitcase. The porthole fittings were caked with verdigris, and there was a strong smell of paint. The steward manhandled the suitcase under the bunk, and squeezed out into the alleyway.

"*Favorisca di darmi il suo biglietto ed il suo passaporto, signore. Li portero al Commissario.*"

Graham gave him the ticket and passport, and, pointing to the porthole, made the motions of unscrewing and opening it.

The steward said, "*Subito, signore,*" and went away.

Graham sat down wearily on the bunk. It was the first time for nearly twenty-four hours that he had been left alone to think. He took his right hand carefully out of his overcoat pocket, and looked at the bandages swathed round it. It throbbed and ached abominably. If that was what a bullet graze felt like, he thanked his stars that the bullet had not really hit him.

He looked round the cabin, accepting his presence in it as he had accepted so many other absurdities since he had returned to his hotel in Pera the night before. The acceptance was unquestioning. He felt only as if he had lost something valuable. In fact, he had lost nothing of any value but a sliver of skin and

2

cartilage from the back of his right hand. All that had happened to him was that he had discovered the fear of death.

By the husbands of his wife's friends, Graham was considered lucky. He had a highly paid job with a big armaments manufacturing concern, a pleasant house in the country an hour's drive from his office, and a wife whom everyone liked. Not that he didn't deserve it all. He was, though you would never think it to look at him, a brilliant engineer; quite an important one if some of the things you heard were true; something to do with guns. He went abroad a good deal on business. He was a quiet, likeable sort of chap, and generous with his whisky. You couldn't, of course, imagine yourself getting to know him very well (it was hard to say which was worse—his golf or his bridge), but he was always friendly. Nothing effusive; just friendly; a bit like an expensive dentist trying to take your mind off things. He looked rather like an expensive dentist, too, when you came to think of it: thin and slightly stooping, with well-cut clothes, a good smile, and hair going a bit grey. But if it was difficult to imagine a woman like Stephanie marrying him for anything except his salary, you had to admit that they got on extraordinarily well together. It only went to show . . .

Graham himself also thought that he was lucky. From his father, a diabetic schoolmaster, he had inherited, at the age of seventeen, an easy-going disposition, five hundred pounds in cash from a life insurance policy, and a good mathematical brain. The first legacy had enabled him to endure without resentment the ministrations of a reluctant and cantankerous guardian; the second had made it possible for him to use the scholarship he had won to a university; the third resulted in his securing in his middle twenties a science doctorate. The subject of his thesis had been a problem in ballistics, and an abridged version of it had appeared in a technical journal. By the time he was thirty he was in charge of one of his employers' experimental departments, and a little surprised that he should be paid so much money for doing something that he liked doing. That same year he had married Stephanie.

It never occurred to him to doubt that his attitude towards his wife was that of any other man towards a wife to whom he has been married for ten years. He had married her because he had been tired of living in furnished rooms, and had assumed (correctly) that she had married him to get away from her father—a disagreeable and impecunious doctor. He was pleased by her good looks, her good humour, and her capacity for keeping servants and making friends, and if he sometimes found the friends tiresome, was inclined to blame himself rather than them. She, on her part, accepted the fact that he was more interested in his work than in anyone or anything else as a matter of course and without resentment. She liked her life exactly as it was. They lived in an atmosphere of good-natured affection and mutual tolerance, and thought their marriage as successful as one could reasonably expect a marriage to be.

The outbreak of war in September nineteen thirty-nine had little effect on the Graham household. Having spent the previous two years with the certain knowledge that such an outbreak was as inevitable as the going down of the sun, Graham was neither astonished nor dismayed when it occurred. He had calculated to a nicety its probable effects on his private life, and by October he was able to conclude that his calculations had been correct. For him, the war meant more work; but that was all. It touched neither his economic nor his personal security. He could not, under any circumstances, become liable for combatant military service. The chances of a German bomber unloading its cargo anywhere near either his house or his office were remote enough to be disregarded. When he learned, just three weeks after the signing of the Anglo-Turkish treaty of alliance, that he was to go to Turkey on company business, he was troubled only by the dismal prospect of spending Christmas away from home.

He had been thirty-two when he had made his first business trip abroad. It had been a success. His employers had discovered that, in addition to his technical ability, he had the faculty, unusual in a man with his particular qualifications, of making himself amiable to—and liked by—foreign government officials. In the years that followed, occasional trips abroad had become part of his working life. He enjoyed them. He liked the actual business of getting to a strange city almost as much as he liked discovering its strangeness. He liked meeting men of other nationalities, learning smatterings of their languages, and being appalled at his lack of understanding of both. He had acquired a wholesome dislike of the word "typical."

Towards the middle of November, he reached Istanbul, by train from Paris, and left it almost immediately for Izmir and, later, Gallipoli. By the end of December he had finished his work in those two places, and on the first of January took a train back to Istanbul, the starting point of his journey home.

He had had a trying six weeks. His job had been a difficult one made more difficult by his having to discuss highly technical subjects through interpreters. The horror of the Anatolian earthquake disaster had upset him nearly as much as it had upset his hosts. Finally, the train service from Gallipoli to Istanbul had been disorganized by floods. By the time he arrived back in Istanbul he was feeling tired and depressed.

He was met at the station by Kopeikin, the company's representative in Turkey.

Kopeikin had arrived in Istanbul with sixty-five thousand other Russian refugees in nineteen twenty-four, and had been, by turns, card-sharper, part owner of a brothel, and army clothing contractor before he had secured—the Managing Director alone knew how—the lucrative agency he now held. Graham liked him. He was a plump, exuberant man with large projecting ears, irrepressible high spirits, and a vast fund of low cunning.

He wrung Graham's hand enthusiastically. "Have you had a bad trip? I am so sorry. It is good to see you back again. How did you get on with Fethi?"

"Very well, I think. I imagined something much worse from your description of him."

"My dear fellow, you underrate your charm of manner. He is known to be difficult. But he is important. Now everything will go smoothly. But we will talk business over a drink. I have engaged a room for you—a room with a bath, at the Adler-Palace, as before. For to-night I have arranged a farewell dinner. The expense is mine."

"It's very good of you."

"A great pleasure, my dear fellow. Afterwards we will amuse ourselves a little. There is a box that is very popular at the moment—Le Jockey Cabaret. You will like it, I think. It is very nicely arranged, and the people who go there are quite nice. No riff-raff. Is this your luggage?"

Graham's heart sank. He had expected to have dinner with Kopeikin, but he had been promising himself that about ten o'clock he would have a hot bath and go to bed with a Tauchnitz detective story. The last thing he wanted to do was to "amuse" himself at Le

Jockey Cabaret, or any other night place. He said, as they followed the porter out to Kopeikin's car: "I think that perhaps I ought to get to bed early to-night, Kopeikin. I've got four nights in a train in front of me."

"My dear fellow, it will do you good to be late. Besides, your train does not go until eleven to-morrow morning, and I have reserved a sleeper for you. You can sleep all the way to Paris if you feel tired."

Over dinner at the Pera Palace Hotel, Kopeikin gave war news. For him, the Soviets were still "the July assassins" of Nicholas the Second, and Graham heard much of Finnish victories and Russian defeats. The Germans had sunk more British ships and lost more submarines. The Dutch, the Danes, the Swedes and the Norwegians were looking to their defences. The world awaited a bloody Spring. They went on to talk about the earthquake. It was half-past ten when Kopeikin announced that it was time for them to leave for Le Jockey Cabaret.

It was in the Beyoglu quarter; just off the Grande Rue de Pera, and in a street of buildings obviously designed by a French architect of the middle nine-teen twenties. Kopeikin took his arm affectionately as they went in.

"It is a very nice place, this," he said. "Serge, the proprietor, is a friend of mine, so they will not cheat us. I will introduce you to him."

For the man he was, Graham's knowledge of the night life of cities was surprisingly extensive. For some reason, the nature of which he could never discover, his foreign hosts always seemed to consider that the only form of entertainment acceptable to an English engineer was that to be found in the rather less reputable *Nachtlokalen*. He had been in such places in Buenos Aires and in Madrid, in Valparaiso and in Bucharest, in Rome and in Mexico; and he

7

could not remember one that was very much different from any of the others. He could remember the business acquaintances with whom he had sat far into the early morning hours drinking outrageously expensive drinks; but the places themselves had merged in his mind's eye into one prototypical picture of a smoke-filled basement room with a platform for the band at one end, a small space for dancing surrounded by tables, and a bar with stools, where the drinks were alleged to be cheaper, to one side.

He did not expect Le Jockey Cabaret to be any different. It was not.

The mural decorations seemed to have caught the spirit of the street outside. They consisted of a series of immense vorticisms involving sky-scrapers at camera angles, coloured saxophone players, green all-seeing eyes, telephones, Easter Island masks, and ash-blond hermaphrodites with long cigarette holders. The place was crowded and very noisy. Serge was a sharp-featured Russian with bristly grey hair and the air of one whose feelings were constantly on the point of getting the better of his judgment. To Graham, looking at his eyes, it seemed unlikely that they ever did: but he greeted them graciously enough, and showed them to a table beside the dance floor. Kopeikin ordered a bottle of brandy.

The band brought an American dance tune, which they had been playing with painful zeal, to an abrupt end and began, with more success, to play a rumba.

"It is very gay here," said Kopeikin. "Would you like to dance? There are plenty of girls. Say which you fancy and I will speak to Serge."

"Oh, don't bother. I really don't think I ought to stay long."

"You must stop thinking about your journey. Drink some more brandy and you will feel better." He got to

8

his feet. "I shall dance now and find a nice girl for you."

Graham felt guilty. He should, he knew, be displaying more enthusiasm. Kopeikin was, after all, being extraordinarily kind. It could be no pleasure for him to try to entertain a train-weary Englishman who would have preferred to be in bed. He drank some more brandy determinedly. More people were arriving. He saw Serge greet them warmly and then, when their backs were turned, issue a furtive instruction to the waiter who was to serve them: a drab little reminder that Le Jockey Cabaret was in business neither for his own pleasure nor for theirs. He turned his head to watch Kopeikin dancing.

The girl was thin and dark and had large teeth. Her red satin evening dress drooped on her as if it had been made for a bigger woman. She smiled a great deal. Kopeikin held her slightly away from him and talked all the time they were dancing. To Graham, he seemed, despite the grossness of his body, to be the only man on the floor who was completely self-possessed. He was the ex-brothel-proprietor dealing with something he understood perfectly. When the music stopped he brought the girl over to their table.

"This is Maria," he said. "She is an Arab. You would not think it to look at her, would you?"

"No, you wouldn't."

"She speaks a little French."

"*Enchanté, Mademoiselle.*"

"*Monsieur.*" Her voice was unexpectedly harsh, but her smile was pleasant. She was obviously good-natured.

"Poor child!" Kopeikin's tone was that of a governess who hoped that her charge would not disgrace her before visitors. "She has only just recovered from a sore throat. But she is a very nice girl and has good manners. *Assieds-toi*, Maria."

9

She sat down beside Graham. *"Je prends du champagne,"* she said.

"Oui, oui, mon enfant. Plus tard," said Kopeikin vaguely. "She gets extra commission if we order champagne," he remarked to Graham, and poured out some brandy for her.

She took it without comment, raised it to her lips, and said, *"Skål!"*

"She thinks you are a Swede," said Kopeikin.

"Why?"

"She likes Swedes, so I said you were a Swede." He chuckled. "You cannot say that the Turkish agent does nothing for the company."

She had been listening to them with an uncomprehending smile. Now, the music began again and, turning to Graham, she asked him if he would like to dance.

She danced well; well enough for him to feel that he, too, was dancing well. He felt less depressed and asked her to dance again. The second time she pressed her thin body hard against him. He saw a grubby shoulder strap begin to work its way out from under the red satin and smelt the heat of her body behind the scent she used. He found that he was getting tired of her.

She began to talk. Did he know Istanbul well? Had he been there before? Did he know Paris? And London? He was lucky. She had never been to those places. She hoped to go to them. And to Stockholm, too. Had he many friends in Istanbul? She asked because there was a gentleman who had come in just after him and his friend who seemed to know him. This gentleman kept looking at him.

Graham had been wondering how soon he could get away. He realised suddenly that she was waiting for him to say something. His mind had caught her last remark.

"Who keeps looking at me?"

"We cannot see him now. The gentleman is sitting at the bar."

"No doubt he's looking at you." There seemed nothing else to say.

But she was evidently serious. "It is in you that he is interested, Monsieur. It is the one with the handkerchief in his hand."

They had reached a point on the floor from which he could see the bar. The man was sitting on a stool with a glass of vermouth in front of him.

He was a short, thin man with a stupid face: very bony with large nostrils, prominent cheekbones, and full lips pressed together as if he had sore gums or were trying to keep his temper. He was intensely pale and his small, deep-set eyes and thinning, curly hair seemed in consequence darker than they were. The hair was plastered in streaks across his skull. He wore a crumpled brown suit with lumpy padded shoulders, a soft shirt with an almost invisible collar, and a new grey tie. As Graham watched him he wiped his upper lip with the handkerchief as if the heat of the place were making him sweat.

"He doesn't seem to be looking at me now," Graham said. "Anyway, I don't know him, I'm afraid."

"I did not think so, Monsieur." She pressed his arm to her side with her elbow. "But I wished to be sure. I do not know him either, but I know the type. You are a stranger here, Monsieur, and you perhaps have money in your pocket. Istanbul is not like Stockholm. When such types look at you more than once, it is advisable to be careful. You are strong, but a knife in the back is the same for a strong man as for a small one."

Her solemnity was ludicrous. He laughed; but he looked again at the man by the bar. He was sipping at his vermouth; an inoffensive creature. The girl was

11

probably trying, rather clumsily, to demonstrate that her own intentions were good.

He said: "I don't think that I need worry."

She relaxed the pressure on his arm. "Perhaps not, Monsieur." She seemed suddenly to lose interest in the subject. The band stopped and they returned to the table.

"She dances very nicely, doesn't she?" said Kopeikin.

"Very."

She smiled at them, sat down and finished her drink as if she were thirsty. Then she sat back. "We are three," she said and counted round with one finger to make sure they understood; "would you like me to bring a friend of mine to have a drink with us? She is very sympathetic. She is my greatest friend."

"Later, perhaps," said Kopeikin. He poured her out another drink.

At that moment, the band played a resounding "chord-on" and most of the lights went out. A spotlight quivered on the floor in front of the platform.

"The attractions," said Maria. "It is very good."

Serge stepped into the spotlight and pattered off a long announcement in Turkish which ended in a flourish of the hand towards a door beside the platform. Two dark young men in pale blue dinner jackets promptly dashed out on to the floor and proceeded to do an energetic tap dance. They were soon breathless and their hair became dishevelled, but the applause, when they had finished, was lukewarm. Then they put on false beards and, pretending to be old men, did some tumbling. The audience was only slightly more enthusiastic. They retired, rather angrily Graham thought, dripping with perspiration. They were followed by a handsome coloured woman with long thin legs who proved to be a contortionist. Her contortions were ingeniously obscene and evoked gusts of laughter. In response to shouts, she followed her contortions with a snake dance. This was not so successful, as the snake, produced from a gilt wicker crate as cautiously as if it had been a fully grown anaconda, proved to be a small and rather senile python with a tendency to fall asleep in its mistress's hands. It was finally bundled back into its crate while she did some more contortions. When she had gone, the proprietor stepped once more into the spotlight and made an announcement that was greeted with clapping.

The girl put her lips to Graham's ear. "It is Josette and her partner, José. They are dancers from Paris. This is their last night here. They have had a great success."

The spotlight became pink and swept to the entrance door. There was a roll of drums. Then, as the band struck up the Blue Danube waltz, the dancers glided on to the floor.

For the weary Graham, their dance was as much a part of the cellar convention as the bar and the platform for the band: it was something to justify the prices of the drinks: a demonstration of the fact that, by applying the laws of classical mechanics, one small, unhealthy looking man with a broad sash round his waist could handle an eight stone woman as if she were a child. Josette and her partner were remarkable only in that, although they carried out the standard "specialty" routine rather less efficiently than usual, they managed to do so with considerable more effect.

She was a slim woman with beautiful arms and shoulders and a mass of gleaming fair hair. Her heavily lidded eyes, almost closed as she danced, and the rather full lips, fixed in a theatrical half-smile, contradicted in a curious way the swift neatness of her movements. Graham saw that she was not a dancer but a woman who had been trained to dance and who did so with a sort of indolent sensuality, conscious of her young-looking body, her long legs, and the muscles below the smooth surfaces of her thighs and stomach. If her performance did not succeed as a dance, as an *attraction* at Le Jockey Cabaret it succeeded perfectly and in spite of her partner.

He was a dark, preoccupied man with tight, disagreeable lips, a smooth sallow face, and an irritating way of sticking his tongue hard in his cheek as he prepared to exert himself. He moved badly and was clumsy, his fingers shifting uncertainly as he grasped her for the lifts as if he were uncertain of the point of balance. He was constantly steadying himself.

But the audience was not looking at him, and when they had finished called loudly for an encore. It was given. The band played another "chord-on." Mademoiselle Josette took a bow and was presented with a bouquet of flowers by Serge. She returned several times and bowed and kissed her hand.

"She is quite charming, isn't she?" Kopeikin said in English as the lights went up. "I promised you that this place was amusing."

"She's quite good. But it's a pity about the moth-eaten Valentino."

"José? He does well for himself. Would you like to have her to the table for a drink?"

"Very much. But won't it be rather expensive?"

"Gracious no! She does not get commission."

"Will she come?"

"Of course. The *patron* introduced me. I know her well. You might take to her, I think. This Arab is a little stupid. No doubt Josette is stupid, too; but she is very attractive in her way. If I had not learned too much when I was too young, I should like her myself."

Maria stared after him as he went across the floor,

14

and remained silent for a moment. Then she said: "He is very good, that friend of yours."

Graham was not quite sure whether it was a statement, a question, or a feeble attempt to make conversation. He nodded. "Very good."

She smiled. "He knows the proprietor well. If you desire it, he will ask Serge to let me go when you wish instead of when the place closes."

He smiled as regretfully as he could. "I'm afraid, Maria, that I have to pack my luggage and catch a train in the morning."

She smiled again. "It does not matter. But I specially like the Swedes. May I have some more brandy, Monsieur?"

"Of course." He refilled her glass.

She drank half of it. "Do you like Mademoiselle Josette?"

"She dances very well."

"She is very sympathetic. That is because she has a success. When people have a success they are sympathetic. José, nobody likes. He is a Spaniard from Morocco, and very jealous. They are all the same. I do not know how she stands him."

"I thought you said they were Parisians."

"They have danced in Paris. She is from Hungary. She speaks languages—German, Spanish, English—but not Swedish, I think. She has had many rich lovers." She paused. "Are you a business man, Monsieur?"

"No, an engineer." He realised, with some amusement, that Maria was less stupid than she seemed, and that she knew exactly why Kopeikin had left them. He was being warned, indirectly but unmistakably, that Mademoiselle Josette was very expensive, that communication with her would be difficult, and that he would have a jealous Spaniard to deal with.

She drained her glass again, and stared vaguely in

the direction of the bar. "My friend is looking very lonely," she said. She turned her head and looked directly at him. "Will you give me a hundred piastres, Monsieur?"

"What for?"

"A tip, Monsieur." She smiled, but in not quite so friendly a fashion as before.

He gave her a hundred piastre note. She folded it up, put it in her bag, and stood up. "Will you excuse me, please? I wish to speak to my friend. I will come back if you wish." She smiled.

He saw her red satin dress disappear in the crowd gathered round the bar. Kopeikin returned almost immediately.

"Where is the Arab?"

"She's gone to speak to her best friend. I gave her a hundred piastres."

"A hundred! Fifty would have been plenty. But perhaps it is as well. Josette asks us to have a drink with her in her dressing-room. She is leaving Istanbul to-morrow, and does not wish to come out here. She will have to speak to so many people, and she has packing to do."

"Shan't we be rather a nuisance?"

"My dear fellow, she is anxious to meet you. She saw you while she was dancing. When I told her you were an Englishman, she was delighted. We can leave these drinks here."

Mademoiselle Josette's dressing-room was a space about eight feet square, partitioned off from the other half of what appeared to be the proprietor's office by a brown curtain. The three solid walls were covered with faded pink wall-paper with stripes of blue: there were greasy patches here and there where people had leaned against them. The room contained two bent-wood chairs and two rickety dressing tables littered with cream jars and dirty make-up towels.

There was a mixed smell of stale cigarette smoke, face powder, and damp upholstery.

As they went in in response to a grunt of *"Entrez"* from the partner, José, he got up from his dressing table. Still wiping the grease paint from his face, he walked out without a glance at them. For some reason, Kopeikin winked at Graham. Josette was leaning forward in her chair dabbing intently at one of her eyebrows with a swab of damp cotton-wool. She had discarded her costume, and put on a rose velvet house-coat. Her hair hung down loosely about her head as if she had shaken it out and brushed it. It was really, Graham thought, very beautiful hair. She began to speak in slow, careful English, punctuating the words with dabs.

"Please excuse me. It is this filthy paint. It ... *Merde!"*

She threw the swab down impatiently, stood up suddenly, and turned to face them.

In the hard light of the unshaded bulb above her head she looked smaller than she had looked on the dance floor; and a trifle haggard. Graham, thinking of his Stephanie's rather buxom good looks, reflected that the woman before him would probably be quite plain in ten years' time. He was in the habit of comparing other women with his wife. As a method of disguising from himself the fact that other women still interested him, it was usually effective. But Josette was unusual. What she might look like in ten years' time was altogether beside the point. At that moment she was a very attractive, self-possessed woman with a soft, smiling mouth, slightly protuberant blue eyes, and a sleepy vitality that seemed to fill the room.

"This, my dear Josette," said Kopeikin, "is Mr. Graham."

"I enjoyed your dancing very much, Mademoiselle," he said.

"So Kopeikin told me." She shrugged. "It could be better, I think, but it is very good of you to say that you like it. It is nonsense to say that Englishmen are not polite." She flourished her hand round the room. "I do not like to ask you to sit down in this filth, but please try to make yourself comfortable. There is José's chair for Kopeikin, and if you could push José's things away, the corner of his table will be for you. It is too bad that we cannot sit together in comfort outside, but there are so many of these men who make some *chichi* if one does not stop and drink some of their champagne. The champagne here is filthy. I do not wish to leave Istanbul with a headache. How long do you stay here, Mr. Graham?"

"I, too, leave to-morrow." She amused him. Her posturing was absurd. Within the space of a minute she had been a great actress receiving wealthy suitors, a friendly woman of the world, and a disillusioned genius of the dance. Every movement, every piece of affectation was calculated: it was as if she were still dancing.

Now she became a serious student of affairs. "It is terrible, this travelling. And you go back to your war. I am sorry. These filthy Nazis. It is such a pity that there must be wars. And if it is not wars, it is earthquakes. Always death. It is so bad for business. I am not interested in death. Kopeikin is, I think. Perhaps it is because he is a Russian."

"I think nothing of death," said Kopeikin. "I am concerned only that the waiter shall bring the drinks I ordered. Will you have a cigarette?"

"Please, yes. The waiters here are filthy. There must be much better places than this in London, Mr. Graham."

"The waiters there are very bad, too. Waiters are, I think, mostly very bad. But I should have thought you had been to London. Your English . . ."

18

Her smile tolerated his indiscretion, the depths of which he could not know. As well to have asked the Pompadour who paid her bills. "I learned it from an American and in Italy. I have a great sympathy for Americans. They are so clever in business, and yet so generous and sincere. I think it is most important to be sincere. Was it amusing dancing with that little Maria, Mr. Graham?"

"She dances very well. She seems to admire you very much. She says that you have a great success. You do, of course."

"A great success! Here?" The disillusioned genius raised her eyebrows. "I hope you gave her a good tip, Mr. Graham."

"He gave her twice as much as was necessary," said Kopeikin. "Ah, here are the drinks!"

They talked for a time about people whom Graham did not know, and about the war. He saw that behind her posturing she was quick and shrewd, and wondered if the American in Italy had ever regretted his "sincerity." After a while Kopeikin raised his glass.

"I drink," he said pompously, "to your two journeys." He lowered his glass suddenly without drinking. "No, it is absurd," he said, irritably. "My heart is not in the toast. I cannot help thinking that it is a pity that there should be two journeys. You are both going to Paris. You are both friends of mine, and so you have"—he patted his stomach—"much in common."

Graham smiled, trying not to look startled. She was certainly very attractive, and it was pleasant to sit facing her as he was; but the idea that the acquaintance might be extended had simply not occurred to him. He was confused by it. He saw that she was watching him with amusement in her eyes, and had an uncomfortable feeling that she knew exactly what was passing through his mind.

He put the best face on the situation that he could.

"I was hoping to suggest the same thing. I think you should have left me to suggest it, Kopeikin. Mademoiselle will wonder if I am as sincere as an American." He smiled at her. "I am leaving by the eleven o'clock train."

"And in the first class, Mr. Graham?"

"Yes."

She put out her cigarette. "Then there are two obvious reasons why we cannot travel together. I am not leaving by that train and, in any case, I travel in the second class. It is perhaps just as well. José would wish to play cards with you all the way, and you would lose your money."

There was no doubt that she expected them to finish their drinks and go. Graham felt oddly disappointed. He would have liked to stay. He knew, besides, that he had behaved awkwardly.

"Perhaps," he said, "we could meet in Paris."

"Perhaps." She stood up and smiled kindly at him. "I shall stay at the Hotel des Belges near Trinité, if it is still open. I shall hope to meet you again. Kopeikin tells me that as an engineer you are very well known."

"Kopeikin exaggerates—just as he exaggerated when he said that we should not hinder you and your partner in your packing. I hope you have a pleasant journey."

"It has been so good to meet you. It was so kind of you, Kopeikin, to bring Mr. Graham to see me."

"It was his idea," said Kopeikin. "Good-bye, my dear Josette, and bon voyage. We should like to stay, but it is late, and I insisted on Mr. Graham's getting some sleep. He would stay talking until he missed the train if I permitted it."

She laughed. "You are very nice, Kopeikin. When I come next to Istanbul, I shall tell you first. Au 'voir,

Mr. Graham, and *bon voyage.*" She held out her hand.

"The Hotel des Belges near Trinité," he said: "I shall remember." He spoke very little less then the truth. During the ten minutes that his taxi would take to get from the Gare de l'Est to the Gare St. Lazare, he probably would remember.

She pressed his fingers gently. "I'm sure you will," she said. "*Au 'voir*, Kopeikin. You know the way?"

"I think," said Kopeikin, as they waited for their bill, "I think that I am a little disappointed in you, my dear fellow. You made an excellent impression. She was yours for the asking. You had only to ask her the time of her train."

"I am quite sure that I made no impression at all. Frankly, she embarrassed me. I don't understand women of that sort."

"That sort of woman, as you put it, likes a man who is embarrassed by her. Your diffidence was charming."

"Heavens! Anyway, I said that I would see her in Paris."

"My dear fellow, she knows perfectly well that you have not the smallest intention of seeing her in Paris. It is a pity. She is, I know, quite particular. You were lucky, and you chose to ignore the fact."

"Good gracious, man, you seem to forget that I'm a married man!"

Kopeikin threw up his hands. "The English point of view! One cannot reason; one can only stand amazed." He sighed profoundly. "Here comes the bill."

On their way out they passed Maria sitting at the bar with her best friend, a mournful-looking Turkish girl. They received a smile. Graham noticed that the man in the crumpled brown suit had gone.

It was cold in the street. A wind was beginning to moan through the telephone wires bracketed on the wall. At three o'clock in the morning the city of Sulyman the Magnificent was like a railway station after the last train had gone.

"We shall be having snow," said Kopeikin. "Your hotel is quite near. We will walk if you like. It is to be hoped," he went on as they began to walk, "that you will miss the snow on your journey. Last year there was a Simplon Orient express delayed for three days near Salonika."

"I shall take a bottle of brandy with me."

Kopeikin grunted. "Still, I do not envy you the journey. I think perhaps I am getting old. Besides, travelling at this time . . . "

"Oh, I'm a good traveller. I don't get bored easily."

"I was not thinking of boredom. So many unpleasant things can happen in war time."

"I suppose so."

Kopeikin buttoned up his overcoat collar. "To give you only one example . . .

"During the last war an Austrian friend of mine was returning to Berlin from Zürich, where he had been doing some business. He sat in the train with a man who said that he was a Swiss from Lugano. They talked a lot on the journey. This Swiss told my friend about his wife and his children, his business, and his home. He seemed a very nice man. But soon after they had crossed the frontier, the train stopped at a small station and soldiers came on with police. They arrested the Swiss. My friend had also to leave the train as he was with the Swiss. He was not alarmed. His papers were in order. He was a good Austrian. But the man from Lugano was terrified. He turned very pale and cried like a child. They told my friend afterwards that the man was not a Swiss but an Italian spy and that he would be shot. My friend was upset. You see, one can always tell when a man is speaking about something he loves, and there was no doubt that all that this man had said about his wife and children was true: all except one thing—they were in Italy instead of Switzerland. War," he added solemnly, "is unpleasant."

"Quite so." They had stopped outside the Adler-Palace Hotel. "Will you come in for a drink?"

Kopeikin shook his head. "It is kind of you to suggest it, but you must get some sleep. I feel guilty now at having kept you out so late, but I have enjoyed our evening together."

"So have I. I'm very grateful to you."

"A great pleasure. No farewells now. I shall take you to the station in the morning. Can you be ready by ten?"

"Easily."

"Then good night, my dear fellow."

"Good night, Kopeikin."

Graham went inside, stopped at the hall porter's desk for his key and to tell the night porter to call him at eight. Then, as the power for the lift was switched off at night, he climbed wearily up the stairs to his room on the second floor.

It was at the end of the corridor. He put the key in the lock, turned it, pushed the door open and, with his right hand, felt along the wall for the light switch.

The next moment there was a splinter of flame in the darkness and an ear-splitting detonation. A piece of plaster from the wall beside him stung his cheek. Before he could move or even think, the flame and the noise came again and it seemed as if a bar of white-hot metal had been suddenly pressed against the back of his hand. He cried out with pain and stumbled forward out of the light from the corridor into the darkness of the room. Another shot scattered plaster behind him.

There was silence. He was half leaning, half crouching against the wall by the bed, his ears singing from the din of the explosions. He was dimly aware that the window was open and that someone was moving by it. His hand seemed to be numb, but he could feel blood beginning to trickle between his fingers.

He remained motionless, his heart hammering at his head. The air reeked of cordite fumes. Then, as his eyes became used to the darkness, he saw that whoever had been at the window had left by it.

There would, he knew, be another light switch beside the bed. With his left hand he fumbled along the wall towards it. Then his hand touched the telephone. Hardly knowing what he was doing, he picked it up.

He heard a click as the night porter plugged in at the switchboard.

"Room thirty-six," he said and was surprised to find that he was shouting. "Something has happened. I need help."

He put the telephone down, blundered towards the bathroom and switched on the light there. The blood was pouring from a great gash across the back of his hand. Through the waves of nausea flowing from his stomach to his head, he could hear doors being flung open and excited voices in the corridor. Someone started hammering at the door.

CHAPTER II

THE STEVEDORES had finished loading and were battening down. One winch was still working but it was hoisting the steel bearers into place. The bulkhead against which Graham was leaning vibrated as they thudded into their sockets. Another passenger had come aboard and the steward had shown him to a cabin farther along the alleyway. The newcomer had a low, grumbling voice and had addressed the steward in hesitant Italian.

Graham stood up and with his unbandaged hand fumbled in his pocket for a cigarette. He was beginning to find the cabin oppressive. He looked at his watch. The ship would not be sailing for another hour. He wished he had asked Kopeikin to come aboard with him. He tried to think of his wife in England, to picture her sitting with her friends having tea; but it was as if someone behind him were holding a stereoscope to his mind's eyes; someone who was steadily sliding picture after picture between him and the rest of his life to cut him off from it; pictures of Kopeikin and Le Jockey Cabaret, of Maria and the man in the crumpled suit, of Josette and her partner, of stabbing flames in a sea of darkness and of pale, frightened faces in the hotel corridor. He had not known then what he knew now, what he learnt in the cold, beastly dawn that had followed. The whole thing had seemed different then: unpleasant, decidedly unpleasant, but reasonable, accountable. Now he felt as if a doctor had told him that he was suffering from some horrible and deadly disease; as if he had become part of a different world, a world of which he knew nothing but that it was detestable.

The hand holding the match to his cigarette was trembling. "What I need," he thought, "is sleep."

As the waves of nausea subsided and he stood there in the bathroom, shivering, sounds began once more to penetrate the blanket of cotton wool that seemed to have enveloped his brain. There was a sort of irregular thudding coming from a long distance. He realised that someone was still knocking at the bedroom door.

He wrapped a face towel round his hand, went back into the bedroom and switched on the light. As he did so, the knocking ceased and there was a clinking of metal. Someone had got a pass key. The door burst open.

It was the night porter who came in first, blinking round uncertainly. Behind him in the corridor were the people from the neighbouring rooms, drawing back now for fear of seeing what they hoped to see. A small, dark man in a red dressing gown over blue striped pyjamas pushed past the night porter. Graham recognised the man who had shown him to his room.

"There were shots," he began in French. Then he saw Graham's hand and went white. "I ... You are wounded. You are ... "

Graham sat down on the bed. "Not seriously. If you will send for a doctor to bandage my hand properly, I will tell you what has happened. But first: the man who fired the shots left through the window. You might try and catch him. What is below the window?"

"But . . . " began the man shrilly. He stopped, visibly pulling himself together. Then he turned to the night porter and said something in Turkish. The porter went out, shutting the door behind him. There was a burst of excited chatter from outside.

"The next thing," said Graham, "is to send for the manager."

"Pardon, Monsieur, he has been sent for. I am the Assistant Manager." He wrung his hands. "What has happened? Your hand, Monsieur. . . . But the doctor will be here immediately."

"Good. You'd better know what happened. I have been out this evening with a friend. I returned a few minutes ago. As I opened the door here, someone standing there just inside the window fired three shots at me. The second one hit my hand. The other two hit the wall. I heard him moving but I did not see his face. I imagine that he was a thief and that my unexpected return disturbed him."

"It is an outrage!" said the Assistant Manager hotly. His face changed. "A thief! Has anything been stolen, Monsieur?"

"I haven't looked. My suitcase is over there. It was locked."

The Assistant Manager hurried across the room and went down on his knees beside the suitcase. "It is still locked," he reported with a sigh of relief.

Graham fumbled in his pocket. "Here are the keys. You'd better open it."

The man obeyed. Graham glanced at the contents of the case. "It has not been touched."

27

"A blessing!" He hesitated. He was obviously thinking fast. "You say that your hand is not seriously hurt, Monsieur?"

"I don't think it is."

"It is a great relief. When the shots were heard, Monsieur, we feared an unbelievable horror. You may imagine. . . . But this is bad enough." He went to the window and looked out. "The pig! He must have escaped through the gardens immediately. Useless to search for him." He shrugged despairingly. "He is gone now, and there is nothing to be done. I need not tell you, Monsieur, how profoundly we regret that this thing should happen to you in the Adler-Palace. Never before has such a thing happened here." He hesitated again and then went on quickly: "Naturally, Monsieur, we shall do everything in our power to alleviate the distress which has been caused to you. I have told the porter to bring some whisky for you when he has telephoned for the doctor. English whisky! We have a special supply. Happily, nothing has been stolen. We could not, of course, have foreseen that an accident of such a kind should happen; but we shall ourselves see that the best medical attention is given. And there will, of course, be no question of any charge for your stay here. But . . . "

"But you don't want to call in the police and involve the hotel. Is that it?"

The Assistant Manager smiled nervously. "No good can be done, Monsieur. The police would merely ask questions and make inconveniences for all." Inspiration came to him. "For all, Monsieur," he repeated emphatically. "You are a business man. You wish to leave Istanbul this morning. But if the police are brought in, it might be difficult. There would be, inevitably, delays. And for what purpose?"

"They might catch the man who shot me."

"But how, Monsieur? You did not see his face. You

cannot identify him. There is nothing stolen by which he could be traced."

Graham hesitated. "But what about this doctor you are getting? Supposing he reports to the police the fact that there is someone here with a bullet wound."

"The doctor's services, Monsieur, will be paid for liberally by the management."

There was a knock at the door and the porter came in with whisky, soda water, and glasses which he set down on the table. He said something to the Assistant Manager who nodded and then motioned him out.

"The doctor is on his way, Monsieur."

"Very well. No, I don't want any whisky. But drink some yourself. You look as though you need it. I should like to make a telephone call. Will you tell the porter to telephone the Crystal Apartments in the rue d'Italie? The number is forty-four, nine hundred and seven, I think. I want to speak to Monsieur Kopeikin."

"Certainly, Monsieur. Anything you wish." He went to the door and called after the porter. There was another incomprehensible exchange. The Assistant Manager came back and helped himself generously to the whisky.

"I think," he said, returning to the charge, "that you are wise not to invoke the police, Monsieur. Nothing has been stolen. Your injury is not serious. There will be no trouble. It is thus and thus with the police here, you understand."

"I haven't yet decided what to do," snapped Graham. His head was aching violently and his hand was beginning to throb. He was getting tired of the Assistant Manager.

The telephone bell rang. He moved along the bed and picked up the telephone.

"Is that you, Kopeikin?"

He heard a mystified grunt. "Graham? What is it? I have only just this moment come in. Where are you?"

"Sitting on my bed. Listen! Something stupid has happened. There was a burglar in my room when I got up here. He took pot shots at me with a gun before escaping via the window. One of them hit me in the hand."

"Merciful God! Are you badly hurt?"

"No. It just took a slice off the back of my right hand. I don't feel too good, though. It gave me a nasty shock."

"My dear fellow! Please tell me exactly what has happened."

Graham told him. "My suitcase was locked," he went on, "and nothing is missing. I must have got back just a minute or so too soon. But there are complications. The noise seems to have roused half the hotel, including the Assistant Manager who is now standing about drinking whisky. They've sent for a doctor to bandage me up, but that's all. They made no attempt to get out after the man. Not, I suppose, that it would have done any good if they had, but at least they might have seen him. I didn't. They say he must have got away by the gardens. The point is that they won't call in the police unless I turn nasty and insist. Naturally, they don't want police tramping about the place, giving the hotel a bad name. They put it to me that the police would prevent my travelling on the eleven o'clock train if I lodged a complaint. I expect they would. But I don't know the laws of this place; and I don't want to put myself in a false position by failing to lodge a complaint. They propose, I gather, to square the doctor. But that's their look-out. What do I do?"

There was a short silence. Then: "I think," said Kopeikin, slowly, "that you should do nothing at the moment. Leave the matter to me. I will speak to a

30

friend of mine about it. He is connected with the police, and has great influence. As soon as I have spoken to him, I will come to your hotel."

"But there's no need for you to do that, Kopeikin. I . . ."

"Excuse me, my dear fellow, there is every need. Let the doctor attend to your wound and then stay in your room until I arrive."

"I wasn't going out," said Graham acidly; but Kopeikin had rung off.

As he hung up the telephone, the doctor arrived. He was thin and quiet, with a sallow face, and wore an overcoat with a black lamb's wool collar over his pyjamas. Behind him came the Manager, a heavy, disagreeable-looking man who obviously suspected that the whole thing was a hoax concocted expressly to annoy him.

He gave Graham a hostile stare, but before he could open his mouth his assistant was pouring out an account of what had occurred. There was a lot of gesturing and rolling of eyes. The Manager exclaimed as he listened, and looked at Graham with less hostility and more apprehension. At last the assistant paused, and then broke meaningly into French.

"Monsieur leaves Istanbul by the eleven o'clock train, and so does not wish to have the trouble and inconvenience of taking this matter to the police. I think you will agree, Monsieur le Directeur, that his attitude is wise."

"Very wise," agreed the Manager pontifically, "and most discreet." He squared his shoulders. "Monsieur, we infinitely regret that you should have been put to such pain, discomfort and indignity. But not even the most luxurious hotel can fortify itself against thieves who climb through windows. Nevertheless," he went on, "the Hotel Adler-Palace recognises its responsibili-

31

ties towards its guests. We shall do everything humanly possible to arrange the affair."

"If it would be humanly possible to instruct the doctor then to attend to my hand, I should be grateful."

"Ah yes. The doctor. A thousand pardons."

The doctor, who had been standing gloomily in the background, now came forward and began snapping out instructions in Turkish. The windows were promptly shut, the heating turned up, and the Assistant Manager dispatched on an errand. He returned, almost immediately, with an enamel bowl which was then filled with hot water from the bathroom. The doctor removed the towel from Graham's hand, sponged the blood away, and inspected the wound. Then he looked up and said something to the Manager.

"He says, Monsieur," reported the manager, complacently, "that it is not serious—no more than a little scratch."

"I already knew that. If you wish to go back to bed, please do so. But I should like some hot coffee. I am cold."

"Immediately, Monsieur." He snapped his fingers to the Assistant Manager, who scuttled out. "And if there is anything else, Monsieur?"

"No, thank you. Nothing. Good night."

"At your service, Monsieur. It is all most regrettable. Good night."

He went. The doctor cleaned the wound carefully, and began to dress it. Graham wished that he had not telephoned Kopeikin. The fuss was over. It was now nearly four o'clock. But for the fact that Kopeikin had promised to call in to see him, he might have had a few hours' sleep. He was yawning repeatedly. The doctor finished the dressing, patted it reassuringly, and looked up. His lips worked.

"*Maintenant*," he said laboriously, "*il faut dormir.*"

Graham nodded. The doctor got to his feet and repacked his bag with the air of a man who has done everything possible for a difficult patient. Then he looked at his watch and sighed. "*Trèstard,*" he said. "*Giteceg-im Adiyo, efendi.*"

Graham mustered his Turkish. "*Adiyo, hekim efendi. Cok tesekkür ederim.*"

"*Birsey degil. Adiyo.*" He bowed and went.

A moment later, the Assistant Manager bustled in with the coffee, set it down with a businesslike flourish clearly intended to indicate that he, too, was about to return to his bed, and collected the bottle of whisky.

"You may leave that," said Graham; "a friend is on his way to see me. You might tell the porter . . . "

But as he spoke, the telephone rang, and the night porter announced that Kopeikin had arrived. The Assistant Manager retired.

Kopeikin came into the room looking preternaturally grave.

"My dear fellow!" was his greeting. He looked round. "Where is the doctor?"

"He's just left. Just a graze. Nothing serious. I feel a bit jumpy but, apart from that, I'm all right. It's really very good of you to turn out like this. The grateful management has presented me with a bottle of whisky. Sit down and help yourself. I'm having coffee."

Kopeikin sank into the arm-chair. "Tell me exactly how it happened."

Graham told him. Kopeikin heaved himself out of the arm-chair and walked over to the window. Suddenly he stooped and picked something up. He held it up: a small brass cartridge case.

"A nine millimetre calibre self-loading pistol," he remarked. "An unplesant thing!" He dropped it on the floor again, opened the window and looked out.

Graham sighed. "I really don't think it's any good playing detectives, Kopeikin. The man was in the room; I disturbed him, and he shot at me. Come in, shut that window, and drink some whisky."

"Gladly, my dear fellow, gladly. You must excuse my curiosity."

Graham realised that he was being a little ungracious. "It's extremely kind of you, Kopeikin, to take so much trouble. I seem to have made a lot of fuss about nothing."

"It is good that you have." He frowned. "Unfortunately a lot more fuss must be made."

"You think we ought to call in the police? I don't see that it can do any good. Besides, my train goes at eleven. I don't want to miss it."

Kopeikin drank some whisky and put his glass down with a bang. "I am afraid, my dear fellow, that you cannot under any circumstances leave on the eleven o'clock train."

"What on earth do you mean? Of course I can. I'm perfectly all right."

Kopeikin looked at him curiously. "Fortunately you are. But that does not alter facts."

"Facts?"

"Did you notice that both your windows and the shutters outside have been forced open?"

"I didn't. I didn't look. But what of it?"

"If you will look out of the window you will see that there is a terrace below which gives on the garden. Above the terrace there is a steel framework which reaches almost to the second floor balconies. In the summer it is covered with straw matting so that people can eat and drink on the terrace, out of the sun. This man obviously climbed up by the framework. It would be easy. I could almost do it myself. He could reach the balconies of all the rooms on this floor of the hotel that way. But can you tell me why he chooses to break into one of the few rooms with both shutters and windows locked?"

"Of course I can't. I've always heard that criminals were fools."

"You say nothing was stolen. Your suitcase was not even opened. A coincidence that you should return just in time to prevent him."

"A lucky coincidence. For goodness' sake, Kopeikin, let's talk about something else. The man's escaped. That's the end of it."

Kopeikin shook his head. "I'm afraid not, my dear fellow. Does he not seem to you to have been a very curious thief? He behaves like no other hotel thief ever behaved. He breaks in, and through a locked window as well. If you had been in bed, he would certainly have awakened you. He must, therefore, have known beforehand that you were not there. He must also have discovered your room number. Have you anything so obviously valuable that a thief finds it worth his while to make such preparations? No. A curious thief! He carries, too, a pistol weighing at least a kilogramme with which he fires three shots at you."

"Well?"

Kopeikin bounced angrily out of his chair. "My dear fellow, does it not occur to you that this man was shooting to kill you, and that he came here for no other purpose?"

Graham laughed. "Then all I can say is that he was a pretty bad shot. Now you listen to me carefully, Kopeikin. Have you ever heard the legend about Americans and Englishmen? It persists in every country in the world where English isn't spoken. The story is that all Americans and Englishmen are millionaires, and that they always leave vast amounts of loose cash about the place. And now, if you don't mind, I'm going to try to snatch a few hours' sleep. It was very good of you to come round, Kopeikin, and I'm very grateful, but now ... "

"Have you ever," demanded Kopeikin, "tried firing a heavy pistol in a dark room at a man who's just come through the door? There's no direct light from the corridor outside. Merely a glow of light. Have you ever tried? No. You might be able to see the man, but it's quite another thing to hit him. Under these circumstances even a good shot might miss first time as this man missed. That miss would unnerve him. He does not perhaps know that Englishmen do not usually carry firearms. You may fire back. He fires again, quickly, and clips your hand. You probably cry out with the pain. He probably thinks that he has wounded you seriously. He fires another shot for luck, and goes."

"Nonsense, Kopeikin! You must be out of your senses. What conceivable reason could anyone have for wanting to kill me? I'm the most harmless man alive."

Kopeikin glared at him stonily. "Are you?"

"Now what does *that* mean?"

But Kopeikin ignored the question. He finished his whisky. "I told you that I was going to telephone a friend of mine. I did so." He buttoned up his coat deliberately. "I am sorry to tell you, my dear fellow, that you must come with me to see him immediately. I have been trying to break the news to you gently, but now I must be frank. A man tried to murder you to-night. Something must be done about it at once."

Graham got to his feet. "Are you mad?"

"No, my dear fellow, I am not. You ask me why anyone should want to murder you. There is an excellent reason. Unfortunately, I cannot be more explicit. I have my official instructions."

Graham sat down. "Kopeikin, I shall go crazy in a minute. Will you kindly tell me what you are babbling about? Friend? Murder? Official instructions? What is all this nonsense?"

Kopeikin was looking acutely embarrassed. "I am sorry, my dear fellow. I can understand your feelings. Let me tell you this much. This friend of mine is not, strictly speaking, a friend at all. In fact, I dislike him. But his name is Colonel Haki, and he is the head of the Turkish secret police. His office is in Galata, and he is expecting us to meet him there now to discuss this affair. I may also tell you that I anticipated that you might not wish to go, and told him so. He said, forgive me, that if you did not go you would be fetched. My dear fellow, it is no use your being angry. The circumstances are exceptional. If I had not known that it was necessary both in your interests and in mine to telephone him, I would not have done so. Now then, my dear fellow, I have a taxi outside. We ought to be going."

Graham got slowly to his feet again. "Very well. I must say, Kopeikin, that you have surprised me. Friendly concern, I could understand and appreciate. But this ... Hysteria is the last thing I should have expected from you. To get the head of the secret police out of bed at this hour seems to me a fantastic thing to do. I can only hope that he doesn't object to being made a fool of."

Kopeikin flushed. "I am neither hysterical nor fantastic, my friend. I have something unpleasant to do, and I am doing it. If you will forgive my saying so, I think ... "

"I can forgive almost anything except stupidity," snapped Graham. "However, this is your affair. Do you mind helping me on with my overcoat?"

They drove to Galata in grim silence. Kopeikin was sulking. Graham sat hunched up in his corner staring out miserably at the cold, dark streets, and wishing that he had not telephoned Kopeikin. It was, he kept telling himself, absurd enough to be shot at by a hotel sneak thief: to be bundled out in the early hours of the morning to tell the head of the secret police about it was worse than absurd; it was ludicrous. He felt, too, concerned on Kopeikin's account. The man might be behaving like an idiot; but it was not very pleasant to think of him making an ass of himself before a man who might well be able to do him harm in his business. Besides, he, Graham, had been rude.

He turned his head. "What's this Colonel Haki like?"

Kopeikin grunted. "Very *chic* and polished—a ladies' man. There is also a legend that he can drink two bottles of whisky without getting drunk. It may be true. He was one of Ataturk's men, a deputy in the provisional government of nineteen nineteen. There is also another legend—that he killed prisoners by tying them together in pairs and throwing them into the river to save both food and ammunition. I do not believe everything I hear, nor am I a prig, but, as I told you, I do not like him. He is, however, very clever. But you will be able to judge for yourself. You can speak French to him."

"I still don't see ... "

"You will."

They pulled up soon afterwards behind a big American car which almost blocked the narrow street into which they had turned. They got out. Graham found himself standing in front of a pair of double doors which might have been the entrance to a cheap hotel. Kopeikin pressed a bell push.

One of the doors was opened almost immediately by a sleepy-looking caretaker who had obviously only just been roused from his bed.

"*Haki efendi evde midir,*" said Kopeikin.

"*Efendi var-dir. Yokari.*" The man pointed to the stairs.

They went up.

Colonel Haki's office was a large room at the end of a corridor on the top floor of the building. The Colonel himself walked down the corridor to meet them.

He was a tall man with lean, muscular cheeks, a small mouth and grey hair cropped Prussian fashion. A narrow frontal bone, a long beak of a nose and a slight stoop gave him a somewhat vultural air. He wore a very well-cut officer's tunic with full riding breeches and very tight, shiny cavalry boots; he walked with the slight swagger of a man who is used to riding. But for the intense pallor of his face and the fact that it was unshaven, there was nothing about him to show that he had recently been asleep. His eyes were grey and very wide-awake. They surveyed Graham with interest.

"Ah! *Nasil-siniz. Fransizca konus-abilir misin.* Yes? Delighted, Mr. Graham. Your wound, of course." Graham found his unbandaged hand being gripped with considerable force by long rubbery fingers. "I hope that it is not too painful. Something must be done about this rascal who tries to kill you."

"I'm afraid," said Graham, "that we have disturbed your rest unnecessarily, Colonel. The man stole nothing."

Colonel Haki looked quickly at Kopeikin.

"I have told him nothing," said Kopeikin placidly. "At your suggestion, Colonel, you may remember. I regret to say that he thinks that I am either mad or hysterical."

Colonel Haki chuckled. "It is the lot of you Russians to be misunderstood. Let us go into my office where we can talk."

They followed him: Graham with the growing conviction that he was involved in a nightmare and that he would presently wake up to find himself at his dentist's. The corridor was, indeed, as bare and

39

featureless as the corridors of a dream. It smelt strongly, however, of stale cigarette smoke.

The Colonel's office was large and chilly. They sat down facing him across his desk. He pushed a box of cigarettes towards them, lounged back in his chair and crossed his legs.

"You must realise, Mr. Graham," he said suddenly, "that an attempt was made to kill you to-night."

"Why?" demanded Graham irritably. "I'm sorry, but I don't see it. I returned to my room to find that a man had got in through the window. Obviously he was some sort of thief. I disturbed him. He fired at me and then escaped. That is all."

"You have not, I understand, reported the matter to the police."

"I did not consider that reporting it could do any good. I did not see the man's face. Besides, I am leaving for England this morning on the eleven o'clock train. I did not wish to delay myself. If I have broken the law in any way I am sorry."

"*Zarar yok!* It does not matter." The Colonel lit a cigarette and blew smoke at the ceiling. "I have a duty to do, Mr. Graham," he said. "That duty is to protect you. I am afraid that you cannot leave on the eleven o'clock train."

"But protect me from *what?*"

"I will ask you questions, Mr. Graham. It will be simpler. You are in the employ of Messrs. Cator and Bliss, Ltd., the English armament manufacturers?"

"Yes. Kopeikin here is the company's Turkish agent."

"Quite so. You are, I believe, Mr. Graham, a naval ordnance expert."

Graham hesitated. He had the engineer's dislike of the word "expert." His managing director sometimes applied it to him when writing to foreign naval authorities; but he could, on those occasions, console himself with the reflection that his managing director would describe him as a full-blooded Zulu to impress a customer. At other times he found the word unreasonably irritating.

"Well, Mr. Graham?"

"I'm an engineer. Naval ordnance happens to be my subject."

"As you please. The point is that Messrs. Cator and Bliss, Ltd., have contracted to do some work for my Government. Good. Now, Mr. Graham, I do not know exactly what that work is"—he waved his cigarette airily—"that is the affair of the Ministry of Marine. But I have been told some things. I know that certain of our naval vessels are to be rearmed with new guns and torpedo tubes and that you were sent to discuss the matter with our dockyard experts. I also know that our authorities stipulated that the new equipment should be delivered by the spring. Your company agreed to that stipulation. Are you aware of it?"

"I have been aware of nothing else for the past two months."

"*Iyi dir!* Now I may tell you, Mr. Graham, that the reason for that stipulation as to time was not mere caprice on the part of our Ministry of Marine. The international situation demands that we have that new equipment in our dockyards by the time in question."

"I know that, too."

"Excellent. Then you will understand what I am about to say. The naval authorities of Germany and Italy and Russia are perfectly well aware of the fact that these vessels are being rearmed and I have no doubt that the moment the work is done, or even before, their agents will discover the details known at the moment only to a few men, yourself among them. That is unimportant. No navy can keep that sort of secret: no navy expects to do so. We might even consider it advisable, for various reasons, to publish the details ourselves. But"—he raised a long, well-manicured finger—"at the moment you are in a curious position, Mr. Graham."

"That, at least, I can believe."

The Colonel's small grey eyes rested on him coldly. "I am not here to make jokes, Mr. Graham."

"I beg your pardon."

"Not at all. Please take another cigarette. I was saying that at the moment your position is curious. Tell me! Have you ever regarded yourself as indispensable in your business, Mr. Graham?"

Graham laughed. "Certainly not. I could tell you the names of dozens of other men with my particular qualifications."

"Then," said Colonel Haki, "allow me to inform you, Mr. Graham, that for once in your life you *are* indispensable. Let us suppose for the moment that your thief's shooting had been a little more accurate and that at this moment you were, instead of sitting talking with me, lying in hospital on an operating table with a bullet in your lungs. What would be the effect on this business you are engaged in now?"

"Naturally, the company would send another man out immediately."

Colonel Haki affected a look of theatrical astonishment. "So? That would be splendid. So typically British! Sporting! One man falls—immediately another, undaunted, takes his place. But wait!" The Colonel held up a forbidding arm. "Is it necessary? Surely, Mr. Kopeikin here could arrange to have your papers taken to England. No doubt your colleagues there could find out from your notes, your sketches, your drawings, exactly what they wanted to know even though your company did not build the ships in question, eh?"

Graham flushed. "I gather from your tone that you

know perfectly well that the matter could not be dealt with so simply. I was forbidden, in any case, to put certain things on paper."

Colonel Haki tilted his chair. "Yes, Mr. Graham"—he smiled cheerfully—"I do know that. Another expert would have to be sent out to do some of your work over again." His chair came forward with a crash. "And meanwhile," he said through his teeth, "the spring would be here and those ships would still be lying in the dockyards of Izmir and Gallipoli, waiting for their new guns and torpedo tubes. Listen to me, Mr. Graham! Turkey and Great Britain are allies. It is in the interests of your country's enemies that, when the snow melts and the rain ceases, Turkish naval strength should be exactly what it is now. *Exactly what it is now!* They will do anything to see that it is so. *Anything*, Mr. Graham! Do you understand?"

Graham felt something tightening in his chest. He had to force himself to smile. "A little melodramatic, aren't you? We have no proof that what you say is true. And, after all, this is real life, not . . ." He hesitated.

"Not what, Mr. Graham?" The Colonel was watching him like a cat about to streak after a mouse.

" . . . the cinema, I was going to say, only it sounded a little impolite."

Colonel Haki stood up quickly. "Melodrama! Proof! Real life! The cinema! Impolite!" His lips curled round the words as if they were obscene. "Do you think I care what you say, Mr. Graham? It's your carcass I am interested in. Alive, it's worth something to the Turkish Republic. I'm going to see that it stays alive as long as I've any control over it. There is a war on in Europe. Do you understand *that?*"

Graham said nothing.

The Colonel stared at him for a moment and then

went on quietly. "A little more than a week ago, while you were still in Gallipoli, we discovered—that is, my agents discovered—a plot to murder you there. The whole thing was very clumsy and amateurish. You were to be kidnapped and knifed. Fortunately, we are not fools. *We* do not dismiss as melodramatic anything that does not please us. We were able to persuade the arrested men to tell us that they had been paid by a German agent in Sofia—a man named Moeller about whom we have known for some time. He used to call himself an American until the American Legion objected. His name was Fielding then. I imagine that he claims any name and nationality that happens to suit him. However, I called Mr. Kopeikin in to see me and told him about it but suggested that nothing should be said about it to you. The less these things are talked about the better and, besides, there was nothing to be gained by upsetting you while you were so hard at work. I think I made a mistake. I had reason to believe that this Moeller's further efforts would be directed elsewhere. When Mr. Kopeikin, very wisely, telephoned me immediately he knew of this fresh attempt, I realised that I had underestimated the determination of this gentleman in Sofia. He tried again. I have no doubt that he will try a third time if we give him a chance." He leaned back in his chair. "Do you understand now, Mr. Graham? Has your excellent brain grasped what I have been trying to say? It is perfectly simple! Someone is trying to kill you."

CHAPTER III

On the rare occasions—when matters concerned with insurance policies had been under consideration—on which Graham had thought about his own death, it had been to reaffirm the conviction that he would die of natural causes and in bed. Accidents did happen, of course; but he was a careful driver, an imaginative pedestrian and a strong swimmer; he neither rode horses nor climbed mountains; he was not subject to attacks of dizziness; he did not hunt big game and he had never had even the smallest desire to jump in front of an approaching train. He had felt, on the whole, that the conviction was not unreasonable. The idea that anyone else in the world might so much as hope for his death had never occurred to him. If it had done so he would probably have hastened to consult a nerve specialist. Confronted by the proposition that someone was, in fact, not merely hoping for his death but deliberately trying to murder him, he was as profoundly shocked as if he had been presented with incontrovertible proofs that a^2 no longer equalled b^2+c^2 or that his wife had a lover.

He was a man who had always been inclined to

think well of his fellow creatures; and the first involuntary thought that came into his head was that he must have done something particularly reprehensible for anyone to want to murder him. The mere fact that he was doing his job could not be sufficient reason. He was not dangerous. Besides, he had a wife dependent on him. It was impossible that anyone should wish to kill him. There must be some horrible mistake.

He heard himself saying: "Yes. I understand."

He didn't understand, of course. It was absurd. He saw Colonel Haki looking at him with a frosty little smile on his small mouth.

"A shock, Mr. Graham? You do not like it, eh? It is not pleasant. War is war. But it is one thing to be a soldier in the trenches: the enemy is not trying to kill you in particular because you are Mr. Graham: the man next to you will do as well: it is all impersonal. When you are a marked man it is not so easy to keep your courage. I understand, believe me. But you have advantages over the soldier. You have only to defend yourself. You do not have to go into the open and attack. And you have no trench or fort to hold. You may run away without being a coward. You must reach London safely. But it is a long way from Istanbul to London. You must, like the soldier, take precautions against surprise. You must know your enemy. You follow me?"

"Yes. I follow you."

His brain was icily calm now, but it seemed to have lost control of his body. He knew that he must try to look as if he were taking it all very philosophically, but his mouth kept filling with saliva, so that he was swallowing repeatedly, and his hands and legs were trembling. He told himself that he was behaving like a schoolboy. A man had fired three shots at him. What difference did it make whether the man had been a thief or as intending murderer? He had fired three

46

shots, and that was that. But all the same, it did somehow make a difference . . .

"Then," Colonel Haki was saying, "let us begin with what has just happened." He was obviously enjoying himself. "According to Mr. Kopeiken, you did not see the man who shot at you."

"No, I didn't. The room was in darkness."

Kopeikin chipped in. "He left cartridge cases behind him. Nine millimetre calibre ejected from a self-loading pistol."

"That does not help a great deal. You noticed nothing about him, Mr. Graham?"

"Nothing, I'm afraid. It was all over so quickly. He had gone before I realised it."

"But he had probably been in the room for some time waiting for you. You didn't notice any perfume in the room?"

"All I could smell was cordite."

"What time did you arrive in Istanbul?"

"At about six p.m."

"And you did not return to your hotel until three o'clock this morning. Please tell me where you were during that time."

"Certainly. I spent the time with Kopeikin. He met me at the station, and we drove in a taxi to the Adler-Palace, where I left my suitcase and had a wash. We then had some drinks and dined. Where did we have drinks, Kopeikin?"

"At the Rumca Bar."

"Yes, that was it. We went on to the Pera Palace to dine. Just before eleven we left there, and went on to Le Jockey Cabaret."

"Le Jockey Cabaret! You surprise me! What did you do there?"

"We danced with an Arab girl named Maria, and saw the cabaret."

"We? Was there, then, only one girl between you?"

47

"I was rather tired, and did not want to dance much. Later we had a drink with one of the cabaret dancers, Josette, in her dressing-room." To Graham it all sounded rather like the evidence of detectives in a divorce case.

"A nice girl, this Josette?"

"Very attractive."

The Colonel laughed: the doctor keeping the patient's spirits up. "Blonde or brunette?"

"Blonde."

"Ah! I must visit Le Jockey. I have missed something. And what happened then?"

"Kopeikin and I left the place. We walked back to the Adler-Palace together where Kopeikin left me to go on to his apartment."

The Colonel looked humorously astonished. "You left this dancing blonde?"—he snapped his fingers—"just like that? There were no—little games?"

"No. No little games."

"Ah, but you have told me that you were tired." He swung round suddenly in his chair to face Kopeikin. "These women—this Arab and this Josette—what do you know of them?"

Kopeikin stroked his chin. "I know Serge, the proprietor of Le Jockey Cabaret. He introduced me to Josette some time ago. She is a Hungarian, I believe. I know nothing against her. The Arab girl is from a house in Alexandria."

"Very well. We will see about them later." He turned again to Graham. "Now, Mr. Graham, we shall see what we can find out from you about the enemy. You were tired, you say?"

"Yes."

"But you kept your eyes open, eh?"

"I suppose so."

"Let us hope so. You realise that you must have been followed from the moment you left Gallipoli?"

"I hadn't realised that."

"It must be so. They knew your hotel and your room in it. They were waiting for you to return. They must have known of every movement you made since you arrived."

He got up suddenly and, going to a filing cabinet in the corner, extracted from it a yellow manilla folder. He brought it back and dropped it on the desk in front of Graham. "Inside that folder, Mr. Graham, you will find photographs of fifteen men. Some of the photographs are clear; most are very blurred and indistinct. You will have to do the best you can. I want you to cast your mind back to the time you boarded the train at Gallipoli yesterday, and remember every face you saw, even casually, between that time and three o'clock this morning. Then I want you to look at those photographs and see if you recognise any of the faces there. Afterwards Mr. Kopeikin can look at them, but I wish you to see them first."

Graham opened the folder. There was a series of thin white cards in it. Each was about the size of the folder, and had a photograph gummed to the top half of it. The prints were all the same size, but they had obviously been copied from original photographs of varying sizes. One was an enlargement of part of a photograph of a group of men standing in front of some trees. Underneath each print was a paragraph or two of typewritten matter in Turkish: presumably the description of the man in question.

Most of the photographs were, as the Colonel had said, blurred. One or two of the faces were, indeed, no more than blobs of grey with dark patches marking the eyes and mouths. Those that were clear looked like prison photographs. The men in them stared sullenly at their tormentors. There was one of a negro wearing a tarboosh with his mouth wide open as if he were shouting at someone to the right of the

49

camera. Graham turned the cards over, slowly and hopelessly. If he had ever seen any of these men in his life, he could not recognise them now.

The next moment his heart jolted violently. He was looking at a photograph taken in very strong sunshine of a man in a hard straw hat standing in front of what might have been a shop, and looking over his shoulder at the camera. His right arm and his body below the waist were out of the picture, and what was in was rather out of focus; in addition the photograph looked as if it had been taken at least ten years previously; but there was no mistaking the doughy, characterless features, the long-suffering mouth, the small deep-set eyes. It was the man in the crumpled suit.

"Well, Mr. Graham!"

"This man. He was at Le Jockey Cabaret. It was the Arab girl who drew my attention to him while we were dancing. She said that he came in just after Kopeikin and me, and that he kept looking at me. She warned me against him. She seemed to think that he might stick a knife in my back and take my wallet."

"Did she know him?"

"No. She said that she recognized the type."

Colonel Haki took the card and leaned back. "That was very intelligent of her. Did you see this man, Mr. Kopeikin?"

Kopeikin looked, and then shook his head.

"Very well." Colonel Haki dropped the card on the desk in front of him. "You need not trouble to look at any more of the photographs, gentlemen. I know now what I wanted to know. This is the only one of the fifteen that interests us. The rest I put with it merely to make sure that you identified this one of your own accord."

"Who is he?"

"He is a Roumanian by birth. His name is supposed to be Petre Banat; but as Banat is the name of a Roumanian province, I think it very probable that he never had a family name. We know, indeed, very little about him. But what we do know is enough. He is a professional gunman. Ten years ago he was convicted, in Jassy, of helping to kick a man to death, and was sent to prison for two years. Soon after he came out of prison he joined Codreanu's Iron Guard. In nineteen thirty-three he was charged with the assassination of a police official at Bucova. It appears that he walked into the official's house one Sunday afternoon, shot the man dead, wounded his wife, and then calmly walked out again. He is a careful man, but he knew that he was safe. The trial was a farce. The court-room was filled with Iron Guards with pistols, who threatened to shoot the judge and everyone connected with the trial if Banat were convicted. He was acquitted. There were many such trials in Roumania at that time. Banat was afterwards responsible for at least four other murders in Roumania. When the Iron Guard was proscribed, however, he escaped from the country, and has not returned there. He spent some time in France until the French police deported him. Then he went to Belgrade. But he got into trouble there, too, and has since moved about Eastern Europe.

"There are men who are natural killers. Banat is one of them. He is very fond of gambling, and is always short of money. At one time it was said that his price for killing a man was as little as five thousand French francs and expenses.

"But all that is of no interest to you, Mr. Graham. The point is that Banat is here in Istanbul. I may tell you that we receive regular reports on the activities of this man Moeller in Sofia. About a week ago it was reported that he had been in touch with Banat, and that Banat had afterwards left Sofia. I will admit to you, Mr. Graham, that I did not attach any importance to the fact. To be frank, it was another aspect of this agent's activities which was interesting me at the time. It was not until Mr. Kopeikin telephoned me that I remembered Banat and wondered if, by any chance, he had come to Istanbul. We know now that he is here. We know also that Moeller saw him just after those other arrangements for killing you had been upset. There can be no doubt, I think, that it was Banat who was waiting for you in your room at the Adler-Palace."

Graham strove to seem unimpressed. "He looked harmless enough."

"That," said Colonel Haki, sagely, "is because you are not experienced, Mr. Graham. The real killer is not a mere brute. He may be quite sensitive. Have you studied abnormal psychology?"

"I'm afraid not."

"It is very interesting. Apart from detective stories, Krafft-Ebing and Stekel are my favourite reading. I have my own theory about men such as Banat. I believe that they are perverts with an *idée fixe* about the father whom they identify not with a virile god"—he held up a cautionary finger—"but with their own impotence. When they kill, they are thus killing their own weakness. There is no doubt of it, I think."

"Very interesting, I feel sure. But can't you arrest this man?"

Colonel Haki cocked one gleaming boot over the arm of his chair, and pursed his lips. "That raises an awkward problem, Mr. Graham. In the first place, we have to find him. He will certainly be travelling with a false passport and under a false name. I can and, of course, will circulate his description to the frontier posts so that we shall know if he leaves the country, but as for arresting him . . . You see, Mr. Graham, the

so-called democratic forms of government have serious drawbacks for a man in my position. It is impossible to arrest and detain people without absurd legal
formalities." He threw up his hands—a patriot be-
moaning his country's decadence. "On what charge
can we arrest him? We have no evidence against him.
We could, no doubt, invent a charge and then apologise, but what good will it do? No! I regret it, but we
can do nothing about Banat. I do not think it matters
a great deal. What we must think of now is the future.
We must consider how to get you home safely."

"I have, as I have already told you, a sleeping berth
on the eleven o'clock train. I fail to see why I
shouldn't use it. It seems to me that the sooner I leave
here the better."

Colonel Haki frowned. "Let me tell you, Mr. Graham, that if you were to take that or any other train,
you would be dead before you reached Belgrade.
Don't imagine for one moment that the presence of
other travellers would deter them. You must not underrate the enemy, Mr. Graham. It is a fatal mistake.
In a train you would be caught like a rat in a trap.
Picture it for yourself! There are innumerable stops
between the Turkish and French frontiers. Your assas-
sin might get on the train at any of them. Imagine
yourself sitting there for hour after hour trying to stay
awake lest you should be knifed while you slept; not
daring to leave the compartment for fear of being
shot down in the corridor; living in terror of everyone
—from the man sitting opposite to you in the restaurant car to the Customs officials. Picture it, Mr. Graham, and then reflect that a transcontinental train is
the safest place in the world in which to kill a man.
Consider the position! These people do not wish you
to reach England. So they decide, very wisely and
logically, to kill you. They have tried twice and
failed. They will wait now to see what you will do.

They will not try again in this country. They will know that you will now be too well protected. They will wait until you come out in the open. No! I am afraid that you cannot travel by train."

"Then I don't see . . ."

"If," continued the Colonel, "the air line services had not been suspended we could send you by aeroplane to Brindisi. But they *are* suspended—the earthquake, you understand. Everything is disorganized. The planes are being used for relief work. But we can do without them. It will be best if you go by sea."

"But surely . . ."

"There is an Italian shipping line which runs a weekly service of small cargo boats between here and Genoa. Sometimes, when there is a cargo, they go up as far as Constanza, but usually they run only as far as here, calling at the Piræus on the way. They carry a few passengers, fifteen at the most, and we can make sure that every one of them is harmless before the boat is given its clearance papers. When you get to Genoa, you will have only the short train journey between Genoa and the French frontier to put you out of reach of German agents."

"But as you yourself pointed out, time is an important factor. To-day is the second. I am due back on the eighth. If I have to wait for boats I shall be days late. Besides, the journey itself will take at least a week."

"There will be no delay, Mr. Graham," sighed the Colonel. "I am not stupid. I telephoned the port police before you arrived. There is a boat leaving in two days' time for Marseilles. It would have been better if you could have travelled on that even though it does not ordinarily take passengers. But the Italian boat leaves to-day at four-thirty in the afternoon. You will be able to stretch your legs in Athens to-morrow afternoon. You will dock in Genoa early

Saturday morning. You can, if you wish and if your visas are in order, be in London by Monday morning. As I have told you, a marked man has advantages over his enemies: he can run away—disappear. In the middle of the Mediterranean, you will be as safe as you are in this office."

Graham hesitated. He glanced at Kopeikin; but the Russian was staring at his fingernails.

"Well, I don't know, Colonel. This is all very good of you, but I can't help thinking that, in view of the circumstances which you have explained to me, I ought to get in touch with the British Consul here, or with the British Embassy, before deciding anything."

Colonel Haki lit a cigarette. "And what do you expect the Consul or the Ambassador to do? Send you home in a cruiser?" He laughed unpleasantly. "My dear Mr. Graham, I am not asking you to decide anything. I am telling you what you must do. You are, I must again remind you, of great value to my country in your present state of health. You must allow me to protect my country's interests in my own way. I think that you are probably tired now and a little upset. I do not wish to harass you, but I must explain that, if you do not agree to follow my instructions, I shall have no alternative but to arrest you, have an order issued for your deportation and put you on board the *Sestri Levante* under guard. I hope that I make myself clear."

Graham felt himself reddening. "Quite clear. Would you like to handcuff me now? It will save a lot of trouble. You need ... "

"I think," put in Kopeikin hastily, "that I should do as the Colonel suggests, my dear fellow. It is the best thing."

"I prefer to be my own judge of that, Kopeikin." He looked from one to the other of them angrily. He felt confused and wretched. Things had been moving too quickly for him. Colonel Haki he disliked intensely. Kopeikin seemed to be no longer capable of thinking for himself. He felt that they were making decisions with the glib irresponsibility of schoolboys planning a game of Red Indians. And yet the devil of it was that those conclusions were inescapably logical. His life was threatened. All they were asking him to do was to go home by another and safer route. It was a reasonable request but. . . . Then he shrugged his shoulders. "All right. I seem to have no choice."

"Exactly, Mr. Graham." The Colonel smoothed out his tunic with the air of one who has reasoned wisely with a child. "Now we can make our arrangements. As soon as the shipping company's offices are open Mr. Kopeikin can arrange for your passage and obtain a refund for your railway ticket. I will see that the names and particulars of the other passengers are submitted to me for approval before the ship sails. You need have no fears, Mr. Graham, of your fellow travellers. But I am afraid that you will not find them very *chic* or the boat very comfortable. This line is actually the cheapest route to and from Istanbul if you live in the west. But you will not, I am sure, mind a little discomfort if you have peace of mind to compensate for it."

"As long as I get back to England by the eighth, I don't care how I travel."

"That is the right spirit. And now I suggest that you remain in this building until it is time for you to leave. We will make you as comfortable as possible. Mr. Kopeikin can collect your suitcase from the hotel. I will see that a doctor looks at your hand later on to see that it is still all right." He looked at his watch. "The concièrge can make us some coffee now. Later, he can get some food for you from the restaurant round the corner." He stood up. "I will go and see about it now. We cannot save you from bullets to let you die of starvation, eh?"

"It's very kind of you," said Graham; and then, as the Colonel disappeared down the corridor: "I owe you an apology, Kopeikin. I behaved badly."

Kopeikin looked distressed. "My dear fellow! You cannot be blamed. I am glad everything has been settled so quickly."

"Quickly, yes." He hesitated. "Is this man Haki to be trusted?"

"You do not like him either, eh?" Kopeikin chuckled. "I would not trust him with a woman; but with you—yes."

"You approve of my going on this boat?"

"I do. By the way, my dear fellow," he went on mildly, "have you a gun in your luggage?"

"Good heavens, no!"

"Then you had better take this." He pulled a small revolver out of his overcoat pocket. "I put it in my pocket when I came out after you telephoned. It is fully loaded."

"But I shan't need it."

"No, but it will make you feel better to have it."

"I doubt that. Still. . . ." He took the revolver and stared at it distastefully. "I've never fired one of these things, you know."

"It is easy. You release the safety catch, point it, pull the trigger and hope for the best."

"All the same . . ."

"Put it in your pocket. You can give it to the French Customs officials at Modano."

Colonel Haki returned. "The coffee is being prepared. Now, Mr. Graham, we will decide how you are to amuse yourself until it is time for you to go." He caught sight of the revolver in Graham's hand. "Ah-ha! You are arming yourself!" He grinned. "A little melodrama is sometimes unavoidable, eh, Mr. Graham?"

The decks were silent now and Graham could hear the sounds within the ship: people talking, doors slamming, quick businesslike footsteps in the alleyways. There was not long to wait now. Outside it was getting dark. He looked back upon a day which had seemed interminable, surprised that he could remember so little of it.

Most of it he had spent in Colonel Haki's office, his brain hovering uncertainly on the brink of sleep. He had smoked innumerable cigarettes and read some fortnight-old French newspapers. There had been an article in one of them, he remembered, about the French mandate in the Cameroons. A doctor had been, reported favourably on the state of his wound, dressed it and gone. Kopeikin had brought him his suitcase and he had made a bloody attempt to shave with his left hand. In the absence of Colonel Haki they had shared a cool and soggy meal from the restaurant. The Colonel had returned at two to inform him that there were nine other passengers travelling on the boat, four of them women, that none of them had booked for the journey less than three days previously, and that they were all harmless.

The gangway was down now and the last of the nine, a couple who sounded middle-aged and spoke French, had come aboard and were in the cabin next to his. Their voices penetrated the thin wooden bulkhead with dismaying ease. He could hear almost every sound they made. They had argued incessantly, in whispers at first as if they had been in church; but the novelty of their surroundings soon wore off and they spoke in ordinary tones.

"The sheets are damp."

58

"No, it is simply that they are cold. In any case it does not matter."

"You think not? You think not?" She made a noise in her throat. "You may sleep as you wish, but do not complain to me about your kidneys."

"Cold sheets do not harm the kidneys, *chérie*."

"We have paid for our tickets. We are entitled to comfort."

"If you never sleep in a worse place you will be lucky. This is not the *Normandie*."

"That is evident." The washing cabinet clicked open. "Ah! Look at this. Look! Do you expect me to wash in it?"

"It is only necessary to run the water. A little dust."

"Dust! It is *dirty*. Filthy! It is for the steward to clean it. I will not touch it. Go and fetch him while I unpack the luggage. My dresses will be crushed. Where is the W.C.?"

"At the end of the corridor."

"Then find the steward. There is no room for two while I unpack. We should have gone by train."

"Naturally. But it is I who must pay. It is I who must give the steward a tip."

"It is you who make too much noise. Quickly. Do you want to disturb everyone?"

The man went out and the woman sighed loudly. Graham wondered whether they would talk all night. And one or both of them might snore. He would have to cough loudly once or twice so that they would realise how thin the partition was. But it was strangely comforting to hear people talking about damp sheets and dirty wash basins and W.C.'s as if—the phrase was in his mind before he realised it—as if they were matters of life and death.

Life and death! He got to his feet and found himself staring at the framed instructions for lifeboat drill.

"CINTURE DI SALVATAGGIO, CEINTURES DE SAUVETAGE, RETTUNGSGÜRTEL. LIFEBELTS. . . . *In case of danger, the signal will be given by six short blasts on the whistle followed by one long blast and the ringing of alarm bells. Passengers should then put on their lifebelts and assemble at boat station number 4."*

He had seen the same sort of thing dozens of times before but now he read it carefully. The paper it was printed on was yellow with age. The lifebelt on top of the washing cabinet looked as if it had not been moved for years. It was all ludicrously reassuring. *"In case of danger. . . ."* In case! But you couldn't get away from danger! It was all about you, all the time. You could live in ignorance of it for years: you might go to the end of your days believing that some things couldn't possibly happen to *you,* that death could only come to you with the sweet reason of disease or an "act of God": but it was there just the same, waiting to make nonsense of all your comfortable ideas about your relations with time and chance, ready to remind you—in case you had forgotten—that civilisation was a word and that you still lived in the jungle.

The ship swayed gently. There was a faint clanging from the engine room telegraph. The floor began to vibrate. Through the smeared glass of the porthole he saw a light begin to move. The vibration ceased for a moment or two; then the engines went astern and the water glass rattled in its bracket on the wall. Another pause and then the engines went ahead again, slowly and steadily. They were free of the land. With a sigh of relief he opened the cabin door and went up on deck.

It was cold but the ship had turned and was taking the wind on her port side. She seemed stationary on the oily water of the harbour but the dock lights were sliding past them and receding. He drew the cold air into his lungs. It was good to be out of the cabin. His thoughts no longer seemed to worry him. Istanbul, Le Jockey Cabaret, the man in the crumpled suit, the Adler-Palace and its manager, Colonel Haki—they were all behind him. He could forget about them.

He began to pace slowly along the deck. He would, he told himself, be able to laugh at the whole business soon. It was already half-forgotten; there was already an air of the fantastic about it. He might almost have dreamed it. He was back in the ordinary world: he was on his way home.

He passed one of his fellow passengers, the first he had seen, an elderly man leaning on the rail staring at the lights of Istanbul coming into view as they cleared the mole. Now, as he reached the end of the deck and turned about, he saw that a woman in a fur coat had just come out of the saloon door and was walking towards him.

The light on the deck was dim and she was within a few yards of him before he recognised her.

It was Josette.

CHAPTER IV

FOR A MOMENT they stared blankly at one another. Then she laughed. "Merciful God! It is the Englishman. Excuse me, but this is extraordinary."

"Yes, isn't it."

"And what happened to your first-class compartment on the Orient Express?"

He smiled. "Kopeikin thought that a little sea air would do me good."

"And you needed doing good?" The straw-coloured hair was covered with a woollen scarf tied under the chin, but she held her head back to look at him as if she were wearing a hat that shaded her eyes.

"Evidently." On the whole, he decided, she looked a good deal less attractive than she had looked in her dressing-room. The fur coat was shapeless, and the scarf did not suit her. "Since we are talking about trains," he added, "what happened to your second-class compartment?"

She frowned with a smile at the corners of her mouth. "This way is so much less expensive. Did I say I was travelling by train?"

Graham flushed. "No, of course not." He realised

that he was being rather rude. "In any case, I am delighted to see you again so soon. I have been wondering what I should do if I found that the Hotel des Belges was closed."

She looked at him archly. "Ah! You were really going to telephone me, then?"

"Of course. It was understood, wasn't it?"

She discarded the arch look and replaced it with a pout. "I do not think that you are sincere after all. Tell me truthfully why you are on this boat."

She began to walk along the deck. He could do nothing but fall in step beside her.

"You don't believe me?"

She lifted her shoulders elaborately. "You need not tell me if you do not wish to. I am not inquisitive."

He thought he saw her difficulty. From her point of view there could be only two explanations of his presence on the boat: either his claim to be travelling first class on the Orient Express had been a pretentious lie intended to impress her—in which case he would have very little money—or he had somehow discovered that she was travelling on the boat, and had abandoned the luxury of the Orient Express in order to pursue her—in which case he would probably have plenty of money. He had a sudden absurd desire to startle her with the truth.

"Very well," he said. "I am travelling this way to avoid someone who is trying to shoot me."

She stopped dead. "I think it is too cold out here," she said calmly. "I shall go in."

He was so surprised that he laughed.

She turned on him quickly. "You should not make such stupid jokes."

There was no doubt about it; she was genuinely angry. He held up his bandaged hand. "A bullet grazed it."

She frowned. "You are very bad. If you have hurt

your hand I am sorry, but you should not make jokes about it. It is very dangerous."

"Dangerous!"

"You will have bad luck, and so shall I. It is very bad luck to joke in that way."

"Oh, I see." He grinned. "I am not superstitious."

"That is because you do not know. I would sooner see a raven flying than joke about killing. If you wish me to like you, you must not say such things."

"I apologise," said Graham, mildly. "Actually I cut my hand with a razor."

"Ah, they are dangerous things! In Algiers José saw a man with his throat cut from ear to ear with a razor."

"Suicide?"

"No, no! It was his *petite amie* who did it. There was a lot of blood. José will tell you about it if you ask him. It was very sad."

"Yes, I can imagine. José is travelling with you, then?"

"Naturally." And then, with a sidelong look: "He is my husband."

Her husband! That explained why she "put up with" José. It also explained why Colonel Haki had omitted to tell him that the "dancing blonde" was travelling on the boat. Graham remembered the promptitude with which José had retired from the dressing-room. That, no doubt, had been a matter of business. *Attractions* at a place like Le Jockey Cabaret were not quite so attractive if they were known to have husbands in the vicinity. He said: "Kopeikin didn't tell me that you were married."

"Kopeikin is very nice, but he does not know everything. But I will tell you confidentially that with José and me it is an arrangement. We are partners, nothing more. He is jealous about me only when I neglect business for pleasure."

She said it indifferently, as if she were discussing a clause in her contract.

"Are you going to dance in Paris now?"

"I do not know. I hope so; but so much is closed on account of the war."

"What will you do if you can't get an engagement?"

"What do you think? I shall starve. I have done it before." She smiled bravely. "It is good for the figure." She pressed her hands on her hips and looked at him, inviting his considered opinion. "Do you not think it would be good for my figure to starve a little? One grows fat in Istanbul." She posed. "You see?"

Graham nearly laughed. The picture being presented for his approval had all the simple allure of a full-page drawing in *La Vie Parisienne*. Here was the "business man's" dream come true: the beautiful blonde dancer, married but unloved, in need of protection: something expensive going cheap.

"A dancer's must be a very hard life," he said dryly.

"Ah, yes! Many people think that it is so gay. If they knew!"

"Yes, of course. It is getting a little cold, isn't it? Shall we go inside and have a drink?"

"That would be nice." She added with a tremendous air of candour: "I am so glad we are travelling together. I was afraid that I was going to be bored. Now, I shall enjoy myself."

He felt that his answering smile was probably rather sickly. He was beginning to have an uncomfortable suspicion that he was making a fool of himself. "We go this way, I think," he said.

The *salone* was a narrow room about thirty feet long, with entrances from the shelter deck and from the landing at the head of the stairs to the cabins. There were grey upholstered *banquettes* round the walls and, at one end, three round dining tables bolted down. Evidently there was no separate dining-room. Some chairs, a card table, a shaky writing desk, a radio, a piano and a threadbare carpet completed the furnishings. Opening off the room at the far end was a cubby hole with half doors. The lower door had a strip of wood screwed to the top of it to make a counter. This was the bar. Inside it, the steward was opening cartons of cigarettes. Except for him, the place was deserted. They sat down.

"What would you like to drink, Mrs. ... ," began Graham tentatively.

She laughed. "José's name is Gallindo, but I detest it. You must call me Josette. I would like some English whisky and a cigarette, please."

"Two whiskies," said Graham.

The steward put his head out and frowned at them. "Viski? *E molto caro*," he said warningly; "*très cher. Cinque lire*. Five lire each. Vair dear."

"Yes, it is, but we will have them just the same."

The steward retired into the bar, and made a lot of noise with the bottles.

"He is very angry," said Josette. "He is not used to people who order whisky." She had obviously derived a good deal of satisfaction from the ordering of the whisky, and the discomfiture of the steward. In the light of the saloon her fur coat looked cheap and old; but she had unbuttoned it and arranged it round her shoulders as if it had been a thousand guinea mink. He began, against his better judgment, to feel sorry for her.

"How long have you been dancing?"

"Since I was ten. That is twenty years ago. You see," she remarked, complacently, "I do not lie to you about my age. I was born in Serbia, but I say that I am Hungarian because it sounds better. My mother and father were very poor."

"But honest, no doubt."

She looked faintly puzzled. "Oh no, my father was

66

not at all honest. He was a dancer, and he stole some money from someone in the troupe. They put him in prison. Then the war came, and my mother took me to Paris. A very rich man took care of us for a time, and we had a very nice apartment." She gave a nostalgic sigh: an impoverished *grande dame* lamenting past glories. "But he lost his money, and so my mother had to dance again. My mother died when we were in Madrid, and I was sent back to Paris, to a convent. It was terrible there. I do not know what happened to my father. I think perhaps he was killed in the war."

"And what about José?"

"I met him in Berlin when I was dancing there. He did not like his partner. She was," she added simply, "a terrible bitch."

"Was this long ago?"

"Oh, yes. Three years. We have been to a great many places." She examined him with affectionate concern. "But you are tired. You look tired. You have cut your face, too."

"I tried to shave with one hand."

"Have you got a very nice house in England?"

"My wife likes it."

"*Oh là-là!* And do you like your wife?"

"Very much."

"I do not think," she said reflectively, "that I would like to go to England. So much rain and fog. I like Paris. There is nothing better to live in than an apartment in Paris. It is not expensive."

"No?"

"For twelve hundred francs a month one can have a very nice apartment. In Rome it is not so cheap. I had an apartment in Rome that was very nice, but it cost fifteen hundred lire. My fiancé was very rich. He sold automobiles."

"That was before you married José?"

"Of course. We were going to be married but there

was some trouble about his divorce from his wife in America. He always said that he would fix it, but in the end it was impossible. I was very sorry. I had that apartment for a year."

"And that was how you learned English?"

"Yes, but I had learned a little in that terrible convent." She frowned. "But I tell you everything about myself. About you I know nothing except that you have a nice house and a wife, and that you are an engineer. You ask questions, but you tell me nothing. I still do not know why you are here. It is very bad of you."

But he did not have to reply to this. Another passenger had entered the saloon, and was advancing towards them, clearly with the intention of making their acquaintance.

He was short, broad-shouldered and unkempt, with a heavy jowl and a fringe of scurfy grey hair round a bald pate. He had a smile, fixed like that of a ventriloquist's doll: a standing apology for the iniquity of his existence.

The boat had begun to roll slightly; but from the way he clutched for support at the backs of chairs as he crossed the room, it might have been riding out a full gale.

"There is lot of movement, eh?" he said in English, and subsided into a chair. "Ah! That is better, eh?" He looked at Josette with obvious interest, but turned to Graham before he spoke again. "I hear English spoken so I am interested at once," he said. "You are English, sir?"

"Yes. And you?"

"Turkish. I also go to London. Trade is very good. I go to sell tobacco. My name is Mr. Kuvetli, sir."

"My name is Graham. This is Señora Gallindo."

"So good," said Mr. Kuvetli. Without getting up

from his chair, he bowed from the waist. "I don't speak English very well," he added, unnecessarily.

"It is a very difficult language," said Josette, coldly. She was obviously displeased by the intrusion.

"My wife," continued Mr. Kuvetli, "does not speak English any. So I do not bring her with me. She has not been to England."

"But you have?"

"Yes, sir. Three times, and to sell tobacco. I do not sell much before, but now I sell lot. It is war. United States ships do not come to England any more. English ships bring guns and aeroplanes from U.S. and have no room for tobacco, so England now buys lot of tobacco from Turkey. It is good business for my boss. Firm of Pazar and Co."

"It must be."

"He would come to England himself, but cannot speak English any. Or he cannot write. He is very ignorant. I reply to all favours from England and elsewhere abroad. But he knows lot about tobacco. We produce best." He plunged his hand into his pocket and produced a leather cigarette case. "Please try cigarette made from tobacco by Pazar and Co." He extended the case to Josette.

She shook her head. *"Tesekkür ederim."*

The Turkish phrase irritated Graham. It seemed to belittle the man's polite efforts to speak a language foreign to him.

"Ah!" said Mr. Kuvetli, "you speak my language. That is very good. You have been long in Turkey?"

"Dört ay." She turned to Graham. "I would like one of *your* cigarettes, please."

It was a deliberate insult but Mr. Kuvetli only smiled a little more. Graham took one of the cigarettes.

"Thank you very much. It's very good of you. Will you have a drink, Mr. Kuvetli?"

"Ah, no, thank you. I must go to arrange my cabin before it is dinner."

"Then later, perhaps."

"Yes, please." With a broadened smile and a bow to each of them he got to his feet and made his way to the door.

Graham lit his cigarette. "Was it absolutely necessary to be so rude? Why drive the man away?"

She frowned. "Turks! I do not like them. They are"—she ransacked the automobile salesman's vocabulary for an epithet—"they are goddamned dagoes. See how thick his skin is! He does not get angry. He only smiles."

"Yes, he behaved very well."

"I do not understand it," she burst out angrily. "In the last war you fought with France against the Turks. In the convent they told me much about it. They are heathen animals, these Turks. There were the Armenian atrocities and the Syrian atrocities and the Smyrna atrocities. Turks killed babies with their bayonets. But now it is all different. You like the Turks. They are your allies and you buy tobacco from them. It is the English hypocrisy. I am a Serb. I have a longer memory."

"Does your memory go back to nineteen twelve? I was thinking of the Serbian atrocities in Turkish villages. Most armies commit what are called atrocities at some time or other. They usually call them reprisals."

"Including the British army, perhaps?"

"You would have to ask an Indian or an Afrikander about that. But every country has its madmen. Some countries have more than others. And when you give such men a license to kill they are not always particular about the way they kill. But I am afraid that the rest of their fellow countrymen remain human beings. Personally, I like the Turks."

She was clearly angry with him. He suspected that her rudeness to Mr. Kuvetli had been calculated to earn his approval and that she was annoyed because he had not responded in the way she had expected. "It is stuffy in here," she said, "and there is a smell of cooking. I should like to walk outside again. You may come with me if you wish."

Graham seized the opportunity. He said, as they walked towards the door: "I think that I should unpack my suitcase. I shall hope to see you at dinner."

Her expression changed quickly. She became an international beauty humouring, with a tolerant smile, the extravagances of a love-sick boy. "As you wish. José will be with me later. I shall introduce you to him. He will want to play cards."

"Yes, I remember you told me that he would. I shall have to try to remember a game that I can play well."

She shrugged. "He will win in any case. But I have warned you."

"I shall remember that when I lose."

He returned to his cabin and stayed there until the steward came round beating a gong to announce dinner. When he went upstairs he was feeling better. He had changed his clothes. He had managed to complete the shave which he had begun in the morning. He had an appetite. He was prepared to take an interest in his fellow passengers.

Most of them were already in their places when he entered the saloon.

The ship's officers evidently ate in their own quarters. Only two of the dining tables were laid. At one of them sat Mr. Kuvetli, a man and woman who looked as if they might be the French couple from the cabin next to his, Josette, and with her a very sleek José. Graham smiled courteously at the assembly and received in return a loud "good evening"

71

from Mr. Kuvetli, a lift of the eyebrows from Josette, a cool nod from José, and a blank stare from the French couple. There was about them an air of tension which seemed to him to be more than the ordinary restraint of passengers on a boat sitting down together for the first time. The steward showed him to the other table.

One of the places was already filled by the elderly man whom he had passed on his walk round the deck. He was a thick, round-shouldered man with a pale heavy face, white hair and a long upper lip. As Graham sat down next to him he looked up. Graham met a pair of prominent pale blue eyes.

"Mr. Graham?"

"Yes. Good evening."

"My name is Haller. Doctor Fritz Haller. I should explain that I am a German, a good German, and that I am on my way back to my country." He spoke very good, deliberate English in a deep voice.

Graham realised that the occupants of the other table were staring at them in breathless silence. He understood now their air of tension.

He said calmly: "I am an Englishman. But I gather you knew that."

"Yes, I knew it." Haller turned to the food in front of him. "The Allies seem to be here in force and unhappily the steward is an imbecile. The two French people at the next table were placed here. They objected to eating with the enemy, insulted me and moved. If you wish to do the same I suggest that you do so now. Everyone is expecting the scene."

"So I see." Graham cursed the steward silently.

"On the other hand," Haller continued, breaking his bread, "you may find the situation humorous. I do myself. Perhaps I am not as patriotic as I should be. No doubt I should insult you before you insult me; but, quite apart from the unfair differences in our ages, I can think of no effective way of insulting you. One must understand a person thoroughly before one can insult him effectively. The French lady, for example, called me a filthy Bosche. I am unmoved. I bathed this morning and I have no unpleasant habits."

"I see your point. But . . ."

"But there is a matter of etiquette involved. Quite so. Fortunately, I must leave that to you. Move or not, as you choose. Your presence here would not embarrass me. If it were understood that we were to exclude international politics from our conversation we might even pass the next half-hour in a civilised manner. However, as the newcomer on the scene, it is for you to decide."

Graham picked up the menu. "I believe it is the custom for belligerents on neutral ground to ignore each other if possible and in any case to avoid embarrassing the neutrals in question. Thanks to the steward, we cannot ignore each other. There seems to be no reason why we should make a difficult situation unpleasant. No doubt we can rearrange the seating before the next meal."

Haller nodded approval. "Very sensible. I must admit that I am glad of your company to-night. My wife suffers from the sea and will stay in her cabin this evening. I think that Italian cooking is very monotonous without conversation."

"I am inclined to agree with you." Graham smiled intentionally and heard a rustle from the next table. He also heard an exclamation of disgust from the Frenchwoman. He was annoyed to find that the sound made him feel guilty.

"You seem," said Haller, "to have earned some disapproval. It is partly my fault. I am sorry. Perhaps it is that I am old, but I find it extremely difficult to identify men with their ideas. I can dislike, even hate

73

an idea, but the man who has it seems to be still a man."

"Have you been long in Turkey?"

"A few weeks. I came there from Persia."

"Oil?"

"No, Mr. Graham, archeology. I was investigating the early pre-Islamic cultures. The little I have been able to discover seems to suggest that some of the tribes who moved westward to the plains of Iran about four thousand years ago assimilated the Sumerian culture and preserved it almost intact until long after the fall of Babylon. The form of perpetuation of the Adonis myth alone was instructive. The weeping for Tammuz was always a focal point of the pre-historic religions—the cult of the dying and risen god. Tammuz, Osiris and Adonis are the same Sumerian deity personified by three different races. But the Sumerians called this god Dumuzida. So did some of the pre-Islamic tribes of Iran! And they had a most interesting variation of the Sumerian epic of Gilgamish and Enkidu which I had not heard about before. But forgive me, I am boring you already."

"Not at all," said Graham politely. "Were you in Persia for long?"

"Two years only. I would have stayed another year but for the war."

"Did it make so much difference?"

Haller pursed his lips. "There was a financial question. But even without that I think that I might not have stayed. We can learn only in the expectation of life. Europe is too preoccupied with its destruction to concern itself with such things: a condemned man is interested only in himself, the passage of hours and such intimations of immorality as he can conjure from the recesses of his mind."

"I should have thought that a preoccupation with the past. . . ."

"Ah yes, I know. The scholar in his study can ignore the noise in the market place. Perhaps—if he is a theologian or a biologist or an antiquarian. I am none of those things. I helped in the search for a logic of history. We should have made of the past a mirror with which to see round the corner that separates us from the future. Unfortunately, it no longer matters what we could have seen. We are returning the way we came. Human understanding is re-entering the monastery."

"Forgive me but I thought you said that you were a *good* German."

He chuckled. "I am old. I can afford the luxury of despair."

"Still, in your place, I think that I should have stayed in Persia and luxuriated at a distance."

"The climate, unfortunately, is not suitable for any sort of luxuriating. It is either very hot or very cold. My wife found it particularly trying. Are you a soldier, Mr. Graham?"

"No, an engineer."

"That is much the same thing. I have a son in the army. He has always been a soldier. I have never understood why he should be my son. As a lad of fourteen he disapproved of me because I had no duelling scars. He disapproved of the English, too, I am afraid. We lived for some time in Oxford while I was doing some work there. A beautiful city! Do you live in London?"

"No, in the North."

"I have visited Manchester and Leeds. I preferred Oxford. I live in Berlin myself. I don't think it is any uglier than London." He glanced at Graham's hand. "You seem to have had an accident."

"Yes. Fortunately it's just as easy to eat ravioli with the left hand."

75

"There is that to be said for it, I suppose. Will you have some of this wine?"

"I don't think so, thank you."

"Yes, you're wise. The best Italian wines never leave Italy." He dropped his voice. "Ah! Here are the other two passengers."

They looked like mother and son. The woman was about fifty and unmistakably Italian. Her face was very hollow and pale and she carried herself as if she had been seriously ill. Her son, a handsome lad of eighteen or so, was very attentive to her and glared defensively at Graham, who had risen to draw back her chair for her. They both wore black.

Haller greeted them in Italian to which the boy replied briefly. The woman inclined her head to them but did not speak. It was obvious that they wished to be left to themselves. They conferred in whispers over the menu. Graham could hear José talking at the next table.

"War!" he was saying in thick, glutinous French; "it makes it very difficult for all to earn money. Let Germany have all the territory she desires. Let her choke herself with territory. Then let us go to Berlin and enjoy ourselves. It is ridiculous to fight. It is not businesslike."

"Ha!" said the Frenchman. "You, a Spaniard, say that! Ha! That is very good. Magnificent!"

"In the civil war," said José, "I took no sides. I had my work to do, my living to earn. It was madness. I did not go to Spain."

"War is terrible," said Mr. Kuvetli.

"But if the Reds had won . . ." began the Frenchman.

"Ah yes!" exclaimed his wife. "If the Reds had won. . . . They were anti-Christ. They burnt churches and broke sacred images and relics. They violated nuns and murdered priests."

76

"It was all very bad for business," repeated José obstinately. "I know a man in Bilbao who had a big business. It was all finished by the war. War is very stupid."

"The voice of the fool," murmured Haller, "with the tongue of the wise. I think that I will go and see how my wife is. Will you excuse me, please?"

Graham finished his meal virtually alone. Haller did not return. The mother and son opposite to him ate with their heads bent over their plates. They seemed to be in communion over some private sorrow. He felt as if he were intruding. As soon as he had finished he left the saloon, put on his overcoat and went out on deck to get some air before going to bed.

The lights on the land were distant now, and the ship was rustling through the sea before the wind. He found the companionway up to the boat deck and stood for a time in the lee of a ventilator idly watching a man with a lamp on the well-deck below tapping the wedges which secured the hatch tarpaulins. Soon the man finished his task, and Graham was left to wonder how he was going to pass the time on the boat. He made up his mind to get some books in Athens the following day. According to Kopeikin, they would dock at the Piræus at about two o'clock in the afternoon, and sail again at five. He would have plenty of time to take the tram into Athens, buy some English cigarettes and books, send a telegram to Stephanie and get back to the dock.

He lit a cigarette, telling himself that he would smoke it and then go to bed; but, even as he threw the match away, he saw that Josette and José had come on to the deck, and that the girl had seen him. It was too late to retreat. They were coming over to him.

"So you are here," she said accusingly. "This is José."

José, who was wearing a very tight black overcoat and a grey soft hat with a curly brim, nodded reluctantly and said: *"Enchanté, Monsieur,"* with the air of a busy man whose time is being wasted.

"José does not speak English," she explained.

"There is no reason why he should. It is a pleasure to meet you, Señor Gallindo," he went on in Spanish. "I very much enjoyed the dancing of you and your wife."

José laughed rudely. "It is nothing. The place was impossible."

"José was angry all the time because Coco—the negress with the snake, you remember?—had more money from Serge than we did, although we were the principal attraction."

José said something unprintable, in Spanish.

"She was," said Josette, "Serge's lover. You smile, but it is true. Is it not true, José?"

José made a loud noise with his lips.

"José is very vulgar," commented Josette. "But it is true about Serge and Coco. It is a very *drôle* story. There was a great joke about Fifi, the snake. Coco was very fond of Fifi, and always used to take it to bed with her. But Serge did not know that until he became her lover. Coco says that when he found Fifi in the bed, he fainted. She made him increase her wages to double before she would consent to Fifi's sleeping alone in its basket. Serge is no fool: even José says that Serge is no fool; but Coco treats him like dirt. It is because she has a very great temper that she is able to do it."

"He needs to hit her with his fist," said José.

"Ah! *Salop!*" She turned to Graham. "And you! Do you agree with José?"

"I have no experience of snake dancers."

"Ah! You do not answer. You are brutes, you men!"

She was obviously amusing herself at his expense. He said to José: "Have you made this trip before?"

José stared suspiciously. "No. Why? Have you?"

"Oh no."

José lit a cigarette. "I am already very tired of this ship," he announced. "It is dull and dirty, and it vibrates excessively. Also the cabins are too near the lavabos. Do you play poker?"

"I *have* played. But I don't play very well."

"I told you!" cried Josette.

"She thinks," said José sourly, "that because I win I cheat. I do not care a damn what she thinks. People are not compelled by law to play cards with me. Why should they squeal like stuck pigs when they lose?"

"It is," Graham admitted, tactfully, "illogical."

"We will play now if you like," said José, as if someone had accused him of refusing a challenge.

"If you don't mind, I'd sooner leave it until to-morrow. I'm rather tired to-night. In fact, I think that if you will excuse me I shall get to bed now."

"So soon!" Josette pouted, and broke into English. "There is only one interesting person on the boat, and he goes to bed. It is too bad. Ah yes, you are being very bad. Why did you sit next to that German at dinner?"

"He did not object to my sitting beside him. Why should *I* object? He is a very pleasant and intelligent old fellow."

"He is a German. For you no German should be pleasant or intelligent. It is as the French people were saying. The English are not serious about these things."

José turned suddenly on his heel. "It is very boring to listen to English," he said, "and I am cold. I shall go and drink some brandy."

Graham was beginning to apologise when the girl cut him short. "He is very unpleasant to-day. It is

79

because he is disappointed. He thought there were going to be some pretty little girls for him to roll his eyes at. He always has a great success with pretty little girls—and old women."

She had spoken loudly, and in French. José, who had reached the top of the companionway, turned and belched deliberately before descending.

"He is gone," said Josette. "I am glad. He has very bad manners." She drew in her breath, and looked up at the clouds. "It is a lovely night. I do not see why you wish to go to bed. It is early."

"I'm very tired."

"You cannot be too tired to walk across the deck with me."

"Of course not."

There was a corner of the deck below the bridge where it was very dark. She stopped there, turned abruptly and leaned with her back to the rail so that he was facing her.

"I think you are angry with me?"

"Good gracious, no! Why should I be?"

"Because I was rude to your little Turk."

"He's not *my* little Turk."

"But you are angry?"

"Of course not."

She sighed. "You are very mysterious. You have still not told me why you are travelling on this boat. I am very interested to know. It cannot be because it is cheap. Your clothes are expensive!"

He could not see her face, only a vague outline of her but he could smell the scent she was using, and the mustiness of the fur coat. He said: "I can't think why you should be interested."

"But you know perfectly well that I am."

She had come an inch or two nearer to him. He knew that, if he wanted to do so, he could kiss her and that she would return the kiss. He knew also that it would be no idle peck, but a declaration that their relationship was to be the subject of discussion. He was surprised to find that he did not reject the idea instantaneously, that the immediate prospect of feeling her full smooth lips against his was more than attractive. He was cold and tired: she was near, and he could sense the warmth of her body. It could do no one any harm if . . . He said: "Are you travelling to Paris via Modane?"

"Yes. But why ask? It is the way to Paris."

"When we get to Modane I will tell you exactly why I travelled this way, if you are still interested."

She turned and they walked on. "Perhaps it is not so important," she said. "You must not think I am inquisitive." They reached the companionway. Her attitude towards him had changed perceptibly. She looked at him with friendly concern. "Yes, my dear sir, you are tired. I should not have asked you to stay up here. I shall finish my walk alone. Good night."

"Good night, Señora."

She smiled. "Señora! You must not be so unkind. Good night."

He went below amused and irritated by his thoughts. Outside the door of the saloon he came face to face with Mr. Kuvetli.

Mr. Kuvetli broadened his smile. "First officer says we shall have good weather, sir."

"Splendid." He remembered with a sinking heart that he had invited the man to have a drink. "Will you join me in a drink?"

"Oh no, thank you. Not now." Mr. Kuvetli placed one hand on his chest. "Matter of fact, I have pain because of wine at table. Very strong acid stuff!"

"So I should imagine. Until to-morrow, then."

"Yes, Mr. Graham. You will be glad to arrive back at your home, eh?" He seemed to want to talk.

"Oh yes, very glad."

81

"You go to Athens when we stop to-morrow?"

"I was thinking of doing so."

"Do you know Athens well, I suppose?"

"I've been there before."

Mr. Kuvetli hesitated. His smile became oily. "You are in a position to do me service, Mr. Graham."

"Oh yes?"

"I do not know Athens. I have never been. Would you allow me to go with you?"

"Yes, of course. I should be glad of company. But I was only going to buy some English books and cigarettes."

"I am most grateful."

"Not at all. We get in just after lunch, don't we?"

"Yes, yes. That is quite right. But I will find out exact time. You leave that to me."

"Then that's settled. I think I shall go to bed now. Good night, Mr. Kuvetli."

"Good night, sir. And I thank you for your favour."

"Not at all. Good night."

He went to his cabin, rang for the steward and said that he wanted his breakfast coffee in his cabin at nine-thirty. Then he undressed and got into his bunk.

For a few minutes he lay on his back enjoying the gradual relaxing of his muscles. Now, at last, he could forget Haki, Kopeikin, Banat, and the rest of it. He was back in his own life, and could sleep. The phrase "asleep almost as soon as his head touched the pillow" passed through his mind. That was how it would be with him. God knew he was tired enough. He turned on his side. But sleep did not come so easily. His brain would not stop working. It was as if the needle were trapped in one groove on the record. He'd made a fool of himself with that wretched woman Josette. He'd made a fool . . . He jerked his thoughts forward. Ah yes! He was committed to three unalloyed hours of Mr. Kuvetli's company. But that was to-morrow. And now, sleep. But his hand was throbbing again, and there seemed to be a lot of noise going on. That boor José was right. The vibration *was* excessive. The cabins *were* too near the lavatories. There were footsteps overhead, too: people walking round the shelter deck. Round and round. Why, for Heaven's sake, must people always be walking?

He had been lying awake for half an hour when the French couple entered their cabin.

They were quiet for a minute or two, and he could only hear the sounds they made as they moved about the cabin, and an occasional grunted comment. Then the woman began.

"Well, that is the first evening over! Three more! It is too much to think of."

"It will pass." A yawn. "What is the matter with the Italian woman and her son?"

"You did not hear? Her husband was killed in the earthquake at Erzurum. The first officer told me. He is very nice, but I had hoped that there would be at least one French person to talk to."

"There are people who speak French. The little Turk speaks it very well. And there are the others."

"They are not French. That girl and that man—the Spaniard. They say that they are dancers, but I ask you."

"She is pretty."

"Certainly. I do not dispute it. But you need not think little thoughts. She is interested in the Englishman. I do not like him. He does not look like an Englishman."

"You think the English are all *milords* with sporting clothes and monocles. Ha! I saw the Tommies in nineteen fifteen. They are all small and ugly with very loud voices. They talk very quickly. This type is more like the officers who are thin and slow, and look as if things do not smell very nice."

"This type is not an English officer. He likes the Germans."

"You exaggerate. An old man like that! I would have sat with him myself."

"Ah! So you say. I will not believe it."

"No? When you are a soldier you do not call the Bosche 'the filthy Bosche.' That is for the women, the civilians."

"You are mad. They are filthy. They are beasts like those in Spain who violated nuns and murdered priests."

"But, my little one, you forget that there were many of Hitler's Bosches who fought *against* the Reds in Spain. You forget. You are not logical."

"They are not the same as those who attack France. They were Catholic Germans."

"You are ridiculous! Was I not hit in the guts by a bullet fired by a Bavarian Catholic in 'seventeen? You make me tired. You are ridiculous. Be silent."

"No, it is you who ... "

They went on. Graham heard little more. Before he could make up his mind to cough loudly, he was asleep.

He awoke only once in the night. The vibration had ceased. He looked at his watch, saw that the time was half-past two, and guessed that they had stopped at Chanaq to drop the pilot. A few minutes later, as the engines started again, he went to sleep again.

It was not until the steward brought his coffee seven hours later that he learned that the pilot cutter from Chanaq had brought a telegram for him.

It was addressed: "GRAHAM, VAPUR SESTRI LEVANTE, CANAKKALE." He read:

"H. REQUESTS ME INFORM YOU B. LEFT FOR SOFIA HOUR
AGO. ALL WELL. BEST WISHES. KOPEIKIN."

It had been handed in at Beyoglu at seven o'clock
the previous evening.

CHAPTER V

IT WAS an Ægean day: intensely coloured in the sun and with small pink clouds drifting in a bleached indigo sky. A stiff breeze was blowing and the amethyst of the sea was broken and white. The *Sestri Levante* was burying her stem in it and lifting clouds of spray which the breeze whipped across the well-deck like hail. The steward had told him that they were within sight of the island of Makronisi and as he went out on deck he saw it: a thin golden line shimmering in the sun and stretched out ahead of them like a sand bar at the entrance to a lagoon.

There were two other persons on that side of the deck. There was Haller and with him, on his arm, a small desiccated woman with thin grey hair, who was evidently his wife. They were steadying themselves at the rail and he was holding his head up to the wind as if to draw strength from it. He had his hat off and the white hair quivered with the air streaming through it.

Evidently they had not seen him. He made his way up to the boat deck. The breeze there was stronger. Mr. Kuvetli and the French couple stood by the rail clutching at their hats and watching the gulls following the ship. Mr. Kuvetli saw him immediately and waved. He went over to them.

"Good morning. *Madame. Monsieur.*"

They greeted him guardedly but Mr. Kuvetli was enthusiastic.

"It *is* good morning, eh? You sleep well? I look forward to our excursion this afternoon. Permit me to present Monsieur and Madame Mathis. Monsieur Graham."

There was handshaking. Mathis was a sharp-featured man of fifty or so with lean jaws and a permanent frown. But his smile, when it came, was good and his eyes were alive. The frown was the badge of his ascendancy over his wife. She had bony hips and wore an expression which said that she was determined to keep her temper however sorely it were tried. She was like her voice.

"Monsieur Mathis," said Mr. Kuvetli, whose French was a good deal more certain than his English, "is from Eskeshehir, where he has been working with the French railway company."

"It is a bad climate for the lungs," said Mathis. "Do you know Eskeshehir, Monsieur Graham?"

"I was there for a few minutes only."

"That would have been quite enough for me," said Madame Mathis. "We have been there three years. It was never any better than the day we arrived."

"The Turks are a great people," said her husband. "They are hard and they endure. But we shall be glad to return to France. Do you come from London, Monsieur?"

"No, the North of England. I have been in Turkey for a few weeks on business."

"To us, war will be strange after so many years. They say that the towns in France are darker than the last time."

"The towns are damnably dark both in France and in England. If you do not have to go out at night it is better to stay in."

"It is war," said Mathis sententiously.

"It is the filthy Bosche," said his wife.

"War," put in Mr. Kuvetli, stroking an unshaven chin, "is a terrible thing. There is no doubt of it. But the Allies must win."

"The Bosche is strong," said Mathis. "It is easy to say that the Allies must win, but they yet have the fighting to do. And do we yet know whom we are going to fight or where? There is a front in the East as well as in the West. We do not yet know the truth. When that is known the war will be over."

"It is not for us to ask questions," said his wife.

His lips twisted and in his brown eyes was the bitterness of years. "You are right. It is not for us to ask questions. And why? Because the only people who can give us the answers are the bankers and the politicians at the top, the boys with the shares in the big factories which make war materials. They will not give us answers. Why? Because they know that if the soldiers of France and England knew those answers they would not fight."

His wife reddened. "You are mad! Naturally the men of France would fight to defend us from the filthy Bosche." She glanced at Graham. "It is bad to say that France would not fight. We are not cowards."

"No, but neither are we fools." He turned quickly to Graham. "Have you heard of Briey, Monsieur? From the mines of the Briey district comes ninety per cent. of France's iron ore. In nineteen fourteen those mines were captured by the Germans, who worked them for the iron they needed. They worked them hard. They have admitted since that without the iron they mined at Briey they would have been finished in nineteen seventeen. Yes, they worked Briey hard. I, who was at Verdun, can tell you that. Night after night we watched the glare in the sky from the blast furnaces of Briey a few kilometres away; the blast furnaces that were feeding the German guns. Our artillery and our bombing aeroplanes could have blown those furnaces to pieces in a week. But our artillery remained silent; an airman who dropped one bomb on the Briey area was court-martialled. Why?" His voice rose. "I will tell you why, Monsieur. Because there were orders that Briey was not to be touched. Whose orders? Nobody knew. The orders came from someone at the top. The Ministry of War said that it was the generals. The generals said that it was the Ministry of War. We did not find out the facts until after the war. The orders had been issued by Monsieur de Wendel of the Comité des Forges who owned the Briey mines and blast furnaces. We were fighting for our lives, but our lives were less important than that the property of Monsieur de Wendel should be preserved to make fat profits. No, it is not good for those who fight to know too much. Speeches, yes! The truth, no!"

His wife sniggered. "It is always the same. Let someone mention the war and he begins to talk about Briey—something that happened twenty-four years ago."

"And why not?" he demanded. "Things have not changed so much. Because we do not know about such things until after they have happened it does not mean that things like it are not happening now. When I think of war I think also of Briey and the glare of the blast furnaces in the sky to remind myself that I am an ordinary man who must not believe all that he is told. I see the newspapers from France with the blanks in them to show where the censor has been at work. They tell me certain things, these newspapers. France, they say, is fighting with England against Hitler and the Nazis for democracy and liberty."

"And you don't believe that?" Graham asked.

"I believe that *the peoples* of France and England are so fighting, but is that the same thing? I think of Briey and wonder. Those same newspapers once told me that the Germans were not taking ore from the Briey mines and that all was well. I am an invalid of the last war. I do not have to fight in this one. But I can think."

His wife laughed again. "Ha! It will be different when he gets to France again. He talks like a fool but you should take no notice, Messieurs. He is a good Frenchman. He won the Croix de Guerre."

He winked. "A little piece of silver outside the chest to serenade the little piece of steel inside, eh? It is the women, I think, who should fight these wars. They are more ferocious as patriots than the men."

"And what do you think, Mr. Kuvetli?" said Graham.

"Me? Ah, please!" Mr. Kuvetli looked apologetic. "I am neutral, you understand. I know nothing. I have no opinion." He spread out his hands. "I sell tobacco. Export business. That is enough."

The Frenchman's eyebrows went up. "Tobacco? So? I arranged a great deal of transport for the tobacco companies. What company is that?"

"Pazar of Istanbul."

"Pazar?" Mathis looked slightly puzzled. "I don't think . . ."

But Mr. Kuvetli interrupted him. "Ah! See! There is Greece!"

They looked. There, sure enough, was Greece. It looked like a low bank of cloud on the horizon beyond the end of the golden line of Makronisi, a line that was contracting slowly as the ship ploughed on its way through the Zea channel.

"Beautiful day!" enthused Mr. Kuvetli. "Magnificent!" He drew a deep breath and exhaled loudly. "I anticipate very much to see Athens. We get to Piræus at two o'clock."

"Are you and Madame going ashore?" said Graham to Mathis.

"No, I think not. It is too short a time." He turned his coat collar up and shivered. "I agree that it is a beautiful day, but it is cold."

"If you did not stand talking so much," said his wife, "you would keep warm. And you have no scarf."

"Very well, very well!" he said irritably. "We will go below. Excuse us, please."

"I think that I, too, will go," said Mr. Kuvetli. "Are you coming down, Mr. Graham?"

"I'll stay a little." He would have enough of Mr. Kuvetli later.

"Then at two o'clock."

"Yes."

When they had gone he looked at his watch, saw that it was eleven-thirty, and made up his mind to walk round the boat deck ten times before he went down for a drink. He was, he decided as he began to walk, a good deal better for his night's rest. For one thing, his hand had ceased throbbing and he could bend the fingers a little, without pain. More important, however, was the fact that the feeling of moving in a nightmare which he had had the previous day had now gone. He felt whole again and cheerful. Yesterday was years away. There was, of course, his bandaged hand to remind him of it but the wound no longer seemed significant. Yesterday it had been a part of something horrible. To-day it was a cut on the back of his hand, a cut which would take a few days to heal. Meanwhile he was on his way home, back to his work. As for Mademoiselle Josette, he had had, fortunately, enough sense left not to behave really stupidly. That he should actually have wanted, even momentarily, to kiss her was fantastic enough. However, there were extenuating circumstances. He had been tired and confused; and, while she was a woman whose needs and methods of fulfilling them were only too apparent, she was undeniably attractive in a blowzy way.

He had completed his fourth circuit when the subject of these reflections appeared on the deck. She had on a camel hair coat instead of the fur, a green cotton scarf round her head in place of the woollen one, and wore sports shoes with cork "platform" soles. She waited for him to come over to her.

He smiled and nodded. "Good morning."

She raised her eyebrows. "Good morning! Is that all you have to say?"

He was startled. "What should I say?"

"You have disappointed me. I thought that all Englishmen got out of bed early to eat a great English breakfast. I get out of bed at ten but you are nowhere to be found. The steward says that you are still in your cabin."

"Unfortunately they don't serve English breakfasts on this boat. I made do with coffee and drank it in bed."

She frowned. "Now, you do not ask why I wished to see you. Is it so natural that I should wish to see you as soon as I left my bed?"

The mock severity was appalling. Graham said: "I'm afraid I didn't take you seriously. Why *should* you want to find me?"

"Ah, that is better. It is not good but it is better. Are you going into Athens this afternoon?"

"Yes."

"I wished to ask you if you would let me come with you."

"I see. I should be ... "

"But now it is too late."

"I'm so sorry," said Graham happily. "I should have been delighted to take you."

She shrugged. "It is too late. Mr. Kuvetli, the little Turk, has asked me and, *faut de mieux*, I accepted. I do not like him but he knows Athens very well. It will be interesting."

"Yes, I should think it would be."

"He is a very interesting man."

"Evidently."

"Of course, I might be able to persuade him ... "

"Unfortunately, there is a difficulty. Last night Mr. Kuvetli asked me if I minded his going with me as he had never been in Athens before."

It gave him a great deal of pleasure to say it; but she was disconcerted only momentarily. She burst out laughing.

"You are not at all polite. Not at all. You let me say what you know to be untrue. You do not stop me. You are unkind." She laughed again. "But it is a good joke."

"I'm really very sorry."

"You are too kind. I wished only to be friendly to you. I do not care whether I go to Athens or not."

"I'm sure Mr. Kuvetli would be delighted if you came with us. So should I, of course. You probably know a great deal more about Athens than I do."

Her eyes narrowed suddenly. "What, please, do you mean by that?"

He had not meant anything at all beyond the plain statement. He said, with a smile that he intended to be reassuring: "I mean that you have probably danced there."

She stared at him sullenly for a moment. He felt the

smile, still clinging fatuously to his lips, fading. She said slowly: "I do not think I like you as much as I thought. I do not think that you understand me at all."

"It's possible. I've known you for such a short time."

"Because a woman is an artiste," she said angrily, "you think that she must be of the *milieu*."

"Not at all. The idea hadn't occurred to me. Would you like to walk round the deck?"

She did not move. "I am beginning to think that I do not like you at all."

"I'm sorry. I was looking forward to your company on the journey."

"But you have Mr. Kuvetli," she said viciously.

"Yes, that's true. Unfortunately, he's not as attractive as you are."

She laughed sarcastically. "Oh, you have seen that I am attractive? That is very good. I am so pleased. I am honoured."

"I seem to have offended you," he said. "I apologise."

She waved one hand airily. "Do not trouble. I think that it is perhaps because you are stupid. You wish to walk. Very well, we will walk."

"Splendid."

They had taken three steps when she stopped and faced him. "Why do you have to take this little Turk to Athens?" she demanded. "Tell him that you cannot go. If you were polite you would do that."

"And take you? Is that the idea?"

"If you asked me, I would go with you. I am bored with this ship and I like to speak English."

"I'm afraid that Mr. Kuvetli might not think it so polite."

"If you liked me it would not matter to you about Mr. Kuvetli." She shrugged. "But I understand. It does not matter. I think that you are very unkind, but it does not matter. I am bored."

"I'm sorry."

"Yes, you are sorry. That is all right. But I am still bored. Let us walk." And then, as they began to walk: "José thinks that you are indiscreet."

"Does he? Why?"

"That old German you talked to. How do you know that he is not a spy?"

He laughed outright. "A spy! What an extraordinary idea!"

She glanced at him coldly. "And why is it extraordinary?"

"If you had talked to him you would know quite well that he couldn't possibly be anything of the sort."

"Perhaps not. José is always very suspicious of people. He always believes that they are lying about themselves."

"Frankly, I should be inclined to accept José's disapproval of a person as a recommendation."

"Oh, he does not disapprove. He is just interested. He likes to find things out about people. He thinks that we are all animals. He is never shocked by anything people do."

"He sounds very stupid."

"You do not understand José. He does not think of good things and evil things as they do in the convent, but only of things. He says that a thing that is good for one person may be evil for another, so that it is stupid to talk of good and evil."

"But people sometimes do good things simply because those things *are* good."

"Only because they feel nice when they do them—that is what José says."

"What about the people who stop themselves from doing evil because it *is* evil?"

"José says that if a person *really* needs to do something he will not trouble about what others may think of him. If he is really hungry, he will steal. If he is in real danger, he will kill. If he is really afraid, he will be cruel. He says that it was people who were safe and well fed who invented good and evil so that they would not have to worry about the people who were hungry and unsafe. What a man does depends on what he needs. It is simple. You are not a murderer. You say that murder is evil. José would say that you are as much a murderer as Landru or Weidmann and that it is just that fortune has not made it necessary for you to murder anyone. Someone once told him that there was a German proverb which said that a man is an ape in velvet. He always likes to repeat it."

"And do you agree with José? I don't mean about my being a potential murderer. I mean about why people are what they are."

"I do not agree or disagree. I do not care. For me, some people are nice, some people are sometimes nice and others are not at all nice." She looked at him out of the corners of her eyes. "You are sometimes nice."

"What do you think about yourself?"

She smiled. "Me? Oh, I am sometimes nice, too. When people are nice to me, I am a little angel." She added: "José thinks that he is as clever as God."

"Yes, I can see that he would."

"You do not like him. I am not surprised. It is only the old women who like José."

"Do *you* like him?"

"He is my partner. With us it is business."

"Yes, you told me that before. But do you *like* him?"

"He makes me laugh sometimes. He says amusing things about people. You remember Serge? José said that Serge would steal straw from his mother's kennel. It made me laugh very much."

"It must have done. Would you like a drink now?"

She looked at a small silver watch on her wrist and said that she would.

They went down. One of the ship's officers was leaning by the bar with a beer in his hand, talking to the steward. As Graham ordered the drinks, the officer turned his attention to Josette. He obviously counted on being successful with women: his dark eyes did not leave hers while he was talking to her. Graham, listening to the Italian with bored incomprehension, was ignored. He was content to be ignored. He got on with his drink. It was not until the gong sounded for lunch and Haller came in that he remembered that he had done nothing about changing his place at table.

The German nodded in a friendly way as Graham sat down beside him. "I did not expect to have your company to-day."

"I completely forgot to speak to the steward. If you . . ."

"No, please. I take it as a compliment."

"How is your wife?"

"Better, though she is not yet prepared to face a meal. But she took a walk this morning. I showed her the sea. This is the way Xerxes' great ships sailed to their defeat at Salamis. For those Persians that grey mass on the horizon was the country of Themistocles and the Attic Greeks of Marathon. You will think that it is my German sentimentality but I must say that the fact that for me that grey mass is the country of Venizelos and Metaxas is as regrettable as it could be. I was at the German Institute in Athens for several years when I was young."

"Shall you go ashore this afternoon?"

"I do not think so. Athens can only remind me of

what I know already—that I am old. Do you know the city?"

"A little. I know Salamis better."

"That is now their big naval base, isn't it?"

Graham said yes rather too carelessly. Haller glanced sideways and smiled slightly. "I beg your pardon. I see that I am on the point of being indiscreet."

"I shall go ashore to get some books and cigarettes. Can I get anything for you?"

"It is very kind of you, but there is nothing. Are you going alone?"

"Mr. Kuvetli, the Turkish gentleman at the next table, has asked me to show him round. He has never been to Athens."

Haller raised his eyebrows. "Kuvetli? So that is his name. I talked with him this morning. He speaks German quite well and knows Berlin a little."

"He speaks English, too, and very good French. He seems to have travelled a lot."

Haller grunted. "I should have thought that a Turk who had travelled a lot would have been to Athens."

"He sells tobacco. Greece grows its own tobacco."

"Yes, of course. I had not thought of that. I am apt to forget that most people who travel do so not to see but to sell. I talked with him for twenty minutes. He has a way of talking without saying anything. His conversation consists of agreements or indisputable statements."

"I suppose it's something to do with his being a salesman. 'The world is my customer and the cutomer is always right.'"

"He interests me. In my opinion he is too simple to be true. The smile is a little too stupid, the conversation a little too evasive. He tells you some things about himself within the first minutes of your meeting him and then tells you no more. That is curious. A man

98

who begins by telling you about himself usually goes on doing so. Besides, who ever heard of a simple Turkish business man? No, he makes me think of a man who has set out to create a definite impression of himself in people's minds. He is a man who wishes to be underrated."

"But why? He's not selling us tobacco."

"Perhaps, as you suggest, he regards the world as his cutomer. But you will have an opportunity of probing a little this afternoon." He smiled. "You see, I assume, quite unwarrantably, that you are interested. I must ask your pardon. I am a bad traveller who has had to do a great deal of travelling. To pass the time I have learned to play a game. I compare my own first impressions of my fellow travellers with what I can find out about them."

"If you are right you score a point? If you are wrong you lose one?"

"Precisely. Actually I enjoy losing more than winning. It is an old man's game, you see."

"And what is your impression of Señor Gallindo?"

Haller frowned. "I am afraid that I am only too right about that gentleman. He is not really very interesting."

"He has a theory that all men are potential murderers and is fond of quoting a German proverb to the effect that a man is an ape in velvet."

"It does not surprise me," was the acid reply. "Every man must justify himself somehow."

"Aren't you a little severe?"

"Perhaps. I regret to say that I find Señor Gallindo a very ill-mannered person."

Graham's reply was interrupted by the entrance of the man himself, looking as if he had just got out of bed. He was followed by the Italian mother and son. The conversation became desultory and over-polite.

The *Sestri Levante* was tied up alongside the new

wharf on the north side of the harbour of the Piræus soon after two o'clock. As, with Mr. Kuvetli, Graham stood on the deck waiting for the passenger gangway to be hoisted into position, he saw that Josette and José had left the saloon and where standing behind him. José nodded to them suspiciously as if he were afraid that they were thinking of borrowing money from him. The girl smiled. It was the tolerant smile that sees a friend disregarding good advice.

Mr. Kuvetli spoke up eagerly. "Are you going ashore, Monsieur-dame?"

"Why should we?" demanded José. "It is a waste of time to go."

But Mr. Kuvetli was not sensitive. "Ah! Then you know Athens, you and your wife?"

"Too well. It is a dirty town."

"I have not seen it. I was thinking that if you and Madame were going, we might all go together." He beamed round expectantly.

José set his teeth and rolled his eyes as if he were being tortured. "I have already said that we are *not* going."

"But it is very kind of you to suggest it," Josette put in graciously.

The Mathises came out of the saloon. "Ah!" he greeted them. "The adventurers! Do not forget that we leave at five. We shall not wait for you."

The gangway thudded into position and Mr. Kuvetli clambered down it nervously. Graham followed. He was beginning to wish that he had decided to stay on board. At the foot of the gangway he turned and looked up—the inevitable movement of a passenger leaving a ship. Mathis waved his hand.

"He is very amiable, Monsieur Mathis," said Mr. Kuvetli.

"Very."

Beyond the Customs shed there was a fly-blown old

Fiat landaulet with a notice on it in French, Italian, English and Greek, saying that an hour's tour of the sights and antiquities of Athens for four persons cost five hundred drachmes.

Graham stopped. He thought of the electric trains and trams he would have to clamber on to, of the hill up to the Acropolis, of the walking he would have to do, of the exhausting boredom of sightseeing on foot. Any way of avoiding the worst of it was, he decided, worth thirty shillingsworth of drachmes.

"I think," he said, "that we will take this car."

Mr. Kuvetli looked worried. "There is no other way? It is very expensive."

"That's all right. I'll pay."

"But it is you who do favour to me. I must pay."

"Oh, I should have taken a car in any case. Five hundred drachmes is not really expensive."

Mr. Kuvetli's eyes opened very wide. "Five hundred? But that is for four persons. We are two."

Graham laughed. "I doubt if the driver will look at it that way. I don't suppose it costs him any less to take two instead of four."

Mr. Kuvetli looked apologetic. "I have little Greek. You will permit me to ask him?"

"Of course. Go ahead."

The driver, a predatory looking man wearing a suit several sizes too small for him and highly polished tan shoes without socks, had leapt out at their approach and was holding the door open. Now he began to shout. "*Allez! Allez! Allez!*" he exhorted them; "*très bon marché. Cinque-cento, solamente.*"

Mr. Kuvetli strode forward, a stout, grubby little Daniel going out to do battle with a lean Goliath in stained blue serge. He began to speak.

He spoke Greek fluently; there was no doubt of it. Graham saw the surprised look on the driver's face replaced by one of fury as a torrent of words poured

101

from Mr. Kuvetli's lips. He was disparaging the car. He began to point. He pointed to every defect in the thing from a patch of rust on the luggage grid to a small tear in the upholstery, from a crack in the windshield to a worn patch on the running board. He paused for breath and the angry driver seized the opportunity of replying. He shouted and thumped the door panels with his fist to emphasise his remarks and made long streamlining gestures. Mr. Kuvetli smiled sceptically and returned to the attack. The driver spat on the ground and counterattacked. Mr. Kuvetli replied with a short, sharp burst of fire. The driver flung up his hands, disgusted, but defeated.

Mr. Kuvetli turned to Graham. "Price," he reported simply, "is now three hundred drachmes. It is too much, I think, but it will take time to reduce more. But if you think . . ."

"It seems a very fair price," said Graham hurriedly.

Mr. Kuvetli shrugged. "Perhaps. It could be reduced more, but . . ." He turned and nodded to the driver, who suddenly grinned broadly. They got into the cab.

"Did you say," said Graham, as they drove off, "that you had never been in Greece before?"

Mr. Kuvetli's smile was bland. "I know little Greek," he said. "I was born in Izmir."

The tour began. The Greek drove fast and with dash, twitching the wheel playfully in the direction of slow moving pedestrians, so that they had to run for their lives, and flinging a running commentary over his right shoulder as he went. They stopped for a moment on the road by the Theseion and again on the Acropolis where they got out and walked round. Here, Mr. Kuvetli's curiosity seemed inexhaustible. He insisted on a century by century history of the Parthenon and prowled round the museum as if he would have liked to spend the rest of the day there;

but at last they got gack into the car and were whisked round to the theatre of Dionysos, the arch of Hadrian, the Olympieion, and the Royal Palace. It was, by now, four o'clock and Mr. Kuvetli had been asking questions and saying "very nice" and "*formidable*" for well over the allotted hour. At Graham's suggestion they stopped in the Syntagma, changed some money and paid off the driver, adding that if he liked to wait in the square he could earn another fifty drachmes by driving them back to the wharf later. The driver agreed. Graham bought his cigarettes and books and sent his telegram. There was a band playing on the terrace of one of the cafés when they got back to the square and at Mr. Kuvetli's suggestion they sat down at a table to drink coffee before returning to the port.

Mr. Kuvetli surveyed the square regretfully. "It is very nice," he said with a sigh. "One would like to stay longer. So many magnificent ruins we have seen!"

Graham remembered what Haller had said at lunch about Mr. Kuvetli's evasions. "What is your favourite city, Mr. Kuvetli?"

"Ah, that is difficult to say. All cities have their magnificences. I like all cities." He breathed the air. "It is most kind of you to bring me here to-day, Mr. Graham."

Graham stuck to the point. "A great pleasure. But surely you have some preference."

Mr. Kuvetli looked anxious. "It is so difficult. I like London very much."

"Personally I like Paris better."

"Ah, yes. Paris is also magnificent."

Feeling rather baffled, Graham sipped his coffee. Then he had another idea. "What do you think of Señor Gallindo, Mr. Kuvetli?"

"Señor Gallindo? It is so difficult. I do not know him. His manner is strange."

103

"His manner," said Graham, "is damnably offensive. Don't you agree?"

"I do not like Señor Gallindo very much," conceded Mr. Kuvetli. "But he is Spanish."

"What can that have to do with it? The Spanish are an exceedingly polite race."

"Ah, I have not been to Spain." He looked at his watch. "It is quarter-past four now. Perhaps we should go, eh? It has been very nice this afternoon."

Graham nodded wearily. If Haller wanted Mr. Kuvetli "probed" he could do the probing hismelf. His, Graham's, personal opinion was that Mr. Kuvetli was an ordinary bore whose conversation, such as it was, sounded a little unreal because he used languages with which he was unfamiliar.

Mr. Kuvetli insisted on paying for the coffee; Mr. Kuvetli insisted on paying the fare back to the wharf. By a quarter to five they were on board again. An hour later Graham stood on deck watching the pilot's boat chugging back towards the greying land. The Frenchman, Mathis, who was leaning on the rail a few feet away, turned his head.

"Well, that's *that!* Two more days and we shall be in Genoa. Did you enjoy your excursion ashore this afternoon, Monsieur?"

"Oh, yes, thank you. It was ... "

But he never finished telling Monsieur Mathis what it was. A man had come out of the saloon door some yards away and was standing blinking at the setting sun which streamed across the sea towards them.

"Ah, yes," said Mathis. "We have acquired another passenger. He arrived while you were ashore this afternoon. I expect that he is a Greek."

Graham did not, could not, answer. He knew that the man standing there with the golden light of the sun on his face was not a Greek. He knew, too, that beneath the dark grey raincoat the man wore there was a crumpled brown suit with lumpy padded shoulders; that below the high-crowned soft hat and above the pale, doughy features with the self-conscious mouth was thinning curly hair. He knew that this man's name was Banat.

CHAPTER VI

GRAHAM stood there motionless. His body was tingling as if some violent mechanical shock had been transmitted to it through his heels. He heard Mathis' voice a long way away, asking him what the matter was.

He said: "I don't feel well. Will you excuse me, please?"

He saw apprehension flicker over the Frenchman's face and thought: "He thinks I'm going to be sick." But he did not wait for Mathis to say anything. He turned and, without looking again at the man by the saloon door, walked to the door at the other end of the deck and went below to his cabin.

He locked the door when he got inside. He was shaking from head to foot. He sat down on the bunk and tried to pull himself together. He told himself: "There's no need to get worried. There's a way out of this. You've got to think."

Somehow Banat had discovered that he was on the *Sestri Levante*. It could not have been very difficult. An inquiry made at the Wagon-Lit and shipping company offices would have been enough. The man had

106

then taken a ticket for Sofia, left the train when it crossed the Greek frontier, and taken another train via Salonika to Athens.

He pulled Kopeikin's telegram out of his pocket and stared at it. "All well!" The fools! The bloody fools! He'd distrusted this ship business from the start. He ought to have relied on his instinct and insisted on seeing the British Consul. If it had not been for that conceited imbecile Haki . . . But now he was caught like a rat in a trap. Banat wouldn't miss twice. My God, no! The man was a professional murderer. He would have his reputation to consider—to say nothing of his fee.

A curious but vaguely familiar feeling began to steal over him: a feeling that was dimly associated with the smell of antiseptics and the singing of a kettle. With a sudden rush of horror, he remembered. It had happened years ago. They had been trying out an experimental fourteen-inch gun on the proving ground. The second time they fired it, it had burst. There had been something wrong with the breech mechanism. It had killed two men outright and badly injured a third. This third man had looked like a great clot of blood lying there on the concrete. But the clot of blood had screamed: screamed steadily until the ambulance had come and a doctor had used a hypodermic. It had been a thin, high, inhuman sound; just like the singing of a kettle. The doctor had said that the man was unconscious even though he was screaming. Before they had examined the remains of the gun, the concrete had been swabbed down with a solution of lysol. He hadn't eaten any lunch. In the afternoon it had begun to rain. He . . .

He realised suddenly that he was swearing. The words were dropping from his lips in a steady stream: a meaningless succession of obscenities. He stood up quickly. He was losing his head. Something had got to

107

be done; and done quickly. If he could get off the ship . . .

He wrenched the cabin door open and went out into the alleyway. The Purser was the man to see first. The Purser's office was on the same deck. He went straight to it.

The door of the office was ajar and the Purser, a tall, middle-aged Italian with the stump of a cigar in his mouth, was sitting in his shirt-sleeves before a typewriter and a stack of copies of Bills of Lading. He was copying details of the Bills on the ruled sheet in the typewriter. He looked up with a frown as Graham knocked. He was busy.

"*Signore?*"

"Do you speak English?"

"No, *signore.*"

"French?"

"Yes. What is it you wish?"

"I want to see the Captain at once."

"For what reason, Monsieur?"

"It is absolutely necessary that I am put ashore immediately."

The Purser put his cigar down and turned in his swivel chair.

"My French is not very good," he said calmly. "Do you mind repeating . . . ?"

"I want to be put ashore."

"Monsieur Graham, is it?"

"Yes."

"I regret, Monsieur Graham. It is too late. The pilot boat has gone. You should have . . . "

"I know. But it is absolutely necessary that I go ashore now. No, I am not mad. I realise that under ordinary circumstances it would be out of the question. But the circumstances are exceptional. I am ready to pay for the loss of time and the inconvenience caused."

The Purser looked bewildered. "But why? Are you ill?"

"No, I . . ." He stopped and could have bitten his tongue off. There was no doctor aboard and the threat of some infectious disease might have been sufficient. But it was too late now. "If you will arrange for me to see the Captain at once, I will explain why. I can assure you that my reasons are good ones."

"I am afraid," said the Purser stiffly, "that it is out of the question. You do not understand . . ."

"All I am asking," interrupted Graham desperately, "is that you put back a short way and ask for a pilot boat. I am willing and able to pay."

The Purser smiled in an exasperated way. "This is a ship, Monsieur, not a taxi. We carry cargo and run to a schedule. You are not ill and . . ."

"I have already said that my reasons are excellent. If you will allow me to see the Captain . . ."

"It is quite useless to argue, Monsieur. I do not doubt your willingness or ability to pay the cost of a boat from the harbour. Unfortunately that is not the important thing. You say that you are not ill but that you have reasons. As you can only have thought of those reasons within the last ten minutes, you must not be angry if I say that they cannot be of very grave importance. Let me assure you, Monsieur, that nothing but proved and evident reasons of life and death will suffice to stop any ship for the convenience of one passenger. Naturally, if you can give me any such reasons I will place them before the Captain immediately. If not, then I am afraid your reasons must wait until we get to Genoa."

"I assure you . . ."

The Purser smiled sorrowfully. "I do not question the good faith of your assurances, Monsieur, but I regret to say that we need more than assurances."

"Very well," snapped Graham, "since you insist on

details I will tell you. I have just found that there is a man on this ship who is here for the express purpose of murdering me."

The Purser's face went blank. "Indeed, Monsieur?"

"Yes, I . . ." Something in the man's eyes stopped him. "I suppose you've decided that I'm either mad or drunk," he concluded.

"Not at all, Monsieur." But what he was thinking was as plain as a pikestaff. He was thinking that Graham was just another of the poor lunatics with whom his work sometimes brought him in contact. They were a nuisance, because they wasted time. But he was tolerant. It was useless to be angry with a lunatic. Besides, dealing with them always seemed to emphasise his own sanity and intelligence: the sanity and intelligence which, had the owners been less short sighted, would long ago have taken him to a seat on the board of directors. And they made good stories to tell his friends when he got home. "Imagine, Beppo! There was this Englishman, looking sane but really mad. He thought that someone was trying to murder him! Imagine! It is the whisky, you know. I said to him . . . " But meanwhile he would have to be humoured, to be dealt with tactfully. "Not at all, Monsieur," he repeated.

Graham began to lose control of his temper. "You asked me for my reasons. I am giving them to you."

"And I am listening carefully, Monsieur."

"There is someone on this ship who is here to murder me."

"And his name, Monsieur?"

"Banat. B-A-N-A-T. He is a Roumanian. He . . . "

"One moment, Monsieur." The Purser got a sheet of paper out of a drawer and ran a pencil down the names on it with ostentatious care. Then he looked up. "There is no one of that name or nationality on the ship, Monsieur."

"I was about to tell you, when you interrupted me, that the man is travelling on a false passport."

"Then, please . . ."

"He is the passenger who came aboard this afternoon."

The Purser looked at the paper again. "Cabin number nine. That is Monsieur Mavrodopoulos. He is a Greek business man."

"That may be what his passport says. His real name is Banat and he is a Roumanian."

The Purser remained polite with obvious difficulty. "Have you any proof of that, Monsieur?"

"If you radio Colonel Haki of the Turkish police at Istanbul, he will confirm what I say."

"This is an Italian ship, Monsieur. We are not in Turkish territorial waters. We can refer such a matter only to the Italian police. In any case, we carry wireless only for navigational purposes. This is not the *Rex* or the *Conte di Savoia*, you understand. This matter must be left until we reach Genoa. The police there will deal with your accusation concerning the passport."

"I don't care a damn about his passport," said Graham violently. "I'm telling you that the man intends to kill me."

"And why?"

"Because he has been paid to do so; that is why. Now do you understand?"

The Purser got to his feet. He had been tolerant. Now the time had come to be firm. "No, Monsieur, I do *not* understand."

"Then if you cannot understand, let me speak to the Captain."

"That will not be necessary, Monsieur. I understand enough." He looked Graham in the eyes. "In my opinion there are two *charitable* explanations of this matter. Either you have mistaken this Monsieur Mavrodopoulos for someone else, or you have had a bad dream. If it is the former, I advise you not to repeat your mistake to anyone else. I am discreet, but if Monsieur Mavrodopoulos should hear of it he might regard it as a reflection upon his honour. If it is the second, I suggest that you lie down in your cabin for a while. And remember that nobody is going to murder you on this ship. There are too many people about."

"But don't you see . . . ?" shouted Graham.

"I see," said the Purser grimly, "that there is another less charitable explanation of this matter. You may have invented this story simply because for some private reason you wish to be put ashore. If that is true, I am sorry. It is a ridiculous story. In any case, the ship stops at Genoa and not before. And now, if you will excuse me, I have work to do."

"I demand to see the Captain."

"If you will close the door as you leave," said the Purser happily.

Almost sick with anger and fear, Graham went back to his cabin.

He lit a cigarette and tried to think reasonably. He should have gone straight to the Captain. He could still go straight to the Captain. For a moment he considered doing so. If he . . . But it would be useless and unnecessarily humiliating. The Captain, even if he could get to him and make him understand, would probably receive his story with even less sympathy. And he would still have no proof that what he said was true. Even if he could persuade the Captain that there was some truth in what he was saying, that he was not, in fact, suffering from some form of delusional insanity, the answer would be the same: "Nobody is going to murder you on this ship. There are too many people about."

Too many people about! They did not know Banat.

The man who had walked into a police official's house in broad daylight, shot the official and his wife and then calmly walked out again, was not going to be unnerved so easily. Passengers had disappeared from ships in mid-ocean before. Sometimes their bodies had been washed ashore, and sometimes they hadn't. Sometimes the disappearances had been explained, and sometimes they hadn't. What would there be to connect this disappearance of an English engineer (who had behaved very queerly) from a ship at sea with Mr. Mavrodopoulos, a Greek business man? Nothing. And even if the body of the English engineer were washed ashore before the fish had rendered it unidentifiable and it were found that he had been killed before he had entered the water, who was going to prove that Mr. Mavrodopoulos—if by that time there were anything left of Mr. Mavrodopoulos but the ashes of his passport—had been responsible for the killing? Nobody.

He thought of the telegram he had sent in Athens that afternoon. "Home Monday," he had said. Home Monday! He looked at his unbandaged hand and moved the fingers of it. By Monday they could be dead and beginning to decompose with the rest of the entity which called itself Graham. Stephanie would be upset, but she'd get over it quickly. She was resilient and sensible. But there wouldn't' be much money for her. She'd have to sell the house. He should have taken out more insurance. If only he'd known. But of course it was just because you *didn't* know, that there *were* such things as insurance companies. Still, he could do nothing now but hope that it would be over quickly, that it wouldn't be painful.

He shivered and began to swear again. Then he pulled himself up sharply. He'd *got* to think of some way out. And not only for his own sake and Stephanie's. There was the job he had to do. "It is in the

interests of your country's enemies that when the
snow melts and the rain ceases, Turkish naval
strength shall be exactly what it is now. They will do
anything to see that it is so." Anything! Behind Banat
was the German agent in Sofia and behind him was
Germany and the Nazis. Yes, he'd *got* to think of
some way out. If other Englishmen could die for their
country, surely he could manage to stay alive for it.
Then another of Colonel Haki's statements came back
to him. "You have advantages over the soldier. You
have only to defend yourself. You do not have to go
into the open. You may run away without being a
coward."

Well he couldn't run away now; but the rest of it
was true enough. He didn't have to go out into the
open. He could stay here in the cabin; have his meals
here; keep the door locked. He could defend himself,
too, if need be. Yes, by God! He had Kopeikin's
revolver.

He had put it among the clothes in his suitcase.
Now, thanking his stars that he had not refused to
take it, he got it out and weighed it in his hand.

For Graham a gun was a series of mathematical
expressions resolved in such a way as to enable one
man, by touching a button, to project an armour-
piercing shell so that it hit a target several miles away
plumb in the middle. It was a piece of machinery no
more and no less significant than a vacuum cleaner or
a bacon slicer. It had no nationality and no loyalties.
It was neither awe-inspiring nor symbolic of anything
except the owner's ability to pay for it. His interest in
the men who had to fire the products of his skill as in
the men who had to suffer their fire (and, thanks to
his employer's tireless internationalism, the same sets
of men often had to do both) had always been de-
tached. To him who knew what even one four-inch
shell could accomplish in the way of destruction, it

114

seemed that they should be—could only be—nerveless cyphers. That they were not was an evergreen source of astonishment to him. His attitude towards them was as uncomprehending as that of the stoker of a crematorium towards the solemnity of the grave.

But this revolver was different. It wasn't impersonal. There was a relationship between it and the human body. It had, perhaps, an effective range of twenty-five yards or less. That meant that you could see the face of the man at whom you fired it both before and after you fired it. You could see and hear his agony. You couldn't think of honour and glory with a revolver in your hand, but only of killing and being killed. There was no machine to serve. Life and death were there in your hand in the shape of an elementary arrangement of springs and levers and a few grammes of lead and cordite.

He had never handled a revolver in his life before. He examined it carefully. Stamped above the trigger guard was "Made in U.S.A." and the name of an American typewriter manufacturer. There were two small sliding bosses on the other side. One was the safety catch. The other, when moved, released the breech which dropped sideways and showed that there were cartridges in all six chambers. It was beautifully made. He took the cartridges out and pulled the trigger once or twice experimentally. It was not easy with his bandaged hand, but it could be done. He put the cartridges back.

He felt better now. Banat might be a professional killer, but he was as susceptible to bullets as any other man. And *he* had to make the first move. One had to look at things from his point of view. He'd failed in Istanbul and he'd had to catch up with the victim again. He'd managed to get aboard the boat on which the victim was travelling. But did that really help him very much? What he had done in Roumania as a member of the Iron Guard was beside the point now. A man could afford to be bold when he was protected by an army of thugs and an intimidated judge. It was true that passengers were sometimes lost off ships at sea; but those ships were big liners, not two thousand ton cargo boats. It really would be very difficult to kill a man on a boat of that size without anyone discovering that you had done so. You might be able to do it; that is if you could get your victim alone on deck at night. You could knife him and push him over the side. But you would have to get him there first, and there was more than a chance that you would be seen from the bridge. Or heard: a knifed man might make a lot of noise before he reached the water. And if you cut his throat there would be a lot of blood left behind to be accounted for. Besides, that was always assuming that you could use a knife so skilfully. Banat was a gunman, not a cut-throat. That confounded Purser was right. There were too many people about for anyone to murder him on the ship. As long as he was careful he would be all right. The real danger would begin when he got off the ship at Genoa.

Obviously the thing for him to do there would be to go straight to the British Consul, explain all the circumstances, and secure police protection as far as the frontier. Yes, that was it. He had one priceless advantage over the enemy. *Banat did not know that he was identified.* He would be assuming that the victim was unsuspecting, that he could bide his time, that he could do his work between Genoa and the French frontier. By the time he discovered his mistake it would be too late for him to do anything about rectifying it. The only thing now was to see that he did not discover the mistake too soon.

Supposing, for instance, that Banat had noticed his

hasty retreat from the deck. His blood ran cold at the idea. But no, the man had not been looking. The supposition showed, though, how careful he had to be. It was out of the question for him to skulk in his cabin for the rest of the trip. That would arouse immediate suspicion. He would have to look as unsuspecting as he could and yet take care not to expose himself to any sort of attack. He must make sure that if he were not in his cabin with the door locked, he was with or near one of the other passengers. He must even be amiable to "Monsieur Mavrodopoulos."

He unbuttoned his jacket and put the revolver in his hip pocket. It bulged absurdly and uncomfortably. He took the wallet out of his breast pocket and put the revolver there. That was uncomfortable, too, and the shape of it could be seen from the outside. Banat must not see that he was armed. The revolver could stay in the cabin.

He put it back in his suitcase and stood up, bracing himself. He'd go straight up to the saloon and have a drink now. If Banat were there, so much the better. A drink would help to ease the strain of the first encounter. He knew that it would be a strain. He had to face a man who had tried once to kill him and who was going to try again, and behave as if he had never seen or heard of him before. His stomach was already responding to the prospect. But he had to keep calm. His life, he told himself, might depend on his behaving normally. And the longer he hung about thinking it over, the less normal he would be. Better get it over with now.

He lit a cigarette, opened the cabin door and went straight upstairs to the saloon.

Banat was not there. He could have laughed aloud with relief. Josette and José were there with drinks in front of them, listening to Mathis.

"And so," he was saying vehemently, "it goes on.

The big newspapers of the Right are owned by those whose interest it is to see that France spends her wealth on arms and that the ordinary people do not understand too much of what goes on behind the scenes. I am glad to be going back to France because it is my country. But do not ask me to love those who have my country in the palms of their hands. Ah, no!"

His wife was listening with tight-lipped disapproval. José was openly yawning. Josette was nodding sympathetically but her face lit up with relief when she saw Graham. "And where has our Englishman been?" she said immediately. "Mr. Kuvetli has told everyone what a magnificent time you both had."

"I've been in my cabin recovering from the afternoon's excitements."

Mathis did not look very pleased at the interruption but said agreeably enough: "I was afraid that you were ill, Monsieur. Are you better now?"

"Oh yes, thanks."

"You have been ill?" demanded Josette.

"I felt tired."

"It is the ventilation," said Madame Mathis promptly. "I myself have felt a nausea and a headache since I got on the ship. We should complain. But"—she made a derogatory gesture in the direction of her husband—"as long as he is comfortable all is well."

Mathis grinned. "Bah! It is seasickness."

"You are ridiculous. If I am sick it is of you."

José made a loud plopping noise with his tongue and leaned back in his chair, his closed eyes and tightened lips calling upon Heaven to deliver him from domesticity.

Graham ordered a whisky.

"Whisky?" José sat up whistling astonishment. "The Englishman drinks whisky?" he announced and then, pursing his lips and screwing up his face to express congenital aristocratic idiocy, added: "Some viskee, pliz, ol' bhoy!" He looked round, grinning, for applause.

"That is his idea of an Englishman," Josette explained. "He is very stupid."

"Oh I don't think so," said Graham; "he has never been to England. A great many English people who have never been to Spain are under the impression that all Spaniards smell of garlic."

Mathis giggled.

José half rose in his chair. "Do you intend to be insulting?" he demanded.

"Not at all. I was merely pointing out that these misconceptions exist. You, for instance, do not smell of garlic at all."

José subsided into his chair again. "I am glad to hear you say so," he said ominously. "If I thought . . ."

"Ah! Be silent!" Josette broke in. "You make yourself look a fool."

To Graham's relief the subject was disposed of by the entrance of Mr. Kuvetli. He was beaming happily.

"I come," he said to Graham, "to ask you to have drink with me."

"That's very good of you but I've just ordered a drink. Supposing you have one with me."

"Most kind. I will take vermouth, please." He sat down. "You have seen we have new passenger?"

"Yes, Monsieur Mathis pointed him out to me." He turned to the steward bringing him his whisky and ordered Mr. Kuvetli's vermouth.

"He is Greek gentleman. Name of Mavrodopoulos. He is business man."

"What business is he in?" Graham found, to his relief, that he could talk of Monsieur Mavrodopoulos quite calmly.

"That I do not know."

"That I do not care," said Josette. "I have just seen him. Ugh!"

119

"What's the matter with him?"

"She likes only men who look clean and simple," said José vindictively. "This Greek looks dirty. He would probably smell dirty too, but he uses a cheap perfume." He kissed his fingers to the air. *"Nuit de Petits Gars! Numero soixante-neuf! Cinq francs la bouteille."*

Madame Mathis' face froze.

"You are disgusting, José," said Josette. "Besides, your own perfume cost only fifty francs a bottle. It is filthy. And you must not say such things. You will offend Madame here who is not used to your jokes."

But Madame Mathis had already taken offence. "It is disgraceful," she said angrily, "that such things should be said when there are women present. With men alone it would not be polite."

"Ah yes!" said Mathis. "My wife and I are not hypocrites but there are some things that should not be said." He looked as if he were pleased to be able, for once, to side with his wife. Her surprise was almost pathetic. They proceeded to make the most of the occasion.

She said: "Monsieur Gallindo should apologise."

"I must insist," said Mathis, "that you apologise to my wife."

José stared at them in angry astonishment. "Apologise? What for?"

"He will apologise," said Josette. She turned to him and broke into Spanish. "Apologise, you dirty fool. Do you want trouble? Don't you see he's showing off to the woman? He would break you in pieces."

José shrugged. "Very well." He looked insolently at the Mathises. "I apologise. What for, I do not know, but I apologise."

"My wife accepts the apology," said Mathis stiffly. "It is not gracious but it is accepted."

"An officer says," remarked Mr. Kuvetli tactfully,

"that we shall not be able to see Messina because it will be dark."

But this elephantine change of subject was unnecessary for at that moment Banat came through the door from the promenade deck.

He stood there for an instant looking at them, his raincoat hanging open, his hat in his hand, like a man who has strayed into a picture gallery out of the rain. His white face was drawn from lack of sleep, there were circles under the small deep-set eyes, the full lips were twisted slightly as if he had a headache.

Graham's heart drummed sickeningly at the base of his skull. This was the executioner. The hand with the hat in it was the hand which had fired the shots which had grazed his own hand, now outstretched to pick up a glass of whisky. This was the man who had killed men for as little as five thousand francs and his expenses.

He felt the blood leaving his face. He had only glanced quickly at the man but the whole picture of him was in his mind; the whole picture from the dusty tan shoes to the new tie with the filthy soft collar and the tired, frowsty, stupid face. He drank some of his whisky and saw that Mr. Kuvetli was bestowing his smile on the newcomer. The others were staring blankly.

Banat walked slowly over to the bar.

"Bon soir, Monsieur," said Mr. Kuvetli.

"Bon soir." It was grunted almost inaudibly as if he were anxious not to commit himself to accepting something he did not want. He reached the bar and murmured something to the steward.

He had passed close to Madame Mathis and Graham saw her frown. Then he himself caught the smell of scent. It was attar of roses and very strong. He remembered Colonel Haki's question as to whether he had noticed any perfume in his room at the Adler-

Palace after the attacks. Here was the explanation. The man reeked of scent. The smell of it would stay with the things he touched.

"Are you going far, Monsieur?" said Mr. Kuvetli.

The man eyed him. "No. Genoa."

"It is a beautiful city."

Banat turned without answering to the drink the steward had poured out for him. He had not once looked at Graham.

"You are not looking well," said Josette severely. "I do not think you are sincere when you say that you are only tired."

"You are tired?" said Mr. Kuvetli in French. "Ah, it is my fault. Always with ancient monuments it is necessary to walk." He seemed to have given Banat up as a bad job.

"Oh, I enjoyed the walk."

"It is the ventilation," Madame Mathis repeated stubbornly.

"There *is*," conceded her husband, "a certain stuffiness." He addressed himself very pointedly to exclude José from his audience. "But what can one expect for so little money?"

"So little!" exclaimed José. "That is very good. It is quite expensive enough for me. I am not a millionaire."

Mathis flushed angrily. "There are more expensive ways of travelling from Istanbul to Genoa."

"There is always a more expensive way of doing anything," retorted José.

Josette said quickly: "My husband always exaggerates."

"Travelling is very expensive to-day," pronounced Kuvetli.

"But . . ."

The argument rambled on, pointless and stupid; a mask for the antagonism between José and the Mathises. Graham listened with half his mind. He knew

122

that sooner or later Banat must look at him and he wanted to see that look. Not that it would tell him anything that he did not already know, but he wanted to see it just the same. He could look at Mathis and yet see Banat out of the corner of his eye. Banat raised the glass of brandy to his lips and drank some of it; then, as he put the glass down, he looked directly at Graham.

Graham leaned back in his chair.

" ... but," Mathis was saying, "compare the service one receives. On the train there is a *couchette* in a compartment with others. One sleeps—perhaps. There is waiting at Belgrade for the coaches from Bucharest and at Trieste for the coaches from Budapest. There are passport examinations in the middle of the night and terrible food in the day. There is the noise and there is the dust and soot. I cannot conceive ..."

Graham drained his glass. Banat was inspecting him: secretly, as the hangman inspects the man whom he is to execute the following morning; mentally weighing him, looking at his neck, calculating the drop.

"Travelling is very expensive to-day," said Mr. Kuvetli again.

At that moment the dinner gong sounded. Banat put his glass down and went out of the room. The Mathises followed. Graham saw that Josette was looking at him curiously. He got to his feet. There was a smell of food coming from the kitchen. The Italian woman and her son came in and sat down at the table. The thought of food made him feel ill.

"You are sure you feel well?" said Josette as they went to the dinner tables. "You do not look it."

"Quite sure." He cast about desperately for something else to say and uttered the first words that came into his head: "Madame Mathis is right. The ventilation is not good. Perhaps we could walk on deck after dinner is over."

She raised her eyebrows. "Ah, now I know that you cannot be well! You are polite. But very well, I will go with you."

He smiled fatuously, went on to his table, and exchanged reserved greetings with the two Italians. It was not until he sat down that he noticed that an extra place had been laid beside them.

His first impulse was to get up and walk out. The fact that Banat was on the ship was bad enough: to have to eat at the same table would be intolerable. But everything depended upon his behaving normally. He would *have* to stay. He must try and think of Banat as Monsieur Mavrodopoulos, a Greek business man, whom he had never seen or heard of before. He must ...

Haller came in and sat down beside him. "Good evening, Mr. Graham. And did you enjoy Athens this afternoon?"

"Yes, thanks. Mr. Kuvetli was suitably impressed."

"Ah, yes, of course. You were doing duty as a guide. You must be feeling tired."

"To tell you the truth, my courage failed me. I hired a car. The chauffeur did the guiding. As Mr. Kuvetli speaks fluent Greek, the whole thing went off quite satisfactorily."

"He speaks Greek and yet he has never been to Athens?"

"It appears that he was born in Smyrna. Apart from that, I regret to say, I discovered nothing. My own private opinion is that he is a bore."

"That is disappointing. I had hopes ... However, it cannot be helped. To tell you the truth, I wished afterwards that I had come with you. You went up to the Parthenon, of course."

"Yes."

Haller smiled apologetically. "When you reach my age you sometimes think of the approach of death. I thought this afternoon how much I would have liked to have seen the Parthenon just once more. I doubt if I shall have another opportunity of doing so. I used to spend hours standing in the shade by the Propylæa looking at it and trying to understand the men who built it. I was young then and did not know how difficult it is for Western man to understand the dream-heavy classical soul. They are so far apart. The god of superlative shape has been replaced by the god of superlative force and between the two conceptions there is all space. The destiny idea symbolised by the Doric columns is incomprehensible to the children of Faust. For us . . . " He broke off. "Excuse me. I see that we have another passenger. I suppose that he is to sit here."

Graham forced himself to look up.

Banat had come in and was standing looking at the tables. The steward, carrying plates of soup, appeared behind him and motioned him towards the place next to the Italian woman. Banat approached, looked round the table, and sat down. He nodded to them, smiling slightly.

"Mavrodopoulos," he said. *"Je parle français un petit peu."*

His voice was toneless and husky and he spoke with a slight lisp. The smell of attar of roses came across the table.

Graham nodded distantly. Now that the moment had come he felt quite calm.

Haller's look of strangled disgust was almost funny. He said pompously: "Haller. Beside you are Signora and Signor Beronelli. This is Monsieur Graham."

Banat nodded to them again and said: "I have travelled a long way to-day. From Salonika."

Graham made an effort. "I should have thought,"

he said, "that it would have been easier to go to Genoa by train from Salonika." He felt oddly breathless as he said it and his voice sounded strange in his own ears.

There was a bowl of raisins in the centre of the table and Banat put some in his mouth before replying. "I don't like trains," he said shortly. He looked at Haller. "You are a German, Monsieur?"

Haller frowned. "I am."

"It is a good country, Germany." He turned his attention to Signora Beronelli. "Italy is good, too." He took some more raisins.

The woman smiled and inclined her head. The boy looked angry.

"And what," said Graham, "do you think about England?"

The small tired eyes stared into his coldly. "I have never seen England." The eyes wandered away round the table. "When I was last in Rome," he said, "I saw a magnificent parade of the Italian army with guns and armoured cars and aeroplanes." He swallowed his raisins. "The aeroplanes were a great sight and made one think of God."

"And why should they do that, Monsieur?" demanded Haller. Evidently he did not like Monsieur Mavrodopoulos.

"They made one think of God. That is all I know. You feel it in the stomach. A thunderstorm makes one think of God, too. But these aeroplanes were better than a storm. They shook the air like paper."

Watching the full self-conscious lips enunciating these absurdities, Graham wondered if an English jury, trying the man for murder, would find him insane. Probably not: he killed for money; and the Law did not think that a man who killed for money was insane. And yet he *was* insane. His was the insanity of the sub-conscious mind running naked, of the "throw back," of the mind which could discover the majesty of God in thunder and lightning, the roar of bombing planes, or the firing of a five-hundred pound shell; the awe-inspired insanity of the primæval swamp. Killing, for this man, *could* be a business. Once, no doubt, he had been surprised that people should be prepared to pay so handsomely for the doing of something they could do so easily for themselves. But, of course, he would have ended by concluding, with other successful business men, that he was cleverer than his fellows. His mental approach to the business of killing would be that of the lavatory attendant to the business of attending to his lavatories or of the stockbroker towards the business of taking his commission: purely practical.

"Are you going to Rome now?" said Haller politely. It was the heavy politeness of an old man with a young fool.

"I go to Genoa," said Banat.

"I understand," said Graham, "that the thing to see at Genoa is the cemetery."

Banat spat out a raisin seed. "That is so? Why?" Obviously, that sort of remark was not going to disconcert him.

"It is supposed to be very large, very well arranged, and planted with very fine cypresses."

"Perhaps I shall go."

The waiter brought soup. Haller turned rather ostentatiously to Graham and began once more to talk about the Parthenon. It seemed that he liked arranging his thoughts aloud. The resultant monologue demanded practically nothing of the listener but an occasional nod. From the Parthenon he wandered to pre-Hellenic remains, the Aryan hero tales, and the Vedic religion. Graham ate mechanically, listened, and watched Banat. The man put his food in his mouth as if he enjoyed it. Then, as he chewed, he would look round the room like a dog over a plate of scraps. There was something pathetic about him. He was—Graham realised it with a shock—pathetic in the way that a monkey, in its likeness to man, could be pathetic. He was not insane. He was an animal and dangerous.

The meal came to an end. Haller, as ususal, went to his wife. Thankful for the opportunity, Graham left at the same time, got his overcoat, and went out on deck.

The wind had dropped and the roll of the ship was long and slow. She was making good speed and the water sliding along her plates was hissing and bubbling as if they were red hot. It was a cold, clear night.

The smell of attar of roses was at the back of his throat and in his nostrils. He drew the fresh unscented air into his lungs with conscious pleasure. He was, he told himself, over the first hurdle. He had sat face to face with Banat and talked to him without giving himself away. The man could not possibly suspect that he was known and understood. The rest of it would be easy. He had only to keep his head.

There was a step behind him and he swung round quickly, his nerves jumping.

It was Josette. She came towards him smiling. "Ah! So this is your politeness. You ask me to walk with you, but you do not wait for me. I have to find you. You are very bad."

"I'm sorry. It was so stuffy in the saloon that ..."

"It is not at all stuffy in the saloon, as you know perfectly well." She linked her arm in his. "Now we will walk and you shall tell me what is *really* the matter."

He looked at her quickly. "What is *really* the matter! What do you mean?"

She became the *grande dame*. "So you are not

going to tell me. You will not tell me how you came to be on this ship. You will not tell me what has happened to-day to make you so nervous."

"Nervous! But . . ."

"Yes, Monsieur Graham, nervous!" She abandoned the *grande dame* with a shrug. "I am sorry but I have seen people who are afraid before. They do not look at all like people who are tired or people who feel faint in a stuffy room. They have a special look about them. Their faces look very small and grey round the mouth and they cannot keep their hands still." They had reached the stairs to the boat deck. She turned and looked at him. "Shall we go up?"

He nodded. He would have nodded if she had suggested that they jump overboard. He could think of only one thing. If *she* knew a frightened man when she saw one, then so did Banat. And if Banat had noticed. . . . But he couldn't have noticed. He couldn't. He . . .

They were on the boat deck now and she took his arm again.

"It is a very nice night," she said. "I am glad that we can walk like this. I was afraid this morning that I had annoyed you. I did not really wish to go to Athens. That officer who thinks he is so nice asked me to go with him but I did not. But I would have gone if you had asked me. I do not say that to flatter you. I tell you the truth."

"It's very kind of you," he muttered.

She mimicked him. " 'It's very kind of you.' Ah, you are so solemn. It is as if you did not like me."

He managed to smile. "Oh, I like you, all right."

"But you do not trust me? I understand. You see me dancing in Le Jockey Cabaret and you say, because you are so experienced: 'Ah! I must be careful of this lady.' Eh? But I am a friend. You are so silly."

"Yes, I am silly."

"But you *do* like me?"

"Yes, I like you." A stupid, fantastic suggestion was taking root in his mind.

"Then you must trust me, also."

"Yes, I must." It was absurd, of course. He couldn't trust her. Her motives were as transparent as the day. He couldn't trust anybody. He was alone; damnably alone. If he had someone to talk to about it, it wouldn't be so bad. Now supposing Banat had seen that he was nervous and concluded that he was on his guard. Had he or hadn't he seen? She could tell him that.

"What are you thinking about?"

"To-morrow." She said that she was a friend. If there was one thing he needed now, it was, God knew, a friend. Any friend. Someone to talk to, to discuss it with. Nobody knew about it but him. If anything happened to him there would be nobody to accuse Banat. He would go scot free to collect his wages. She was right. It was stupid to distrust her simply because she danced in night places. After all, Kopeikin had liked her and he was no fool about women.

They had reached the corner below the bridge structure. She stopped as he had known she would.

"If we stay here," she said, "I shall get cold. It will be better if we go on walking round and round and round the deck."

"I thought you wanted to ask me questions."

"I have told you I am not inquisitive."

"So you did. Do you remember that yesterday evening I told you that I came on this ship to avoid someone who was trying to shoot me and that this"— he held up his right hand—"was a bullet wound?"

"Yes. I remember. It was a bad joke."

"A very bad joke. Unfortunately, it happened to be true."

It was out now. He could not see her face but he heard her draw in her breath sharply and felt her fingers dig into his arm.

"You are lying to me."

"I'm afraid not."

"But you are an engineer," she said accusingly. "You said so. What have you done that someone should wish to kill you?"

"I have done nothing." He hesitated. "I just happen to be on important business. Some business competitors don't want me to return to England."

"Now you are lying."

"Yes, I am lying, but not very much. I *am* on important business and there *are* some people who do not want me to get back to England. They employed men to kill me while I was in Gallipoli but the Turkish police arrested these men before they could try. Then they employed a professional killer to do the job. When I got back to my hotel after I left Le Jockey Cabaret the other night, he was waiting for me. He shot at me and missed everything except my hand."

She was breathing quickly. "It is atrocious! A bestiality! Does Kopeikin know of it?"

"Yes. It was partly his idea that I should travel on this boat."

"But who are these people?"

"I only know of one. His name is Moeller and he lives in Sofia. The Turkish police told me that he is a German agent."

"The *salop!* But he cannot touch you now."

"Unfortunately he can. While I was ashore with Kuvetli this afternoon, another passenger came aboard."

"The little man who smells? Mavrodopoulos? But...."

"His real name is Banat and he is the professional killer who shot at me in Istanbul."

"But how do you know?" she demanded breathlessly.

"He was at Le Jockey Cabaret watching me. He had followed me there to see that I was out of the way before he broke into my room at the hotel. It was dark in the room when he shot at me, but the police showed me his photograph later and I identified him."

She was silent for a moment. Then she said slowly: "It is not very nice. That little man is a dirty type."

"No, it is not very nice."

"You must go to the Captain."

"Thanks. I've tried to see the Captain once. I got as far as the Purser. He thinks I'm either crazy, drunk, or lying."

"What are you going to do?"

"Nothing for the moment. He doesn't know that I know who he is. I think that he will wait until we get to Genoa before he tries again. When we get there I shall go to the British Consul and ask him to advise the police."

"But I think he *does* know that you suspect him. When we were in the *salone* before dinner and the Frenchman was talking about trains, this man was watching you. Mr. Kuvetli was watching you also. You looked so curious, you see."

His stomach turned over. "You mean, I suppose, that I looked frightened to death. I was frightened. I admit it. Why shouldn't I? I am not used to people trying to kill me." His voice had risen. He felt himself shaking with a sort of hysterical anger.

She gripped his arm again. "Ssh! You must not speak so loudly." And then: "Does it matter so much that he knows?"

"If he knows, it means that he will have to act before we get to Genoa."

"On this little ship? He would not dare." She paused. "José has a revolver in his box. I will try to get it for you."

"I've got a revolver."

"Where?"

"It's in my suitcase. It shows in my pocket. I did not want him to see that I knew I was in danger."

"If you carry the revolver you will be in no danger. Let him see it. If a dog sees that you are nervous, he will bite you. With types like that you must show that you are dangerous and then they are afraid." She took his other arm. "Ah, you do not need to worry. You will get to Genoa and you will go to the British Consul. You can ignore this dirty beast with the perfume. By the time you get to Paris you will have forgotten him."

"If I get to Paris."

"You are impossible. Why should you not get to Paris?"

"You think I'm a fool."

"I think perhaps you are tired. Your wound . . ."

"It was only a graze."

"Ah, but it is not the size of the wound. It is the shock."

He wanted suddenly to laugh. It was true what she was saying. He hadn't really got over that hellish night with Kopeikin and Haki. His nerves were on edge. He was worrying unnecessarily. He said: "When we get to Paris, Josette, I shall give you the best dinner it is possible to buy."

She came close to him. "I don't want you to give me anything, *chéri*. I want you to like me. You *do* like me?"

"Of course I like you. I told you so."

"Yes, you told me so."

133

His left hand touched the belt on her coat. Her body moved suddenly pressing against his. The next moment his arms were round her and he was kissing her.

When his arms grew tired, she leaned back, half against him, half against the rail.

"Do you feel better, *chéri?*"

"Yes, I feel better."

"Then I will have a cigarette."

He gave her the cigarette and she looked at him across the light of the match. "Are you thinking of this lady in England who is your wife?"

"No."

"But you *will* think of her?"

"If you keep talking about her I shall have to think about her."

"I see. For you I am part of the journey from Istanbul to London. Like Mr. Kuvetli."

"Not quite like Mr. Kuvetli. I shan't kiss Mr. Kuvetli if I can help it."

"What do you think about me?"

"I think that you're very attractive. I like your hair and your eyes and the scent you use."

"That is very nice. Shall I tell you something, *chéri?*"

"What?"

She began to speak very softly. "This boat is very small; the cabins are very small; the walls are very thin; and there are people everywhere."

"Yes?"

"Paris is very large and there are nice hotels there with big rooms and thick walls. One need not see anyone one does not wish to see. And do you know, *chéri*, that if one is making a journey from Istanbul to London and one arrives in Paris, it is sometimes necessary to wait a week before continuing the journey?"

"That's a long time."

"It is because of the war, you see. There are always difficulties. People have to wait days and days for permission to leave France. There is a special stamp that must be put in your passport, and they will not let you on the train to England until you have that stamp. You have to go to the Préfecture for it and there is a great deal of *chichi*. You have to stay in Paris until the old women in the Préfecture can find time to deal with your application."

"Very annoying."

She sighed. "We could pass that week or ten days very nicely. I do not mean at the Hotel des Belges. That is a dirty place. But there is the Ritz Hotel and the Lancaster Hotel and the Georges Cinque. . . ." She paused and he knew that he was expected to say something.

He said it. "And the Crillon and the Meurice."

She squeezed his arm. "You are very nice. But you understand me? An apartment is cheaper, but for so little time that is impossible. One cannot enjoy oneself in a cheap hotel. All the same I do not like extravagance. There are nice hotels for less than it costs at the Ritz or the Georges Cinque and one has more money to spend on eating and dancing at nice places. Even in war time there are nice places." The burning end of her cigarette made an impatient gesture. "But I must not talk about money. You will make the old women at the Préfecture give you your permit too soon and then I shall be disappointed."

He said: "You know, Josette, I shall begin in a minute to think that you are really serious."

"And you think that I am not?" She was indignant.

"I'm quite sure of it."

She burst out laughing. "You can be rude very politely. I shall tell José that. It will amuse him."

"I don't think I want to amuse José. Shall we go down?"

"Ah, you are angry! You think that I have been making a fool of you."

"Not a bit."

"Then kiss me."

Some moments later she said softly: "I like you very much. I would not mind very much a room for fifty francs a day. But the Hotel des Belges is terrible. I do not want to go back there. You are not angry with me?"

"No, I am not angry with you." Her body was soft and warm and infinitely yielding. She had made him feel as if Banat and the rest of the journey really did not matter. He felt both grateful to and sorry for her. He made up his mind that, when he got to Paris, he would buy her a handbag and slip a thousand franc note in it before he gave it to her. He said: "It's all right. You needn't go back to the Hotel des Belges."

When at last they went down to the saloon it was after ten. José and Mr. Kuvetli were there playing cards.

José was playing with thin-lipped concentration and took no notice of them; but Mr. Kuvetli looked up. His smile was sickly.

"Madame," he said ruefully, "your husband plays cards very well."

"He has had a lot of practice."

"Ah, yes, I am sure." He played a card. José slapped another one on top of it triumphantly. Mr. Kuvetli's face fell.

"It is my game," said José and gathered up some money from the table. "You have lost eighty-four lire. If we had been playing for lire instead of centesimi I should have won eight thousand four hundred lire. That would be interesting. Shall we play another game?"

"I think that I will go to bed now," said Mr. Kuvetli hurriedly. "Good night, Messieurs-dame." He went.

José sucked his teeth as if the game had left an unpleasant taste in his mouth. "Everyone goes to bed early on this filthy boat," he said. "It is very boring." He looked up at Graham. "Do you want to play?"

"I'm sorry to say that I must go to bed, too."

José shrugged. "Very well. Good-bye." He glanced at Josette and began to deal two hands. "I will play a game with you."

She looked at Graham and smiled hopelessly. "If I do not he will be disagreeable. Good night, Monsieur."

Graham smiled and said good night. He was not unrelieved.

He got to his cabin feeling a good deal more cheerful than he had felt when he had left it earlier in the evening.

How sensible she was! And how stupid he'd been! With men like Banat it was dangerous to be subtle. If a dog saw that you were nervous, he bit you. From now on he would carry the revolver. What was more, he would use it if Banat tried any funny business. You had to meet force with force.

He bent down to pull his suitcase from under the bunk. He was going to get the revolver out then and there.

Suddenly he stopped. For an instant his nostrils had caught the sweet cloying smell of attar of roses.

The smell had been faint, almost imperceptible, and he could not detect it again. For a moment he remained motionless, telling himself that he must have imagined it. Then panic seized him.

With shaking fingers he tore at the latches on the suitcase and flung back the lid.

The revolver was gone.

CHAPTER VII

HE UNDRESSED slowly, got into his bunk and lay there staring at the cracks in the asbestos round a steam pipe which crossed the ceiling. He could taste Josette's lipstick in his mouth. The taste was all that was left to remind him of the self-assurance with which he had returned to the cabin; the self-assurance which had been swept away by fear welling up into his mind like blood from a severed artery; fear that clotted, paralysing thought. Only his senses seemed alive.

On the other side of the partition, Mathis finished brushing his teeth and there was a lot of grunting and creaking as he clambered into the upper berth. At last he lay back with a sigh.

"Another day!"

"So much the better. Is the porthole open?"

"Unmistakably. There is a very disagreeable current of air on my back."

"We do not want to be ill like the Englishman."

"That was nothing to do with the air. It was seasickness. He would not admit it because it would not be correct for an Englishman to be seasick. The English like to think that they are all great sailors. He is *drôle* but I like him."

"That is because he listens to your nonsense. He is polite—too polite. He and that German greet each other now as if they were friends. *That* is not correct. If this Gallindo . . ."

"Oh, we have talked enough about him."

"Signora Beronelli said that he knocked against her on the stairs and went on without apologising."

"He is a filthy type."

There was a silence. Then:

"Robert!"

"I am nearly asleep."

"You remember that I said that the husband of Signora Beronelli was killed in the earthquake?"

"What about it?"

"I talked to her this evening. It is a terrible story. It was not the earthquake that killed him. He was shot."

"Why?"

"She does not wish everyone to know. You must say nothing of it."

"Well?"

"It was during the first earthquake. After the great shocks were over they went back to their house from the fields in which they had taken refuge. The house was in ruins. There was part of one wall standing and he made a shelter against it with some boards. They found some food that had been in the house but the tanks had been broken and there was no water. He left her with the boy, their son, and went to look for water. Some friends who had a house near theirs were away in Istanbul. That house, too, had fallen, but he went among the ruins to find the water tanks. He found them and one of them had not been broken. He had nothing to take the water back in so he searched for a jug or a tin. He found a jug. It was of silver and had been partly crushed by the falling stones. After the earthquake, soldiers had been sent to patrol the streets to prevent looting, of which there was a great deal because valuable things were lying everywhere in the ruins. As he was standing there trying to straighten the jug, a soldier arrested him. Signora Beronelli knew nothing of this and when he did not come back she and her son went to look for him. But there was such chaos that she could do nothing. The next day she heard that he had been shot. Is that not a terrible tragedy?"

"Yes, it is a tragedy. Such things happen."

"If the good God had killed him in the earthquake she could bear it more easily. But for him to be shot ... ! She is very brave. She does not blame the soldiers. With so much chaos they cannot be blamed. It was the Will of the good God."

"He is a comedian. I have noticed it before."

"Do not blaspheme."

"It is *you* who blaspheme. You talk of the good God as if He were a waiter with a fly-swatter. He hits at the flies and kills some. But one escapes. Ah, *le salaud!* The waiter hits again and the fly is paste with the others. The good God is not like that. He does not make earthquakes and tragedies. He is of the mind."

"You are insupportable. Have you no pity for the poor woman?"

"Yes, I pity her. But will it help her if we hold another burial service? Will it help her if I stay awake arguing instead of going to sleep as I wish? She told you this because she likes to talk of it. Poor soul! It eases her mind to become the heroine of a tragedy. The fact becomes less real. But if there is no audience, there is no tragedy. If she tells me, I, too, will be a good audience. Tears will come into my eyes. But you are not the heroine. Go to sleep."

"You are a beast without imagaination."

"Beasts must sleep. Good night, *chérie!*"

"Camel!"

There was no answer. After a moment or two he sighed heavily and turned over in his bunk. Soon he began gently to snore.

For a time Graham lay awake listening to the rush of the sea outside and the steady throb of the engines. A waiter with a fly-swatter! In Berlin there was a man whom he had never seen and whose name he did not know, who had condemned him to death; in Sofia there was a man named Moeller who had been instructed to carry out the sentence; and here, a few yards away in cabin number nine, was the executioner with a nine millimetre calibre self-loading pistol, ready, now that he had disarmed the condemned man, to do his work and collect his money. The whole thing was as impersonal, as dispassionate, as justice itself. To attempt to defeat it seemed as futile as to argue with the hangman on the scaffold.

He tried to think of Stephanie and found that he could not. The things of which she was a part, his house, his friends, had ceased to exist. He was a man alone, transported into a strange land with death for its frontiers: alone but for the one person to whom he could speak of its terrors. She was sanity. She was reality. He needed her. Stephanie he did not need. She was a face and a voice dimly remembered with the other faces and voices of a world he had once known.

His mind wandered away into an uneasy doze. Then he dreamed that he was falling down a precipice and awoke with a start. He switched on the light and picked up one of the books he had bought that afternoon. It was a detective story. He read a few pages and then put it down. He was not going to be able to read himself to sleep with news of "neat, slightly bleeding" holes in the right temples of corpses lying "grotesquely twisted in the final agony of death."

He got out of his bunk, wrapped himself in a blanket, and sat down to smoke a cigarette. He would, he decided, spend the rest of the night like that: sitting and smoking cigarettes. Lying prone increased his sense of helplessness. If only he had a revolver.

It seemed to him as he sat there that the having or not having a revolver was really as important to a man as the having or not having of sight. That he should have survived for so many years without one could only be due to chance. Without a revolver a man was as defenceless as a tethered goat in a jungle. What an incredible fool he had been to leave the thing in his suitcase! If only . . .

And then he remembered something Josette had said:

"José has a revolver in his box. I will try to get it for you."

He drew a deep breath. He was saved. José had a revolver. Josette would get it for him. All would be well. She would probably be on deck by ten. He would wait until he was sure of finding her there, tell her what had happened, and ask her to get the revolver there and then. With luck he would have it in his pocket within half an hour or so of his leaving his cabin. He would be able to sit down to luncheon with the thing bulging in his pocket. Banat would get a surprise. Thank goodness for José's suspicious nature!

He yawned and put out his cigarette. It would be stupid to sit there all night: stupid, uncomfortable, and dull. He felt sleepy, too. He put the blanket back on the bunk and lay down once more. Within five minutes he was asleep.

When he again awoke, a crescent of sunlight slanting through the porthole was rising and falling on the white paint of the bulkhead. He lay there watching it until he had to get up to unlock the door for the steward bringing his coffee. It was nine o'clock. He drank the coffee slowly, smoked a cigarette, and had a hot sea water bath. By the time he was dressed it was close on ten o'clock. He put on his coat and left the cabin.

The alleyway on to which the cabins opened was only just wide enough for two persons to pass. It formed three sides of a square, the fourth side of which was taken up by the stairs to the saloon and shelter deck and two small spaces in which stood a pair of dusty palms in earthenware tubs. He was within a yard or two of the end of the alleyway when he came face to face with Banat.

The man had turned into the alleyway from the space at the foot of the stairs, and by taking a pace backwards he could have given Graham room to pass; but he made no attempt to do so. When he saw Graham, he stopped. Then, very slowly, he put his hands in his pockets and leaned against the steel bulkhead. Graham could either turn round and go back the way he had come or stay where he was. His heart pounding at his ribs, he stayed where he was.

Banat nodded. "Good morning, Monsieur. It is very fine weather to-day, eh?"

"Very fine."

"For you, an Englishman, it must be very agreeable to see the sun." He had shaved and his pasty jowl gleamed with unrinsed soap. The smell of attar of roses came from him in waves.

"Most agreeable. Excuse me." He went to push by to the stairs.

Banat moved, as if by accident, blocking the way. "It is so narrow! One person must give way to the other, eh?"

"Just so. Do you want to go by?"

Banat shook his head. "No. There is no hurry. I was so anxious to ask you, Monsieur, about your hand. I noticed it last night. What is the matter with it?"

Graham met the small, dangerous eyes staring insolently into his. Banat knew that he was unarmed and was trying to unnerve him as well. And he was succeeding. Graham had a sudden desire to smash his knuckles into the pale, stupid face. He controlled himself with an effort.

"It is a small wound," he said calmly. And then his pent up feelings got the better of him. "A bullet wound, to be exact," he added. "Some dirty little thief took a shot at me in Istanbul. He was either a bad shot or frightened. He missed."

The small eyes did not flicker but an ugly little smile twisted the mouth. Banat said slowly: "A dirty little thief, eh? You must look after yourself carefully. You must be ready to shoot back next time."

"I shall shoot back. There is not the slightest doubt of that."

The smile widened. "You carry a pistol, then?"

"Naturally. And now, if you will excuse me . . ." He walked forward intending to shoulder the other man out of the way if he did not move. But Banat moved. He was grinning now. "Be very careful, Monsieur," he said, and laughed.

Graham had reached the foot of the stairs. He paused and looked back. "I don't think it will be necessary," he said deliberately. "These scum don't risk their skins with an armed man." He used the word *excrément*.

The grin faded from Banat's face. Without replying he turned and went on to his cabin.

By the time Graham reached the deck, reaction had set in. His legs seemed to have gone to jelly and he was sweating. The unexpectedness of the encounter had helped and, all things considered, he had not come out of it too badly. He'd put up a bluff. Banat might conceivably be wondering if, after all, he had a second revolver. But bluff wasn't going to go very far now. The gloves were off. His bluff might be called. Now, whatever happened, he *must* get José's revolver.

He walked quickly round the shelter deck. Haller was there with his wife on his arm, walking slowly. He said good morning; but Graham did not want to talk to anyone but the girl. She was not on the shelter deck. He went on up to the boat deck.

She was there, but talking to the young officer. The Mathises and Mr. Kuvetli were a few yards away. Out of the corner of his eye he saw them look at him expectantly but he pretended not to have seen them and walked over to Josette.

She greeted him with a smile and a meaning look intended to convey that she was bored with her companion. The young Italian scowled a good morning and made to take up the conversation where Graham had interrupted it.

But Graham was in no mood for courtesies. "You must excuse me, Monsieur," he said in French; "I have a message for Madame from her husband."

The officer nodded and stood aside politely.

Graham raised his eyebrows. "It is a *private* message, Monsieur."

The officer flushed angrily and looked at Josette. She nodded to him in a kindly way and said something to him in Italian. He flashed his teeth at her, scowled once more at Graham and stalked on.

She giggled. "You were really very unkind to that poor boy. He was getting on so nicely. Could you think of nothing better than a message from José?"

"I said the first thing that came into my head. I had to speak to you."

She nodded approvingly. "That is very nice." She

looked at him slyly. "I was afraid that you would spend the night being angry with yourself because of last night. But you must not look so solemn. Madame Mathis is very interested in us."

"I'm feeling solemn. Something has happened."

The smile faded from her lips. "Something serious?"

"Something serious. I . . ."

She glanced over his shoulder. "It will be better if we walk up and down and look as if we are talking about the sea and the sun. Otherwise they will be gossiping. I do not care what people say, you understand. But it would be embarrassing."

"Very well." And then, as they began to walk: "When I got back to my cabin last night I found that my revolver had been stolen from my suitcase."

She stopped. "This is true?"

"Quite true."

She began to walk again. "It may have been the steward."

"No. Banat had been in my cabin. I could smell that scent of his."

She was silent for a moment. Then: "Have you told anyone?"

"It's no use my making a complaint. The revolver will be at the bottom of the sea by now. I have no proof that Banat took it. Besides, they wouldn't listen to me after the scene I made with the Purser yesterday."

"What are you going to do?"

"Ask you to do something for me."

She looked at him quickly. "What?"

"You said last night that José had a revolver and that you might be able to get it for me."

"You are serious?"

"Never more so in all my life."

She bit her lip. "But what am I to say to José if he finds that it is gone?"

"Will he find out?"

"He may do."

He began to get angry. "It was, I think, your idea that you should get it for me."

"It is so necessary that you should have a revolver? There is nothing that he can do."

"It was also your idea that I should carry a revolver."

She looked sullen. "I was frightened by what you said about this man. But that was because it was dark. Now that it is daytime it is different." She smiled suddenly. "Ah, my friend, do not be so serious. Think of the nice time we will have in Paris together. This man is not going to make any trouble."

"I'm afraid he is." He told her about his encounter by the stairs, and added: "Besides, why did he steal my revolver if he doesn't intend to make trouble?"

She hesitated. Then she said slowly: "Very well, I will try."

"Now?"

"Yes, if you wish. It is in his box in the cabin. He is in the *salone* reading. Do you want to wait here for me?"

"No, I'll wait on the deck below. I don't want to have to talk to these people here just now."

They went down and stood for a moment by the rail at the foot of the companionway.

"I'll stay here." He pressed her hand. "My dear Josette, I can't tell you how grateful I am to you for this."

She smiled as if at a small boy to whom she had promised sweets. "You shall tell me that in Paris."

He watched her go and then turned to lean against the rail. She could not be more than five minutes. He stared for a time at the long, curling bow wave

147

streaming out and away to meet the transverse wave from the stern and be broken by it into froth. He looked at his watch. Three minutes. Someone clattered down the companionway.

"Good morning, Mr. Graham. You feel all right to-day, eh?" It was Mr. Kuvetli.

Graham turned his head. "Yes, thanks."

"Monsieur and Madame Mathis are hopeful to play some bridge this afternoon. Do you play?"

"Yes, I play." He was not, he knew, being very gracious but he was terrified lest Mr. Kuvetli should attach himself to him.

"Then perhaps we make party of four, eh?"

"By all means."

"I do not play well. Is very difficult game."

"Yes." Out of the corner of his eye he saw Josette step through the door from the landing on to the deck.

Mr. Kuvetli's eyes flickered in her direction. He leered. "This afternoon then, Mr. Graham."

"I shall look forward to it."

Mr. Kuvetli went. Josette came up to him.

"What was he saying?"

"He was asking me to play bridge." Something in her face set his heart going like a trip hammer. "You've got it?" he said quickly.

She shook her head. "The box was locked. He has the keys."

He felt the sweat prickling out all over his body. He stared at her trying to think of something to say.

"Why do you look at me like that?" she exclaimed angrily. "I cannot help it if he keeps the box locked."

"No, you cannot help it." He knew now that she had not intended to get the revolver. She couldn't be blamed. He couldn't expect her to steal for him. He had asked too much of her. But he had been banking on that revolver of José's. Now, in God's name, what was he going to do?

She rested her hand on his arm. "You are angry with me?"

He shook his head. "Why should I be angry? I should have had the sense to keep my own revolver in my pocket. It's just that I was relying on your getting it. It's my own fault. But, as I told you, I'm not used to this sort of thing."

She laughed. "Ah, you need not worry; I can tell you something. This man does not carry a gun."

"What! How do you know?"

"He was going up the stairs in front of me when I came back just now. His clothes are tight and creased. If he carried a revolver I would have seen the shape of it in his pocket."

"You are sure of this?"

"Of course. I would not tell you if . . ."

"But a *small* gun . . ." He stopped. A nine millimetre self-loading pistol would *not* be a small gun. It would weigh about two pounds and would be correspondingly bulky. It would not be the sort of thing a man would carry about in his pocket if he could leave it in a cabin. If . . .

She was watching his face. "What is it?"

"He'll have left his gun in his cabin," he said slowly.

She looked him in the eyes. "I could see that he does not go to his cabin for a long time."

"How?"

"José will do it."

"José?"

"Be calm. I will not have to tell José anything about you. José will play cards with him this evening."

"Banat would play cards. He is a gambler. But will José ask him?"

"I shall tell José that I saw this man open a wallet

149

with a lot of money in it. José will see that he plays cards. You do not know José."

"You're sure you can do it?"

She squeezed his arm. "Of course. I do not like you to be worried. If you take his gun then you will have nothing at all to fear, eh?"

"No, I shall have nothing at all to fear." He said it almost wonderingly. It seemed so simple. Why hadn't he thought of it before? Ah, but he had not known before that the man did not carry his gun. Take the man's gun away from him and he couldn't shoot. That was logical. And if he couldn't shoot there was nothing to fear. That was logical too. *The essence of all good strategy is simplicity.*

He turned to her. "When can you do this?"

"This evening would be best. José does not like so much to play cards in the afternoon."

"How soon this evening?"

"You must not be impatient. It will be some time after the meal." She hesitated. "It will be better if we are not seen together this afternoon. You do not want him to suspect that we are friends."

"I can play bridge with Kuvetli and the Mathises this afternoon. But how shall I know if it is all right?"

"I will find a way to let you know." She leaned against him. "You are sure that you are not angry with me about José's revolver?"

"Of course I'm not."

"There is no one looking. Kiss me."

"Banking!" Mathis was saying. "What is it but usury? Bankers are money lenders, usurers. But because they lend other people's money or money that does not exist, they have a pretty name. They are still usurers. Once, usury was a mortal sin and an abomination, and to be a usurer was to be a criminal for whom there was a prison cell. To-day the usurers are

150

the gods of the earth and the only mortal sin is to be poor."

"There are so many poor people," said Mr. Kuvetli profoundly. "It is terrible!"

Mathis shrugged impatiently. "There will be more before this war is finished. You may depend upon it. It will be a good thing to be a soldier. Soldiers, at least, will be given food."

"Always," said Madame Mathis, "he talks nonsense. Always, always. But when we get back to France it will be different. His friends will not listen so politely. Banking! What does he know about banking?"

"Ha! That is what the banker likes. Banking is a mystery! It is too difficult for ordinary men to understand." He laughed derisively. "If you make two and two equal five you *must* have a lot of mystery." He turned aggressively to Graham. "The international bankers are the real war criminals. Others do the killing but they sit, calm and collected, in their offices and make money."

"I'm afraid," said Graham, feeling that he ought to say something, "that the only international banker I know is a very harassed man with a duodenal ulcer. He is far from calm. On the contrary, he complains bitterly."

"Precisely," said Mathis triumphantly. "It is the System! I can tell you . . ."

He went on to tell them. Graham picked up his fourth whisky and soda. He had been playing bridge with the Mathises and Mr. Kuvetli for most of the afternoon and he was tired of them. He had seen Josette only once during that time. She had paused by the card-table and nodded to him. He had taken the nod to mean that José had risen to the news that Banat had money in his pocket and that sometime that evening it would be safe to go to Banat's cabin.

The prospect cheered and terrified him alternately.

151

At one moment the plan seemed foolproof. He would go into the cabin, take the gun, return to his own cabin, drop the gun out of the porthole and return to the saloon with a tremendous weight lifted from his shoulders. The next moment, however, doubts would begin to creep in. It was *too* simple. Banat might be insane but he was no fool. A man who earned his living in the way Banat earned his and who yet managed to stay alive and free was not going to be taken in so easily. Supposing he should guess what his victim had in mind, leave José in the middle of the game, and go to his cabin! Supposing he had bribed the steward to keep an eye on his cabin on the grounds that it contained valuables! Supposing ...! But what was the alternative? Was he to wait passively while Banat chose the moment to kill him? It was all very well for Haki to talk about a marked man having only to defend himself; but what had he to defend himself with? When the enemy was as close as Banat was, the best defence was attack. Yes, that was it! Anything was better than just waiting. And the plan might well succeed. It was the simple plans of attack that *did* succeed. It would never occur to a man of Banat's conceit to suspect that two could play at the game of stealing guns, that the helpless rabbit might bite back. He'd soon find out his mistake.

Josette and José came in with Banat. José appeared to be making himself amiable.

"... it is only necessary," Mathis was concluding, "to say one word—Briey! When you have said that you have said all."

Graham drained his glass. "Quite so. Will you all have another drink?"

The Mathises, looking startled, declined sharply; but Mr. Kuvetli nodded happily.

"Thank you, Mr. Graham. I will."

Mathis stood up, frowning. "It is time that we got ready for dinner. Please excuse us."

They went. Mr. Kuvetli moved his chair over.

"That was very sudden," said Graham. "What's the matter with them?"

"I think," said Mr. Kuvetli carefully, "that they thought you are making joke of them."

"Why on earth should they think that?"

Mr. Kuvetli looked sideways. "You ask them to have to drink three times in five minutes. You ask them once. They say no. You ask them again. They say no again. You ask again. They do not understand English hospitality."

"I see. I'm afraid that I was thinking of something else. I must apologise."

"Please!" Mr. Kuvetli was overcome. "It is not necessary to apologise for hospitality. But"—he glanced hesitantly at the clock—"it is now nearly time for dinner. You allow me later to have this drink you so kindly offer?"

"Yes, of course."

"And you will excuse me please, now?"

"By all means."

When Mr. Kuvetli had gone, Graham stood up. Yes, he'd had just one drink too many on an empty stomach. He went out on deck.

The starlit sky was hung with small smoky clouds. In the distance were the lights of the Italian coast. He stood there for a moment letting the icy wind sting his face. In a minute or two the gong would sound for dinner. He dreaded the approaching meal as a sick man dreads the approach of the surgeon with a probe. He would sit, as he had sat at luncheon, listening to Haller's monologues and to the Beronellis whispering behind their misery, forcing food down his throat to his unwilling stomach, conscious all the time of the man opposite to him—of why he was there and of what he stood for.

He turned round and leaned against a stanchion. With his back to the deck he found himself constantly looking over his shoulder to make sure that he was alone. He felt more at ease with no deck space behind him.

Through one of the saloon portholes he could see Banat with Josette and José. They sat like details in a Hogarth group; José tight-lipped and intent, Josette smiling, Banat saying something that brought his lips forward. The air in there was grey with tobacco smoke and the hard light from the unshaded lamps flattened their features. There was about them all the squalor of a flashlight photograph taken in a bar.

Someone turned the corner at the end of the deck and came towards him. The figure reached the light and he saw that it was Haller. The old man stopped.

"Good evening, Mr. Graham. You look as if you are really enjoying the air. I, as you see, need a scarf and a coat before I can face it."

"It's stuffy inside."

"Yes. I saw you this afternoon very gallantly playing bridge."

"You don't like bridge?"

"One's tastes change." He stared out at the lights. "To see the land from a ship or to see a ship from the land, I used to like both. Now I dislike both. When a man reaches my age he grows, I think, to resent subconsciously the movement of everything except the respiratory muscles which keep him alive. Movement is change and for an old man change means death."

"And the immortal soul?"

Haller sniffed. "Even that which we commonly regard as immortal dies sooner or later. One day the last Titian and the last Beethoven quartet will cease to exist. The canvas and the printed notes may remain if they are carefully preserved but the works themselves will have died with the last eye and ear accessible to their messages. As for the immortal soul, that is an eternal truth and the eternal truths die with the men to whom they were necessary. The eternal truths of the Ptolemaic system were as necessary to the mediæval theologians as were the enternal truths of Kepler to the theologians of the Reformation and the eternal truths of Darwin to the nineteenth century materialists. The statement of an eternal truth is a prayer to lay a ghost—the ghost of primitive man defending himself against what Spengler calls the 'dark almightiness.' " He turned his head suddenly as the door of the saloon opened.

It was Josette standing there looking uncertainly from one to the other of them. At that moment the gong began to sound for dinner.

"Excuse me," said Haller; "I must see my wife before dinner. She is still unwell."

"Of course," said Graham hurriedly.

Josette came over to him as Haller went.

"What did he want, that old man?" she whispered.

"He was talking about life and death."

"Ugh! I do not like him. He makes me shudder. But I must not stay. I came only to tell you that it is all right."

"When are they going to play?"

"After dinner." She squeezed his arm. "He is horrible, this man Banat. I would not do this for anyone except you, *chéri*."

"You know I am grateful, Josette. I shall make it up to you."

"Ah, stupid!" she smiled at him fondly. "You must not be so serious."

He hesitated. "Are you sure that you can keep him there?"

"You need not worry. I will keep him. But come back to the *salone* when you have been to the cabin so that I shall know that you have finished. It is understood, *chéri?*"

"Yes, it is understood."

It was after nine o'clock and, for the past half hour, Graham had been sitting near the door of the saloon pretending to read a book.

For the hundredth time his eyes wandered to the opposite corner of the room where Banat was talking to Josette and José. His heart began suddenly to beat faster. José had a deck of cards in his hand. He was grinning at something Banat had said. Then they sat down at the card-table. Josette looked across the room.

Graham waited a moment. Then, when he saw them cutting for the deal, he got slowly to his feet and walked out.

He stood on the landing for a moment, bracing himself for what he had to do. Now that the moment had come he felt better. Two minutes—three at the most—and it would be over. He would have the gun and he would be safe. He had only to keep his head.

He went down the stairs. Cabin number nine was beyond his and in the middle section of the alleyway. There was no one about when he reached the palms. He walked on.

He had decided that any sort of stealth was out of the question. He must walk straight to the cabin, open the door and go in without hesitation. If the worst came to the worst and he was seen as he went in by the steward or anyone else, he could protest that he had thought that number nine was an empty cabin and that he was merely satisfying a curiosity to see what the other cabins were like.

But nobody appeared. He reached the door of number nine, paused for barely a second and then, opening the door softly, went in. A moment later he had shut the door behind him and put up the catch. If, for any reason, the steward should try to get in, he would assume that Banat was there when he found the door fastened.

He looked round. The porthole was closed and the air reeked of attar of roses. It was a two-berth cabin and looked strangely bare. Apart from the scent, there were only two indications that the cabin was occupied: the grey raincoat hanging with the soft hat behind the door and a battered composition suitcase under the lower berth.

He ran his hands over the raincoat. There was nothing in the pockets and he turned his attention to the suitcase.

It was unlocked. He pulled it out and threw back the lid.

The thing was crammed with filthy shirts and underwear. There were, besides, some brightly-coloured silk handkerchiefs, a pair of black shoes without laces, a scent spray and a small jar of ointment. The gun was not there.

He shut the case, pushed it back and opened the washing cabinet-cum-wardrobe. The wardrobe part contained nothing but a pair of dirty socks. On the shelf by the tooth-glass was a grey washcloth, a safety razor, a cake of soap and a bottle of scent with a ground glass stopper.

He was getting worried. He had been so sure that the gun would be there. If what Josette had said were true it *must* be there somewhere.

He looked round for other hiding places. There were the mattresses. He ran his hands along the springs beneath them. Nothing. There was the waste compartment below the washing cabinet. Again nothing. He glanced at his watch. He had been there four minutes. He looked round again desperately. It *must* be in there. But he had looked everywhere. He returned feverishly to the suitcase.

Two minutes later he slowly straightened his back. He knew now that the gun was not in the cabin, that the simple plan had been too simple, that nothing was changed. For a second or two he stood there helplessly, putting off the moment when he must finally admit his failure by leaving the cabin. Then the sound of footsteps in the alleyway nearby jarred him into activity.

The footsteps paused. There was the clank of a bucket being put down. Then the footsteps receded. He eased back the door catch and opened the door. The alleyway was empty. A second later he was walking back the way he had come.

He had reached the foot of the stairs before he allowed himself to think. Then he hesitated. He had told Josette that he would go back to the saloon. But that meant seeing Banat. He must have time to steady his nerves. He turned and walked back to his cabin.

He opened the door, took one step forward, and then stopped dead.

Sitting on the bunk with his legs crossed and a book resting on his knee was Haller.

He was wearing a pair of horn-rimmed reading glasses. He removed them very deliberately and looked up. "I've been waiting for you, Mr. Graham," he said cheerfully.

Graham found his tongue. "I don't . . ." he began.

Haller's other hand came from under the book. In it was a large self-loading pistol.

He held it up. "I think," he said, "that this is what you have been looking for, isn't it?"

CHAPTER VIII

GRAHAM looked from the gun to the face of the man who was holding it: the long upper lip, the pale blue eyes, the loose yellowish skin.

"I don't understand," he said, and put out his hand to receive the gun. "How . . . ?" he began and then stopped abruptly. The gun was pointing at him and Haller's forefinger was on the trigger.

Haller shook his head. "No, Mr. Graham. I think I shall keep it. I came for a little talk with you. Supposing you sit down here on the bed and turn sideways so that we can face one another."

Graham strove to conceal the deadly sickness that was stealing over him. He felt that he must be going mad. Amid the flood of questions pouring through his mind there was only one small patch of dry land: Colonel Haki had examined the credentials of all the passengers who had embarked at Istanbul and reported that none of them had booked for the journey less than three days prior to the sailing and that they were all harmless. He clung to it desperately.

"I don't understand," he repeated.

159

"Of course you don't. If you will sit down I will explain."

"I'll stand."

"Ah, yes. I see. Moral support derived from physical discomfort. Remain standing by all means if it pleases you to do so." He spoke with crisp condescension. This was a new Haller, a slightly younger man. He examined the pistol as if he were seeing it for the first time. "You know, Mr. Graham," he went on thoughtfully, "poor Mavrodopoulos was really very upset by his failure in Istanbul. He is not, as you have probably gathered, very intelligent and, like all stupid people, he blames others for his own mistakes. He complains that you moved." He shrugged tolerantly. "Naturally you moved. He could hardly expect you to stand still while he corrected his aim. I told him so. But he was still angry with you, so when he came aboard I insisted on taking care of his pistol for him. He is young, and these Roumanians are so hotheaded. I did not want anything premature to happen."

"I wonder," said Graham, "if your name happens to be Moeller."

"Dear me!" He raised his eyebrows. "I had no idea that you were so well informed. Colonel Haki must have been in a very talkative mood. Did he know that I was in Istanbul?"

Graham reddened. "I don't think so."

Moeller chuckled. "I thought not. Haki is a clever man. I have a great respect for him. But he is human and, therefore, fallible. Yes, after that fiasco in Gallipoli I thought it advisable to attend to things myself. And then, when everything had been arranged, you were inconsiderate enough to move and spoil Mavrodopoulos' shooting. But I bear you no ill will, Mr. Graham. I was irritated at the time, of course. Mavrodopoulos . . ."

"Banat is easier to say."

"Thank you. As I was saying, Banat's failure made more work for me. But now my irritation has passed. Indeed, I am quite enjoying the trip. I like myself as an archeologist. I was a little nervous at first, but as soon as I saw that I had succeeded in boring you I knew that all was well." He held up the book he had been reading. "If you would like a record of my little speeches I can recommend this. It is entitled 'The Sumerian Pantheon' and is by Fritz Haller. His qualifications are given on the title page: ten years with the German Institute in Athens, the period at Oxford, the degrees: it is all here. He seems to be an ardent disciple of Spengler. He quotes the Master a great deal. There is a nostalgic little preface which was most helpful and you will find the piece about eternal truths on page three hundred and forty-one. Naturally I paraphrased a little here and there to suit my own mood. And I drew freely on some of the longer footnotes. You see, the effect I wanted to create was that of an erudite but loveable old bore. I think you will agree that I did well."

"So there *is* a Haller?"

Moeller pursed his lips. "Ah, yes. I was sorry to inconvenience him and his wife, but there was no other way. When I found that you were to leave on this boat I decided that it would be helpful if I travelled with you. Obviously I could not have booked a passage at the last moment without attracting Colonel Haki's attention; I therefore took over Haller's tickets and passport. He and his wife were not pleased. But they are good Germans, and when it was made plain to them that their country's interests must come before their own convenience, they gave no more trouble. In a few days their passport will be returned to them with their own photographs restored to it. My only embarrassment has been the Armenian lady who is doing duty for Frau Professor Haller. She speaks very little German and is virtually a half-wit. I have been forced to keep her out of the way. I had no time to make better arrangements, you see. As it was, the man who found her for me had quite a lot of trouble convincing her that she wasn't being carried off to an Italian *bordello*. Female vanity is sometimes extraordinary." He produced a cigarette-case. "I hope you don't mind my telling you all these little things, Mr. Graham. It's just that I want to be frank with you. I think that an atmosphere of frankness is essential to any business discussion."

"Business?"

"Just so. Now do please sit down and smoke. It will do you good." He held out the cigarette-case. "Your nerves have been a little jumpy to-day, haven't they?"

"Say what you want to say and get out!"

Moeller chuckled. "Yes, certainly a little jumpy!" He looked suddenly solemn. "It is my fault, I'm afraid. You see, Mr. Graham, I could have had this little talk with you before, but I wanted to make sure that you would be in a receptive frame of mind."

Graham leaned against the door. "I think that the best way I can describe my state of mind at the moment is to tell you that I have been seriously considering kicking you in the teeth. I could have done so from here before you could have used your gun."

Moeller raised his eyebrows. "And yet you didn't do it? Was it the thought of my white hairs that stopped you, or was it your fear of the consequences?" He paused. "No answer? You won't mind if I draw my own conclusions, will you?" He settled himself a little more comfortably. "The instinct for self-preservation is a wonderful thing. It is so easy for people to be heroic about laying down their lives for the sake of principles when they do not expect to be called upon to do so. When, however, the smell of danger is in their nostrils they are more practical. They see alternatives not in terms of honour or dishonour, but in terms of greater or lesser evils. I wonder if I could persuade you to see my point of view."

Graham was silent. He was trying to fight down the panic which had seized him. He knew that if he opened his mouth he would shout abuse until his throat ached.

Moeller was fitting a cigarette into a short amber holder as if he had time to waste. Obviously he had not expected any answer to his question. He had the self-contained air of a man who is early for an important appointment. When he finished with the cigarette-holder he looked up. "I like you, Mr. Graham," he said. "I was, I have admitted, irritated when Banat made such a fool of himself in Istanbul. But now that I know you I am glad that he did so. You behaved gracefully over that awkwardness at the dinner-table the night we sailed. You listened politely to my carefully memorised recitations. You are a clever engineer, and yet you are not aggressive. I should not like to think of your being killed—murdered—by any employee of mine." He lit his cigarette. "And yet, the demands made upon us by our life's needs are so uncompromising. I am compelled to be offensive. I must tell you that, as things stand at present, you will be dead within a few minutes of your landing at Genoa on Saturday morning."

Graham had himself in hand now. He said: "I'm sorry to hear that."

Moeller nodded approval. "I am glad to see you take it so calmly. If I were in your place I should be very frightened. But then, of course"—the pale blue eyes narrowed suddenly—"*I* should know that there was no possible chance of my escaping. Banat, in spite of his lapse in Istanbul, is a formidable young

163

man. And when I consider the fact that ready waiting for me in Genoa there would be reinforcements consisting of several other men quite as experienced as Banat, I should realise that there was not the remotest chance of my being able to reach any sort of sanctuary before the end came. I should be left with only one hope—that they did their work so efficiently that I should know very little about it."

"What do you man by 'as things stand at present'?"

Moeller smiled triumphantly. "Ah! I am so glad. You have gone straight to the heart of the matter. I mean, Mr. Graham, that you need not necessarily die. There is an alternative."

"I see. A lesser evil." But his heart leaped in spite of himself.

"Scarcely an evil," Moeller objected. "An alternative and by no means an unpleasant one." He settled himself more comfortably. "I have already said that I liked you, Mr. Graham. Let me add that I dislike the prospect of violence quite as whole-heartedly as you do. I am lily-livered. I admit it freely. I will go out of my way to avoid seeing the results of an automobile accident. So, you see, if there is any way of settling this matter without bloodshed I should be prejudiced in favour of it. And if you are still uncertain of my personal goodwill towards you, let me put the question in another and harder light. The killing would have to be hurried, would consequently subject the killers to additional risks and would, therefore, be expensive. Don't misunderstand me, please. I shall spare no expense if it is necessary. But, naturally enough, I hope it won't be necessary. I can assure you that no one, with the possible exception of yourself, will be more delighted than I am if we can dispose of this whole thing in a friendly way as between business men. I hope you will at least believe that I am sincere in that."

Graham began to get angry. "I don't care a damn whether you're sincere or not."

Moeller looked crestfallen. "No, I suppose you don't. I was forgetting that you have been under some nervous strain. You are naturally interested only in getting home safely to England. That may be possible. It just depends on how calmly and logically you can approach the situation. It is necessary, as you must have gathered, that the completion of the work you are doing should be delayed. Now, if you die before you get back to England, somebody else will be sent to Turkey to do your work over again. I understand that the work as a whole would thus be delayed for six weeks. I also understand that that delay would be sufficient for the purposes of those interested. You might, might you not, conclude from that that the simplest way of dealing with the matter would be to kidnap you in Genoa and keep you under lock and key for the requisite six weeks and then release you, eh?"

"You might."

Moeller shook his head. "But you would be wrong. You would disappear. Your employers and, no doubt, the Turkish Government would make inquiries about you. The Italian police would be informed. The British Foreign Office would address bombastic demands for information to the Italian Government. The Italian Government, conscious that its neutrality was being compromised, would bestir itself. I might find myself in serious difficulties, especially when you were released and could tell your story. It would be most inconvenient for me to be wanted by the Italian police. You see what I mean?"

"Yes, I see."

"The straightforward course is to kill you. There is,

however, a third possibility." He paused and then said: "You are a very fortunate man, Mr. Graham."

"What does *that* mean?"

"In times of peace only the fanatical nationalist demands that a man should surrender himself body and soul to the government of the country in which he was born. Yet, in war time, when men are being killed and there is emotion in the air, even an intelligent man may be so far carried away as to talk of his 'duty to his country.' You are fortunate because you happen to be in a business which sees these heroics for what they are: the emotional excesses of the stupid and brutish. 'Love of country!' There's a curious phrase. Love of a particular patch of earth? Scarcely. Put a German down in a field in Northern France, tell him that it is Hannover, and he cannot contradict you. Love of fellow-countrymen? Surely not. A man will like some of them and dislike others. Love of the country's culture? The men who know most of their countries' cultures are usually the most intelligent and the least patriotic. Love of the country's government? But governments are usually disliked by the people they govern. Love of country, we see, is merely a sloppy mysticism based on ignorance and fear. It has its uses, of course. When a ruling class wishes a people to do something which that people does not want to do, it appeals to patriotism. And, of course, one of the things that people most dislike is allowing themselves to be killed. But I must apologise. These are old arguments and I am sure you are familiar with them."

"Yes, I'm familiar with them."

"I am so relieved. I should not like to think that I had been wrong in judging you to be a man of intelligence. And it makes what I have to say so much easier."

"Well, what *have* you got to say?"

Moeller stubbed his cigarette out. "The third possibility, Mr. Graham, is that you might be induced to retire from business for six weeks of your own free will—that you should take a holiday."

"Are you mad?"

Moeller smiled. "I see your difficulty, believe me. If you simply go into hiding for six weeks, it may be rather awkward to explain matters when you return home. I understand. Hysterical fools might say that in choosing to remain alive instead of choosing to be killed by our friend Banat you did something shameful. The facts that the work would have been delayed in any case and that you were of more use to your country and its allies alive than dead would be ignored. Patriots, in common with other mystics, dislike logical argument. It would be necessary to practise a small deception. Let me tell you how it could be arranged."

"You're wasting your time."

Moeller took no notice. "There are some things, Mr. Graham, which not even patriots can control. One of those things is illness. You have come from Turkey where, thanks to earthquakes and floods, there have been several outbreaks of typhus. What could be more likely than that the moment you get ashore at Genoa a mild attack of typhus should develop? And what then? Well, of course, you will be taken immediately to a private clinic and the doctor there will, at your request, write to your wife and employers in England. Of course, there will be the inevitable delays of war. By the time anyone can get to see you, the crisis will have passed and you will be convalescent: convalescent but much too weak to work or travel. But in six weeks' time you will have recovered sufficiently to do both. All will be well again. How does that appeal to you, Mr. Graham? To me it seems the only solution satisfactory to both of us."

"I see. You don't have the bother of shooting me. I'm out of the way for the requisite six weeks and can't tell tales afterwards without showing myself up. Is that it?"

"That's a very crude way of putting it; but you are quite right. That *is* it. How do you like the idea? Personally I should find the prospect of six weeks' absolute peace and quiet in the place I have in mind very attractive. It is quite near Santa Margherita, overlooking the sea and surrounded by pines. But then, I am old. You might fret."

He hesitated. "Of course," he went on slowly, "if you liked the idea, it might be possible to arrange for Señora Gallindo to share your six weeks' holiday."

Graham reddened. "What on earth do you mean?"

Moeller shrugged. "Come now, Mr. Graham! I am not short-sighted. If the suggestion really offends you, I apologise humbly. If not ... I need hardly say that you would be the only patients there. The medical staff, which would consist of myself, Banat, and another man, apart from the servants, would be unobtrusive unless you were receiving visitors from England. However, that could be discussed later. Now what do you think?"

Graham steeled himself to make an effort. He said with deliberate ease: "I think you're bluffing. Hasn't it occurred to you that I may not be such a fool as you think? I shall, of course, repeat this conversation to the Captain. There will be police inquiries when we reach Genoa. My papers are perfectly genuine. Yours are not. Nor are Banat's. I have nothing to hide. You have plenty to hide. So has Banat. You're relying on my fear of being killed forcing me to agree to this scheme of yours. It won't. It won't keep my mouth shut either. I admit that I have been badly scared. I have had a very unpleasant twenty-four hours. I suppose that's your way of inducing a receptive frame of mind. Well, it doesn't work with me. I'm worried all right; I should be a fool if I weren't; but I'm not worried out of my senses. You're bluffing, Moeller. That's what I think. Now you can get out."

Moeller did not move. He said, as if he were a surgeon musing over some not entirely unforeseen complication: "Yes, I was afraid you might misunderstand me. A pity." He looked up. "And to whom are you going to take your story in the first place, Mr. Graham? The Purser? The third officer was telling me about your curious behaviour over poor Monsieur Mavrodopoulos. Apparently you have been making wild allegations to the effect that he is a criminal named Banat who wants to kill you. The ship's officers, including the Captain, seem to have enjoyed the joke very much. But even the best of jokes become tiresome if it is told too often. There would be a certain unreality about the story that I, too, was a criminal who wanted to kill you. Isn't there a medical name for that sort of delusion? Come now, Mr. Graham! You tell me that you are not a fool. Please do not behave like one. Do you think that I should have approached you in this way if I had thought that you might be able to embarrass me in the way you suggest? I hope not. You are no less foolish when you interpret my reluctance to have you killed as weakness. You may prefer lying dead in a gutter with a bullet in your back to spending six weeks in a villa on the Ligurian Riviera: that is your affair. But please do not deceive yourself: those *are* the inevitable alternatives."

Graham smiled grimly. "And the little homily on patriotism is to still any qualms I might have about accepting the inevitable. I see. Well, I'm sorry, but it doesn't work. I still think you're bluffing. You've bluffed very well. I admit that. You had me worried. I really thought for a moment that I had to choose between possible death and sinking my pride—just like the hero in a melodrama. My real choice was, of course, between using my common senses and letting my stomach do my thinking for me. Well, Mr. Moeller, if that's all you have to say . . ."

Moeller got slowly to his feet. "Yes, Mr. Graham," he said calmly, "that is all I have to say." He seemed to hesitate. Then, very deliberately, he sat down again. "No, Mr. Graham, I have changed my mind. There *is* something else that I should say. It is just possible that on thinking this thing over calmly you may decide that you have been silly and that I may not be as clumsy as you now seem to think. Frankly, I don't expect you to do so. You are pathetically sure of yourself. But in case your stomach should after all take control, I think I should issue a warning."

"Against what?"

Moeller smiled. "One of the many things you don't seem to know is that Colonel Haki considered it advisable to install one of his agents on board to watch over you. I tried hard to interest you in him yesterday, but was unsuccessful. Ihsan Kuvetli is unprepossessing, I agree; but he has the reputation of being a clever little man. If he had not been a patriot, he would have been rich."

"Are you trying to tell me that Kuvetli is a Turkish agent?"

"I am indeed, Mr. Graham!" The pale blue eyes narrowed. "The reason why I approached you this evening instead of to-morrow evening is because I wanted to see you before he made himself known to you. He did not, I think, find out who I was until to-day. He searched my cabin this evening. I think that he must have heard me talking to Banat; the partitions between the cabins are absurdly thin. In any case, I thought it likely that, realising the danger you were in, he would decide that the time had come

170

to approach you. You see, Mr. Graham, with his experience, he is not likely to make the mistake that you are making. However, he has his duty to do and I have no doubt that he will have evolved some laborious plan for getting you to France in safety. What I want to warn you against is telling him of this suggestion I have made to you. You see, if you should after all come round to my way of thinking, it would be embarrassing for both of us if an agent of the Turkish Government knew of our little deception. We could scarcely expect him to keep silent. You see what I mean, Mr. Graham? If you let Kuvetli into the secret you will destroy the only chance of returning to England alive that remains to you." He smiled faintly. "It's a solemn thought, isn't it?" He got up again and went to the door. "That was all I wanted to say. Good night, Mr. Graham."

Graham watched the door close and then sat down on the bunk. The blood was beating through his head as if he had been running. The time for bluffing was over. He should be deciding what he was going to do. He had to think calmly and clearly.

But he could not think calmly and clearly. He was confused. He became conscious of the vibration and movement of the ship and wondered if he had imagined what had just happened. But there was the depression in the bunk where Moeller had been sitting and the cabin was filled with the smoke from his cigarette. It was Haller who was the creature of imagination.

He was conscious now more of humiliation than of fear. He had become almost used to the tight sensation in his chest, the quick hammering of his heart, the dragging at his stomach, the crawling of his spine which were his body's responses to his predicament. In a queer, horrible way it had been stimulating. He had felt that he was pitting his wits against those of

171

an enemy—a dangerous enemy but an intellectual inferior—with a chance of winning. Now he knew that he had been doing nothing of the kind. The enemy had been laughing up their sleeves at him. It had never even occurred to him to suspect "Haller." He had just sat there politely listening to extracts from a book. Heavens, what a fool the man must think him! He and Banat between them had seen through him as if he were made of glass. Not even his wretched little passages with Josette had escaped their notice. Probably they had seen him kissing her. And as a final measure of their contempt for him, it had been Moeller who had informed him that Mr. Kuvetli was a Turkish agent charged with his protection. Kuvetli! It was funny. Josette would be amused.

He remembered suddenly that he had promised to return to the saloon. She would be getting anxious. And the cabin was stifling. He could think better if he had some air. He got up and put on his overcoat.

José and Banat were still playing cards; José with a peculiar intentness as if he suspected Banat of cheating; Banat coolly and deliberately. Josette was leaning back in her chair smoking. Graham realised with a shock that he had left the room less than half an hour previously. It was amazing what could happen to your mind in so short a time; how the whole atmosphere of a place could change. He found himself noticing things about the saloon which he had not noticed before: a brass plate with the name of the builders of the ship engraved on it, a stain on the carpet, some old magazines stacked in a corner.

He stood there for a moment staring at the brass plate. The Mathises and the Italians were sitting there reading and did not look up. He looked past them and saw Josette turning her head back to watch the game. She had seen him. He went across to the farther door and out to the shelter deck.

She would follow him soon to find out if he had been successful. He walked slowly along the deck wondering what he would say to her, whether or not to tell her about Moeller and his "alternative." Yes, he would tell her. She would tell him that he was all right, that Moeller was bluffing. But supposing Moeller *weren't* bluffing! "They will do anything to see that it is so. *Anything*, Mr. Graham! Do you understand?" Haki had not talked about bluffing. The wound under the grimy bandage on his hand did not feel like bluffing. And if Moeller wasn't bluffing, what was he, Graham, going to do?

He stopped and stared out at the lights on the coast. They were nearer now; near enough for him to see the movement of the boat in relation to them. It was incredible that this should be happening to him. Impossible! Perhaps, after all, he had been badly wounded in Istanbul and it was all a fantasy born of anæsthesia. Perhaps he would become conscious again soon to find himself in a hospital bed. But the teak rail, wet with dew, on which his hand rested was real enough. He gripped it in sudden anger at his own stupidity. He should be thinking, cudgelling his brains, making plans, deciding; doing something instead of standing there mooning. Moeller had left him over five minutes ago and here he was still trying to escape from his senses into a fairyland of hospitals and anæsthetics. What was he going to do about Kuvetli? Should he approach him or wait to be approached? What . . . ?

There were quick footsteps on the deck behind him. It was Josette, her fur coat thrown over her shoulders, her face pale and anxious in the dingy glare of the deck light. She seized his arm. "What has happened? Why were you so long?"

"There was no gun there."

"But there must be. Something has happened.

173

When you walked into the *salone* just now you looked as if you had seen a ghost or were going to be sick. What is it, *chéri?*"

"There was no gun there," he repeated. "I searched carefully."

"You were not seen?"

"No, I wasn't seen."

She sighed with relief. "I was afraid when I saw your face . . ." She broke off. "But don't you see? It is all right. He does not carry a gun. There is no gun in his cabin. He has not got a gun." She laughed. "Perhaps he has pawned it. Ah, do not look so serious, *chéri.* He may get a gun in Genoa, but then it will be too late. Nothing can happen to you. You will be all right." She put on a woebegone expression. "I am the one who is in trouble now."

"You?"

"Your smelly little friend plays cards very well. He is winning money from José. José does not like that. He will have to cheat and cheating puts him in a bad temper. He says that it is bad for his nerves. Really it is that he likes to win because he is a better player." She paused and added suddenly: "Please wait!"

They had reached the end of the deck. She stopped and faced him. "What is the matter, *chéri?* You are not listening to what I am saying. You are thinking of something else." She pouted. "Ah, I know. It is your wife. Now that there is no danger you think of her again."

"No."

"You are sure?"

"Yes, I am sure." He knew now that he did not want to tell her about Moeller. He wanted her to talk to him believing that there was no longer any danger, that nothing could happen to him, that he could walk down the gangway at Genoa without fear. Afraid to create his own illusion, he could live in one of her making. He managed to smile. "You mustn't take any notice of me, Josette. I'm tired. You know, it's a very tiring business searching other people's cabins."

Immediately she was all sympathy. "*Mon pauvre chéri.* It is my fault, not yours. I forget how unpleasant things have been for you. Would you like us to go back the the *salone* and have a little drink?"

He would have done almost anything for a drink but go back to the saloon where he could see Banat. "No. Tell me what we shall do first when we arrive in Paris."

She looked at him quickly, smiling. "If we do not walk we shall get cold." She wriggled into her coat and linked her arm in his. "So we are going to Paris together?"

"Of course! I thought it was all arranged."

"Oh yes, but"—she pressed his arm against her side—"I did not think that you were serious. You see," she went on carefully, "so many men like to talk about what will happen, but they do not always like to remember what they have said. It is not that they do not mean what they say but that they do not always feel the same. You understand me, *chéri?*"

"Yes, I understand."

"I want you to understand," she went on, "because it is very important to me. I am a dancer and must think of my career also." She turned to him impulsively. "But you will think that I am selfish and I would not like you to think that. It is just that I like you very much and do not wish you to do anything simply because you have made a promise. As long as you understand that, it is all right. We will not talk about it." She snapped her fingers. "Look! When we get to Paris we will go straight to a hotel which I know of near the St. Philippe du Roule Metro. It is very modern and respectable and if you wish we can have a bathroom. It is not expensive. Then we will have

175

champagne cocktails at the Ritz bar. They are only nine francs. While we have those drinks we can decide where to eat. I am very tired of Turkish foods and the sight of ravioli makes me ill. We must have good French food." She paused and added hesitantly, "I have never been to the Tour d'Argent."

"You shall."

"You mean it? I shall eat until I am as fat as a pig. After that we will begin."

"Begin?"

"There are some little places that are still open late in spite of the police. I will introduce you to a great friend of mine. She was the *sous-maquecée* of the Moulin Galant when Le Boulanger had it and before the gangsters came. You understand *sous-maquecée*?"

"No."

She laughed. "It is very bad of me. I will explain to you another time. But you will like Suzie. She saved a lot of money and now she is very respectable. She had a place in the rue de Liège which was better than Le Jockey Cabaret in Istanbul. She had to close it when the war came but she has opened another place in an impasse off the rue Pigalle and those who are her friends can go there. She had a great many friends and so she is making money again. She is quite old and the police do not trouble her. She shrugs her shoulders at them. Just because there is this filthy war there is no reason why we should all be miserable. I have other friends in Paris, too. You will like them when I introduce you. When they know that you are my friend they will be polite. They are very polite and nice when you are introduced by someone who is known in the quarter."

She went on talking about them. Most of them were women (Lucette, Dolly, Sonia, Claudette, Berthe) but there were one or two men (Jojo, Ventura) who were foreigners and had not been mobilised. She spoke of them vaguely but with an enthusiasm half defensive, half real. They might not be rich as Americans understood being rich, but they were people of the world. Each was remarkable in some particular. One was "very intelligent," another had a friend in the Ministry of the Interior, another was going to buy a villa at San Tropez and invite all his friends there for the summer. All were "amusing" and very useful if one wanted "anything special." She did not say what she meant by "anything special" and Graham did not ask her. He did not object to the picture she was painting. The prospect of sitting in the Café Graf buying drinks for *bizness* men and women from the places up the hill seemed to him at that moment infinitely attractive. He would be safe and free; himself again; able to think his own thoughts, to smile without stretching his nerves to breaking point when he did so. It must happen. It was absurd that he should be killed. Moeller was right about one thing at least. He would be more use to his country alive than dead.

Considerably more! Even if the Turkish contract were delayed for six weeks it would still have to be fulfilled. If he were alive at the end of the six weeks he would be able to go on with it; perhaps he might even make up for some of the lost time. He was, after all, the company's chief designer and it would be difficult to replace him in war time. He had been truthful enough when he had told Haki that there were dozens of other men with his qualifications; but he had not thought it necessary to bolster up Haki's argument by explaining that those dozens were made up of Americans, Frenchmen, Germans, Japanese and Czechs as well as Englishmen. Surely the sensible course would be the safe one. He was an engineer, not a professional secret agent. Presumably, a secret agent would have been equal to dealing with men like Moeller and Banat. He, Graham, was not. It was not for him to decide whether or not Moeller was bluffing. His business was to stay alive. Six weeks on the Ligurian Riviera could not do him any harm. It meant lying, of course: lying to Stephanie and to their friends, to his managing director and to the representatives of the Turkish Government. He couldn't tell them the truth. They would think that he ought to have risked his life. It was the sort of thing people did think when they were safe and snug in their arm-chairs. But if he lied, would they believe him? The people at home would; but what about Haki? Haki would smell a rat and ask questions. And Kuvetli? Moeller would have to do something about putting him off. It would be a tricky business; but Moeller would arrange things. Moeller was used to that sort of thing. Moeller. . . .

He stopped with a jerk. For God's sake, what was he thinking? He must be out of his senses! Moeller was an enemy agent. What he, Graham, had been turning over in his mind was nothing less than treason. And yet. . . . And yet what? He knew suddenly that something had snapped in his mind. The idea of doing a deal with an enemy agent was no longer unthinkable. He could consider Moeller's suggestion on its merits, coolly and calmly. He was becoming demoralised. He could no longer trust himself.

Josette was shaking his arm. "What is it, *chéri?* What is the matter?"

"I've just remembered something," he muttered.

"Ah!" she said angrily, "that is not at all polite. I ask you if you wish to go on walking. You take no notice. I ask you again and you stop as if you were ill. You have not been listening to what I was saying."

He pulled himself together. "Oh yes, I've been listening, but something you said reminded me that if I am to stop in Paris I shall have to write several important business letters so that I can post them immediately I get there." He added with a fair assumption of jauntiness: "I don't want to work while I am in Paris."

"If it is not these *salauds* who tried to kill you, it is business," she grumbled. But she was apparently mollified.

"I apologise, Josette. It shan't happen again. Are you sure you are warm? You wouldn't like a drink?" He wanted to get away now. He knew what he must do and was impatient to do it before he could begin to think.

But she took his arm again. "No, it is all right. I am not angry and I am not cold. If we go up on the top deck you can kiss me to show that we are friends again. Soon I must go back to José. I said that I would only be a few minutes."

Half an hour later he went down to his cabin, took off his coat and went to look for the steward. He found him busy with a mop and bucket in the lavatories.

"Signore?"

"I promised to lend Signor Kuvetli a book. What is the number of his cabin?"

"Three, signore."

Graham walked back to cabin number three and stood for a moment hesitating. Perhaps he should think again before he did anything decisive, anything for which he might be sorry later. Perhaps it would be better if he left it until the morning. Perhaps ...

He set his teeth, raised his hand and knocked on the door.

CHAPTER IX

Mr. Kuvetli opened the door.

He was wearing an old red wool dressing gown over a flannel night-shirt and his fringe of grey hair stood out from the sides of his head in ringlets. He had a book in his hand and looked as if he had been lying in his bunk reading. He stared at Graham blankly for a moment, then his smile returned.

"Mr. Graham! Is very good to see you. What can I do, please?"

At the sight of him, Graham's heart sank. It was to this grubby little man with a stupid smile that he was proposing to commit his safety. But it was too late to turn back now. He said: "I wonder if I could have a talk with you, Mr. Kuvetli."

Mr. Kuvetli blinked a little shiftily. "Talk? Oh, yes. Come in, please."

Graham stepped into the cabin. It was as small as his own and very stuffy.

Mr. Kuvetli smoothed out the blankets on his bunk. "Please take seat."

Graham sat down and opened his mouth to speak, but Mr. Kuvetli forestalled him.

"Cigarette, please, Mr. Graham?"

"Thank you." He took a cigarette. "I had a visit from Herr Professor Haller earlier this evening," he added; and then, remembering that the bulkheads were thin, glanced at them.

Mr. Kuvetli struck a match and held it out. "Herr Professor Haller is very interesting man, eh?" He lit Graham's cigarette and his own and blew the match out. "Cabins on both sides empty," he remarked.

"Then . . ."

"Please," interrupted Mr. Kuvetli, "will you allow me to speak French? My English is not very good, eh? Your French is very good. We understand better each."

"By all means."

"Now, then, we can talk easily." Mr. Kuvetli sat down beside him on the bunk. "Monsieur Graham, I was going to introduce myself to you to-morrow. Now, Monsieur Moeller has saved me the trouble, I think. You know that I am not a tobacco merchant, eh?"

"According to Moeller you are a Turkish agent acting under Colonel Haki's orders. Is that so?"

"Yes, that is so. I will be truthful. I am surprised that you have not dicovered me before this. When the Frenchman asked me what firm I belonged to I had to say Pazar and Co., because I had given that name to you. Unfortunately, the firm of Pazar and Co. does not exist. Naturally he was puzzled. I was able to prevent him from asking more questions then, but I expected him to discuss it with you later." The smile had gone and with it the bright-eyed stupidity which, for Graham, had been the tobacco merchant. In its place was a firm determined mouth, and a pair of steady brown eyes which surveyed him with something very like good-humoured contempt.

"He did not discuss it."

181

"And you did not suspect that I was avoiding his questions?" He shrugged. "One always takes unnecessary precautions. People are so much more trusting than one supposes."

"Why should I suspect?" Graham demanded irritably. "What I cannot understand is why you did not approach me as soon as you knew that Banat was on the ship. I suppose," he added spitefully, "that you *do* know that Banat is on the ship?"

"Yes, I know," said Mr. Kuvetli airily. "I did not approach you for three reasons." He held up podgy fingers. "Colonel Haki instructed me in the first place that your attitude to his efforts to protect you were unsympathetic and that unless it became necessary I would do better to remain unknown to you. Secondly, Colonel Haki has a low opinion of your ability to conceal your feelings and considered that if I wished to keep my true identity secret I had better not tell you of it."

Graham was scarlet. "And what about the third reason?"

"Thirdly," continued Mr. Kuvetli serenely, "I wished to see what Banat and Moeller would do. You tell me that Moeller has talked to you. Excellent. I would like to hear what he had to say."

Graham was angry now. "Before I waste my time doing that," he said coldly, "supposing you show me your credentials. So far I have only Moeller's word and your own that you *are* a Turkish agent. I've already made some silly mistakes on this trip. I don't intend to make any more."

To his surprise, Mr. Kuvetli grinned. "I am pleased to see that you are in such excellent spirits, Monsieur Graham. I was getting a little worried about you this evening. In this sort of situation, whisky does more harm to the nerves than good. Excuse me, please." He turned to his jacket hanging on the hook behind the door and produced from the pocket of it a letter which he handed to Graham. "That was given to me by Colonel Haki to give to you. I think you will find it satisfactory."

Graham looked at it. It was an ordinary letter of introduction written in French on notepaper embossed with the title and address of the Turkish Ministry of the Interior. It was addressed to him personally and signed "Zia Haki." He put it in his pocket. "Yes, Monsieur Kuvetli, it is quite satisfactory. I must apologise for doubting your word."

"It was correct of you to do so," said Mr. Kuvetli primly. "And now, Monsieur, tell me about Moeller. I am afraid Banat's appearance on the ship must have been a shock to you. I felt guilty about keeping you ashore in Athens. But it was for the best. As to Moeller . . ."

Graham looked at him quickly. "Wait a minute! Do you mean to say that you knew Banat was coming aboard? Do you mean that you hung about in Athens asking all those fool questions solely in order to prevent my finding out before we sailed that Banat was on board?"

Mr. Kuvetli looked sheepish. "It was necessary. You must see . . ."

"Of all the damned . . . !" began Graham violently.

"One moment, please," said Mr. Kuvetli sharply. "I have said that it was necessary. At Çanakkale I received a telegram from Colonel Haki saying that Banat had left Turkey, that it was possible that he might try to join the ship at the Piræus and . . ."

"You knew that! And yet . . ."

"Please, Monsieur! I will continue. Colonel Haki added that I was to keep you here on the ship. That was intelligent. On the ship nothing could happen to you. Banat might have been going to the Piræus for the purpose of frightening you on to the land, where

183

very unpleasant things could happen to you. Wait, please! I went to Athens with you partly to see that you were not attacked while you were ashore and partly so that if Banat did join the ship, you would not see him until we had sailed."

"But why, in the name of goodness, didn't Colonel Haki arrest Banat or at least delay him until it was too late for him to reach the ship?"

"Because Banat would certainly have been replaced. We know all about Banat. A strange Monsieur Mavrodopoulos would have been a new problem."

"But you say that Banat's, or, rather, Moeller's idea might have been to scare me off the boat. Banat could not know that I knew him?"

"You told Colonel Haki that Banat was pointed out to you in Le Jockey Cabaret. Banat was watching you then. He would probably know that you had noticed him. He is not an amateur. You see Colonel Haki's point of view? If they were hoping to drive you on to the land and kill you there, it would be better for them to attempt to do so and fail than for the attempt to be frustrated in time for them to make other arrangements. As it happens, however," he went on cheerfully, "their intention was not to drive you on to the land and my precautions were wasted. Banat did join the ship, but he stayed in his cabin until the pilot had been taken off."

"Precisely!" snarled Graham. "I could have gone ashore, taken a train and been safe in Paris by now."

Mr. Kuvetli considered the criticism for a moment and then slowly shook his head. "I do not think so. You have forgotten Monsieur Moeller. I do not think that he and Banat would have stayed on the boat very long if you had not returned by sailing time."

Graham laughed shortly. "Did you know that then?"

Mr. Kuvetli comtemplated dirty fingernails. "I will

be very honest, Monsieur Graham. I did not know it. I knew *of* Monsieur Moeller, of course. I was, through an intermediary, once offered a large sum of money to work for him. I had seen a photograph of him. But photographs are mostly useless. I did not recognise him. The fact that he came aboard at Istanbul prevented my suspecting him. Banat's behaviour made me think that I had overlooked something, and when I saw him talking to the Herr Professor I made some inquiries."

"He says that you searched his cabin."

"I did. I found letters addressed to him in Sofia."

"There has," said Graham bitterly, "been quite a lot of cabin searching. Last night Banat stole my revolver from my suitcase. This evening I went to his cabin and tried to find his gun, the gun he used on me in Istanbul. It was not there. When I returned to my cabin, Moeller was there with Banat's gun."

Mr. Kuvetli had been listening gloomily. "If," he now said, "you will please tell me what Moeller had to say we shall both get to sleep much sooner."

Graham smiled. "You know, Kuvetli, I have had several surprises on this ship. You are the first pleasant one." And then the smile faded. "Moeller came to tell me that unless I agree to delay my return to England for six weeks I shall be murdered within five minutes of my landing in Genoa. He says that apart from Banat, he has other men waiting in Genoa to do the killing."

Mr. Kuvetli did not seem surprised. "And where does he suggest that you should spend the six weeks?"

"In a villa near Santa Margherita. The idea is that I should be certified by a doctor as suffering from typhus and that I should stay in this villa as if it were a clinic. Moeller and Banat would be the medical staff if anyone should come out from England to see me. He proposes, you see, to involve me in the deception so that I cannot tell tales afterwards."

Mr. Kuvetli raised his eyebrows. "And how was I concerned?"

Graham told him.

"And, believing Monsieur Moeller, you decided to ignore his advice and tell me about his suggestion?" Mr. Kuvetli beamed approvingly. "That was very courageous of you, Monsieur."

Graham reddened. "Do you think that I might have agreed?"

Mr. Kuvetli misunderstood. "I think nothing," he said hastily. "But"—he hesitated—"when a person's life is in danger he is not always quite normal. He may do things which he would not do in the ordinary way. He cannot be blamed."

Graham smiled. "I will be frank with you. I came to you now instead of in the morning so that there could be no chance of my thinking things over and deciding to take his advice after all."

"What is important is," said Mr. Kuvetli quietly, "that you *have* in fact come to me. Did you tell him that you were going to do so?"

"No. I told him that I thought he was bluffing."

"And *do* you think that he was?"

"I don't know."

Mr. Kuvetli scratched his armpits thoughtfully. "There are so many things to be considered. And it depends on what you mean by saying that he is bluffing. If you mean that he could not or would not kill you, I think you are wrong. He could and would."

"But how? I have a Consul. What is to prevent my getting into a taxi at the dock and going straight to the Consulate? I could arrange for some sort of protection there."

Mr. Kuvetli lit another cigarette. "Do you know where the British Consulate-General in Genoa is?"

"The taxi-driver would know."

"I can tell you myself. It is at the corner of the Via Ippolito d'Aste. This ship docks at the Ponte San Giorgio in the Vittorio Emanuele basin, several kilometres away from your Consulate. I have travelled this way before and so I know what I am saying. Genoa is a great port. I doubt, Monsieur Graham, whether you would complete one of those kilometres. They will be waiting for you with a car. When you took the taxi they would follow you as far as the Via Francia, then force the taxi on to the pavement and shoot you as you sit there."

"I could telephone to the Consul from the dock."

"Certainly you could. But you would have to go through the Customs shed first. You would then have to wait for the Consul to arrive. *Wait,* Monsieur! Do you understand what that means? Let us suppose that you were to reach the Consul by telephone immediately and convince him that your case was urgent. You would still have to wait at least half an hour for him. Let me tell you that your chances of surviving that half-hour would not be lessened if you spent it drinking prussic acid. To kill an unarmed, unguarded man is never difficult. Among the sheds on the quay it would be simplicity itself. No, I do not think Moeller is bluffing when he says that he can kill you."

"But what about his proposal? He seemed very eager to persuade me to agree."

Mr. Kuvetli fingered the back of his head. "There could be several explanations of that. For instance, it is possible that his intention is to kill you in any case and that he wishes to do so with as little trouble as possible. One cannot deny that it would be easier to kill you on the road to Santa Margherita than on the waterfront at Genoa."

"That's a pleasing idea."

"I am inclined to think that it is the correct one."

187

Mr. Kuvetli frowned. "You see, this proposal of his looks very simple—you are taken ill, there is a forged medical certificate, you get better, you go home. *Voilà!* It is done. But think now of the actuality. You are an Englishman in a hurry to get to England. You land in Genoa. What would you do normally? Take the train for Paris, without a doubt. But what is it necessary to do now? You must, for some mysterious reason, remain in Genoa long enough to discover that you have typhus. Also you must not do what anyone else would do in those circumstances—you must not go to a hospital. You must instead go to a private clinic near Santa Margherita. Is it possible that it would not be thought in England that your behaviour was curious? I think not. Furthermore, typhus is a disease which must be notified to the authorities. That could not be done in this case because there would be no typhus and the medical authorities would soon discover the fact. And supposing your friends discover that your case has not been notified. They might. You are of some importance. The British Consul might be asked to investigate. And then what? No, I cannot see Monsieur Moeller taking such absurd risks. Why should he? It would be easier to kill you."

"He says that he does not like having people killed if he can help it."

Mr. Kuvetli giggled. "He must think you very stupid indeed. Did he tell you what he would do about my presence here?"

"No."

"I am not surprised. For that plan to succeed as he explained it to you, there would be only one thing he could do—kill me. And even when he had killed me I should still embarrass him. Colonel Haki would see to that. I am afraid that Monsieur's proposal is not very honest."

"It sounded convincing. I may say that he was

188

prepared to allow Señora Gallindo to make up the party if I liked to take her along."

Mr. Kuvetli leered: a scurfy faun in a flannel night-shirt. "And did you tell Señora Gallindo that?"

Graham flushed. "She knows nothing of Moeller. I told her about Banat. I'm afraid I gave myself away last night when Banat came into the saloon. She asked me what was wrong and I told her. Anyway," he added defensively but none too truthfully, "I needed her help. It was she who arranged to keep Banat occupied while I searched his cabin."

"By arranging for the good José to play cards with him? Quite so. As to the suggestion that she should accompany you, I think that, if you had accepted it, it would have been withdrawn. It would, no doubt, be explained that difficulties had arisen. Does José know of this business?"

"No. I don't think that she would tell him. She's trustworthy, I think," he added with as much non-chalance as he could muster.

"No woman is trustworthy," gloated Mr. Kuvetli. "But I do not begrudge you your amusements, Monsieur Graham." He moistened his upper lip with the tip of his tongue and grinned. "Señora Gallindo is very attractive."

Graham checked the retort that rose to his lips. "Very," he said tersely. "Meanwhile we have reached the conclusion that I shall be killed if I accept Moeller's proposal and killed if I don't." And then he lost control of himself. "For God's sake, Kuvetli," he burst out in English, "do you think it's pleasant for me to sit here listening to you telling me how easy it would be for these lice to kill me! What am I going to *do?*"

Mr. Kuvetli patted his knee consolingly. "My dear friend, I understand perfectly. I was merely showing you that it would be impossible for you to land in the ordinary way."

189

"But what other way *can* I land? I'm not invisible."

"I will tell you," said Mr. Kuvetli complacently. "It is very simple. You see, although this ship does not actually reach the quayside for the landing of passengers until nine o'clock on Saturday morning, she arrives off Genoa in the early hours, at about four o'clock. Night pilotage is expensive; accordingly, although she takes on a pilot as soon as it begins to get light, she does not move in until sunrise. The pilot boat ..."

"If you're suggesting that I leave by the pilot boat, it's impossible."

"For you, yes. For me, no. I am privileged. I have a diplomatic *laisser passer*." He patted his jacket pocket. "By eight o'clock I can be at the Turkish Consulate. Arrangements can then be made for getting you away safely and taking you to the airport. The international train service is not as good as it used to be, and the Paris train does not leave until two o'clock in the afternoon. It is better that you do not remain so long in Genoa. We will charter a plane to take you to Paris immediately."

Graham's heart began to beat faster. An extraordinary feeling of lightness and ease came over him. He wanted to laugh. He said stolidly: "It sounds all right."

"It will be all right, but precautions must be taken to see that it is so. If Monsieur Moeller suspects that there is a chance of your escaping, something unpleasant will happen. Listen carefully, please." He scratched his chest and then held up a forefinger. "First; you must go to Monsieur Moeller to-morrow and tell him that you agree to his suggestion that you should stay in Santa Margherita."

"What!"

"It is the best way to keep him quiet. I leave you to choose your own opportunity. But I will suggest the following: it is possible that he will approach you again, and so perhaps it will be best if you give him time to do so. Wait until late in the evening. If he has not approached you by then, go to him. Do not appear to be too ingenuous, but agree to do what he wants. When you have done that, go to your cabin, lock the door, and remain there. Do not leave your cabin under any circumstances until eight o'clock the following morning. It might be dangerous.

"Now comes the important part of your instructions. At eight o'clock in the morning you must be ready with your baggage. Call the steward, tip him, and tell him to put your baggage in the Customs shed. There must be no mistake at this point. What you have to do is to remain on the ship until I come to tell you that the preparations have been made and that it is safe for you to land. There are difficulties. If you remain in your cabin the steward will make you go ashore with the rest, including Monsieur Moeller and Banat. If you go on deck, the same thing will happen. You must see that you are not forced to go ashore before it is safe for you to do so."

"But how?"

"I am explaining that. What you must do is to leave your cabin and then, taking care that nobody sees you, to go into the nearest unoccupied cabin. You have cabin number five. Go into cabin number four. That is the next cabin to this. Wait there. You will be quite safe. You will have tipped the steward. If he thinks of you again at all it will be to assume that you have gone ashore. If he is asked about you he will certainly not look in unoccupied cabins. Monsieur Moeller and Banat will naturally be looking for you. You will have agreed to go with them. But they will have to go ashore to wait. By that time we shall be there and able to act."

"Act?"

Mr. Kuvetli smiled grimly. "We shall have two men for every one of theirs. I do not think that they will try to stop us. Are you quite clear about what you have to do?"

"Quite clear."

"There is a small matter. Monsieur Moeller will ask you if I have made myself known to you. You will, of course, say yes. He will ask you what I said. You will tell him that I offered to escort you to Paris myself and that when you insisted on going to the British Consul, I threatened you."

"Threatened me!"

"Yes." Mr. Kuvetli was still smiling, but his eyes had narrowed a little. "If your attitude towards me had been different it might have been necessary for me to threaten you."

"What with?" Graham demanded spitefully. "Death? That would have been absurd, wouldn't it?"

Mr. Kuvetli smiled steadily. "No, Monsieur Graham, not death but with the accusation that you had accepted bribes from an enemy agent to sabotage Turkish naval preparations. You see, Monsieur Graham, it is just as important for me that you return to England without delay as it is for Monsieur Moeller that you should not return."

Graham stared at him. "I see. And this is a gentle reminder that the threat still stands if I should allow myself to be persuaded that Moeller's proposal is, after all, acceptable. Is that it?"

His tone was deliberately offensive. Mr. Kuvetli drew himself up. "I am a Turk, Monsieur Graham," he said with dignity, "and I love my country. I fought with the Gazi for Turkey's freedom. Can you imagine that I would let one man endanger the great work we have done? I am ready to give my life for Turkey. Is it strange that I should not hesitate to do less unpleasant things?"

He had struck an attitude. He was ridiculous and yet, for the very reason that his words were at so odd a variance with his appearance, impressive. Graham was disarmed. He grinned. "Not at all strange. You need have no fears. I shall do exactly what you have told me to do. But supposing he wants to know when our meeting took place?"

"You will tell the truth. It is just possible that you were seen to come to my cabin. You can say that I asked you to do so, that I left a note in your cabin. Remember, too, that we must not be seen in private conversation after this. It will be better if we do not have any sort of conversation. In any case there is nothing more to be said. Everything is arranged. There is only one other matter to be considered—Señora Gallindo."

"What about her?"

"She has part of your confidence. What is her attitude?"

"She thinks that everything is all right now." He reddened. "I said that I would travel with her to Paris."

"And after?"

"She believes that I shall spend some time with her there."

"You did not, of course, intend to do so." He had the air of a schoolmaster dealing with a difficult pupil.

Graham hesitated. "No, I suppose I didn't," he said slowly. "To tell you the truth, it has been pleasant to talk of going to Paris. When you're expecting to be killed . . ."

"But now that you are not expecting to be killed it is different, eh?"

"Yes, it's different." Yet was it so different? He was not quite sure.

Mr. Kuvetli stroked his chin. "On the other hand it would be dangerous to tell her that you have changed

193

your mind," he reflected. "She might be indiscreet—
or angry, perhaps. Say nothing to her. If she discusses
Paris, everything is as it was before. You can explain
that you have business to do in Genoa after the ship
docks and say that you will meet her on the train.
That will prevent her looking for you before she goes
ashore. It is understood?"

"Yes. It is understood."

"She is pretty," Mr. Kuvetli went on thoughtfully.
"It is a pity that your business is so urgent. However,
perhaps you could return to Paris when you have
finished your work." He smiled: the schoolmaster
promising a sweet for good behaviour.

"I suppose I could. Is there anything else?"

Mr. Kuvetli looked up at him slyly. "No. That is all.
Except that I must ask you to continue to look as
distrait as you have been looking since we left the
Piræus. It would be a pity if Monsieur Moeller
should suspect anything from your manner."

"My manner? Oh, yes, I see." He stood up and was
surprised to find that his knees felt quite weak. He
said: "I've often wondered what a condemned man
feels like when they tell him that he has been
reprieved. Now I know."

Mr. Kuvetli smiled patronisingly. "You feel very
well, eh?"

Graham shook his head. "No, Mr. Kuvetli, I don't
feel very well. I feel very sick and very tired and I
can't stop thinking that there must be a mistake."

"A mistake! There is no mistake. You need not
worry. All will be well. Go to bed now, my friend, and
in the morning you will feel better. A mistake!"

Mr. Kuvetli laughed.

CHAPTER X

As Mr. Kuvetli had prophesied, Graham did feel better in the morning. Sitting up in his bunk drinking his coffee, he felt curiously free and competent. The disease from which he had been suffering was cured. He was himself again: well and normal. He had been a fool to worry at all. He ought to have known that everything would be all right. War or no war, men like him weren't shot in the street. That sort of thing just didn't happen. Only the adolescent minds of the Moellers and the Banats could entertain such possibilities. He had no misgivings. Even his hand was better. In the night the bandage had slipped, taking with it the bloody dressing which had been sticking to the wound. He was able to replace it with a piece of lint and two short strips of adhesive plaster. The change, he felt, was symbolic. Not even the knowledge that in the day before him he had some highly disagreeable things to do, could depress him.

The first thing he had to consider was, of course, his attitude towards Moeller. As Mr. Kuvetli had pointed out, it was possible that the man would wait until the evening before making any attempt to find out if the line he had put out the previous evening had caught the fish. That meant that he, Graham, would have to sit through two meals with Moeller and Banat without giving himself away. That, certainly, would not be pleasant. He wondered whether it might not be safer to approach Moeller at once. It would, after all, be far more convincing if the victim made the first move. Or would it be less convincing? Should the fish still be struggling on the hook when the line was reeled in? Evidently Mr. Kuvetli thought that it should. Very well. Mr. Kuvetli's instructions should be followed exactly. The questions of how he was going to behave at lunch and dinner could be left to settle themselves when those times came. As for the actual interview with Moeller, he had ideas about making that convincing. Moeller should not have things all his own way. Rather to his surprise, he found that it was the thought of what he had to do about Josette which worried him most.

He was, he told himself, treating her shabbily. She had been kind to him in her way. Indeed, she could not have been kinder. It was no excuse to say that she had behaved badly over that business of José's revolver. It had been unfair of him to ask her to steal for him: José was, after all, her partner. It would not even be possible now for him to give her that handbag with a thousand-franc note in it, unless he left it for her on his way through Paris, and it was always possible that she would not go to the Hotel des Belges. It was no good protesting that she was out for what she could get. She had made no secret of the fact and he had tacitly accepted it. He was treating her shabbily, he told himself again. It was an attempt to rationalise his feelings about her and it was strangely unsuccessful. He was perplexed.

He did not see her until just before lunch, and then she was with José.

It was a wretched day. The sky was overcast and there was an icy northeast wind with a hint of snow in it. He had spent most of the morning in a corner of the saloon reading some old copies of *L'Illustration* he found there. Mr. Kuvetli had seen and looked through him. He had spoken to no one except the Beronellis, who had given him a defensive "buon giorno," and the Mathises, who had returned his greeting with a frigid bow. He had thought it necessary to explain to the Mathises that his rudeness of the previous evening had been unintentional and due to his feeling ill at the time. The explanation had been accepted by them with some embarrassment and it had occurred to him that they might have preferred a silent feud to an apology. The man had been particularly confused as if he were finding himself in some way ridiculous. They had soon decided that they must go for a walk on deck. Through the porthole Graham had seen them a few minutes later walking with Mr. Kuvetli. The only other person on deck that morning had been Moeller's Armenian demonstrating pathetically, for there was a heavy swell, that her dislike of the sea was no mere figment of her "husband's" imagination. Soon after twelve Graham had collected his hat and coat from his cabin and gone out for the stroll which he had decided should precede the drinking of a large whisky and soda.

He was on his way back to the saloon when he encountered Josette and José.

José stopped with an oath and clutched at his curly soft hat which the wind was trying to snatch from his head.

Josette met Graham's eyes and smiled significantly. "José is angry again. Last night he played cards and lost. It was the little Greek, Mavrodopoulos. The attar of roses was too strong for the California Poppy."

"He is no Greek," said José sourly. "He has the accent of a goat as well as the smell. If he is a Greek I will . . ." He said what he would do.

"But he can play cards, *mon cher caïd.*"

"He stopped playing too soon," said José. "You need not worry. I have not finished with him."

"Perhaps he has finished with you."

"He must be a very good player," Graham put in tactfully.

José eyed him distastefully. "And what do you know about it?"

"Nothing," retorted Graham coldly. "For all I know it may be simply that you are a very bad player."

"You would like to play perhaps?"

"I don't think so. Cards bore me."

José sneered. "Ah, yes! There are better things to do, eh?" He sucked his teeth loudly.

"When he is bad-tempered," Josette explained, "he cannot be polite. There is nothing to be done with him. He does not care what people think."

José pursed up his mouth into an expression of saccharine sweetness. " 'He does not care what people think,' " he repeated in a high, derisive falsetto. Then his face relaxed. "What do I care what they think?" he demanded.

"You are ridiculous," said Josette.

"If they do not like it they can stay in the lavabos," José declared aggressively.

"It would be a small price to pay," murmured Graham.

Josette giggled. José scowled. "I do not understand."

Graham did not see that there was anything to be gained by explaining. He ignored José and said in

English: "I was just going to have a drink. Will you come?"

She looked doubtful. "Do you wish to buy José a drink also?"

"Must I?"

"I cannot get rid of him."

José was glowering at them suspiciously. "It is not wise to insult me," he said.

"No one is insulting you, imbecile. Monsieur here asks us to have drinks. Do you want a drink?"

He belched. "I do not care who I drink with if we can get off this filthy deck."

"He is so polite," said Josette.

They had finished their drinks when the gong sounded. Graham soon found that he had been wise to leave the question of his attitude towards Moeller to answer itself. It was "Haller" who appeared in answer to the gong; a Haller who greeted Graham as if nothing had happened and who embarked almost immediately on a long account of the manifestations of An, the Sumerian sky god. Only once did he show himself to be aware of any change in his relationship with Graham. Soon after he began talking, Banat entered and sat down. Moeller paused and glanced across the table at him. Banat stared back sullenly. Moeller turned deliberately to Graham.

"Monsieur Mavrodopoulos," he remarked, "looks as if he has been frustrated in some way, as if he has been told that he may not be able to do something that he wishes to do very badly. Don't you think so, Mr. Graham? I wonder if he is going to be disappointed."

Graham looked up from his plate to meet a level stare. There was no mistaking the question in the pale blue eyes. He knew that Banat, too, was watching him. He said slowly: "It would be a pleasure to disappoint Monsieur Mavrodopoulos."

Moeller smiled and the smile reached his eyes. "So it would. Now let me see. What was I saying? Ah, yes . . ."

That was all; but Graham went on with his meal, knowing that one at least of the day's problems was solved. He would not have to approach Moeller: Moeller would approach him.

But Moeller was evidently in no hurry to do so. The afternoon dragged intolerably. Mr. Kuvetli had said that they were not to have any sort of conversation and Graham deemed it advisable to plead a headache when Mathis suggested a rubber of bridge. His refusal affected the Frenchman peculiarly. There was a troubled reluctance about his acceptance of it, and he looked as if he had been about to say something important and then thought better of it. There was in his eyes the same look of unhappy confusion that Graham had seen in the morning. But Graham wondered about it only for a few seconds. He was not greatly interested in the Mathises.

Moeller, Banat, Josette and José had gone to their cabins immediately after lunch. Signora Beronelli had been induced to make the fourth with the Mathises and Mr. Kuvetli and appeared to be enjoying herself. Her son sat by her watching her jealously. Graham returned in desperation to the magazines. Towards five o'clock, however, the bridge four showed signs of disintegrating and, to avoid being drawn into a conversation with Mr. Kuvetli, Graham went out on deck.

The sun, obscured since the day before, was pouring a red glow through a thinning of the clouds just above the horizon. To the east the long, low strip of coast which had been visible earlier was already enveloped in a slate grey dusk and the lights of a town had begun to twinkle. The clouds were moving quickly as for the gathering of a storm and heavy drops of rain began to slant in on to the deck. He moved backwards out of the rain and found Mathis at his elbow. The Frenchman nodded.

"Was it a good game?" Graham asked.

"Quite good. Madame Beronelli and I lost. She is enthusiastic, but inefficient."

"Then, except for the enthusiasm, my absence made no difference."

Mathis smiled a little nervously. "I hope that your headache is better."

"Much better, thank you."

It had begun to rain in earnest now. Mathis stared out gloomily into the gathering darkness. "Filthy!" he commented.

"Yes."

There was a pause. Then:

"I was afraid," said Mathis suddenly, "that you did not wish to play with us. I could not blame you if such were the case. This morning you were good enough to make an apology. The true apology was due from me to you."

He was not looking at Graham. "I am quite sure . . ." Graham began to mumble, but Mathis went on as if he were addressing the seagulls following the ship. "I do not always remember," he said bitterly, "that what to some people is good or bad is to others simply boring. My wife has led me to put too much faith in the power of words."

"I'm afraid I don't understand."

Mathis turned his head and smiled wryly. "Do you know the word *encotillonné?*"

"No."

"A man who is governed by his wife is *encotillonné.*"

"In English we say 'hen-pecked.'"

"Ah, yes?" Obviously he did not care what was said in English. "I must tell you a joke about it. Once I was *encotillonné*. Oh, by very badly! Does that surprise you?"

"It does." Graham saw that the man was dramatising himself, and was curious.

"My wife used to have a very great temper. She still has it, I think, but now I do not see it. But for the first ten years of our marriage it was terrible. I had a small business. Trade was very bad and I became bankrupt. It was not my fault, but she always pretended that it was. Has your wife a bad temper, Monsieur?"

"No. Very good."

"You are lucky. For years I lived in misery. And then one day I made a great discovery. There was a socialist meeting in our town and I went to it. I was, you must understand, a Royalist. My family had no money, but they had a title which they would have liked to use without their neighbours sniggering. I was of my family. I went to this meeting because I was curious. The speaker was good, and he spoke about Briey. That interested me because I had been at Verdun. A week later we were with some friends in the café and I repeated what I had heard. My wife laughed in a curious way. Then when I got home I made my great discovery. I found that my wife was a snob and more stupid than I had dreamed. She said that I had humiliated her by saying such things as if I believed them. All her friends were respectable people. I must not speak as if I were a workman. She cried. I knew than that I was free. I had a weapon that I could use against her. I used it. If she displeased me I became a socialist. To the smug little tradesmen whose wives were her friends I would preach the abolition of profit and the family. I bought books and pamphlets to make my arguments more damaging. My wife became very docile. She would cook things that I liked so that I would not disgrace her." He paused.

"You mean that you don't believe all these things you say about Briey and banking and capitalism?" demanded Graham.

Mathis smiled faintly. "That is the joke about which I told you. For a time I was free. I could command my wife and I became more fond of her. I was a manager in a big factory. And then a terrible thing happened. I found that I had begun to believe these things I said. The books I read showed me that I had found a truth. I, a Royalist by instinct, became a socialist by conviction. Worse, I became a socialist martyr. There was a strike in the factory and I, a manager, supported the strikers. I did not belong to a union. Naturally! And so I was dismissed. It was ridiculous." He shrugged. "So here I am! I have become a man in my home at the price of becoming a bore outside it. It is funny, is it not?"

Graham smiled. He had decided that he liked Monsieur Mathis. He said: "It would be funny if it were wholly true. But I can assure you that it was not because I was bored that I did not listen to you last night."

"You are very polite," began Mathis dubiously; "but . . ."

"Oh, there is no question of politeness. You see, I work for an armaments manufacturer, and so I have been more than interested in what you have had to say. On some points I find myself in agreement with you."

A change came over the Frenchman's face. He flushed slightly; a small delighted smile hovered round his lips; for the first time Graham saw the tense frown relax. "On which points do you *not* agree?" he demanded eagerly.

At that moment Graham realised that, whatever

else had happened to him on the *Sestri Levante*, he had made at least one friend.

They were still arguing when Josette came out on deck. Unwillingly, Mathis interrupted what he was saying to acknowledge her presence.

"*Madame.*"

She wrinkled her nose at them. "What are you discussing? It must be very important that you have to stand in the rain to talk about it."

"We were talking politics."

"No, no!" said Mathis quickly. "Not politics, economics! Politics are the effect. We were talking about causes. But you are right. This rain is filthy. If you will excuse me, please, I will see what has happened to my wife." He winked at Graham. "If she suspects that I am making propaganda she will not be able to sleep to-night."

With a smile and a nod he went. Josette looked after him. "He is nice, that man. Why does he marry such a woman?"

"He is very fond of her."

"In the way that you are fond of me?"

"Perhaps not. Would you rather we went in?"

"No. I came out for some air. It will not be so wet round on the other side of the deck."

They began to walk round to the other side. It was dark now and the deck lights had been put on.

She took his arm. "Do you realise that to-day we have not really seen each other until now? No! Of course you do not realise it! You have been amusing yourself with politics. It does not matter that I am worried."

"Worried? What about?"

"This man who wants to kill you, imbecile! You do not tell me what you are going to do at Genoa."

He shrugged. "I've taken your advice. I'm not troubling about him."

"But you will go to the British Consul?"

"Yes." The moment had come when he must do some really steady lying. "I shall go straight there. Afterwards I shall have to see one or two people on business. The train does not leave until two o'clock in the afternoon, so I think that I shall have time. We can meet on the train."

She sighed. "So much business! But I shall see you for lunch, eh?"

"I'm afraid it's unlikely. If we did arrange to meet I might not be able to keep the appointment. It'll be best if we meet on the train."

She turned her head a little sharply. "You are telling me the truth? You are not saying this because you have changed your mind?"

"My dear Josette!" He had opened his mouth to explain again that he had business to attend to, but had stopped himself in time. He must not protest too much.

She pressed his arm. "I did not mean to be disagreeable, *chéri*. It is only that I wish to be sure. We will meet at the train if you wish it. We can have a drink together at Torino. We reach there at four and stop for half an hour. It is because of the coaches from Milano. There are some nice places to drink in Torino. After the ship here it will be wonderful."

"It'll be splendid. What about José?"

"Ah, it does not matter about him. Let him drink by himself. After the way he was rude to you this morning, I do not care what José does. Tell me about the letters you are writing. Are they all finished?"

"I shall finish them this evening."

"And after that, no more work?"

"After that, no more work." He felt that he could not stand much more of this. He said: "You'll get cold if we stay out here much longer. Shall we go inside?"

She stopped and withdrew her arm from his so that

he could kiss her. Her back was taut as she strained her body against his. Seconds later she drew away from him, laughing. "I must remember," she said, "not to say 'whisky-soda,' but 'whisky and soda' now. That is very important, eh?"

"Very important."

She squeezed his arm. "You are nice. I like you very much, *chéri.*"

They began to walk back towards the saloon. He was grateful for the dimness of the lights.

He did not have long to wait for Moeller. The German agent had been in the habit of leaving the table and going to his cabin as soon as a meal was finished. To-night, however, Banat was the first to go, evidently by arrangement; and the monologue continued until the Beronellis had followed him. It was an account of comparisons made between the Sumero-Babylonian liturgies and the ritual forms of certain Mesopotamian fertility cults and it was with unmistakable triumph that he at last brought it to an end. "You must admit, Mr. Graham," he added, lowering his voice, "that I have done extremely well to remember so much. Naturally, I made a few mistakes, and a good deal was lost, I have no doubt, in my translation. The author would probably fail to recognize it. But to the uninitiated I should say it would be most convincing."

"I have been wondering why you have taken so much trouble. You might have been talking Chinese for all the Beronellis knew or cared."

Moeller looked pained. "I was not talking for the Beronellis, but for my own private satisfaction. How stupid it is to say that the memory fails with the approach of old age. Would you think that I am sixty-six?"

"I'm not interested in your age."

"No, of course not. Perhaps we could have a private

talk. I suggest that we take a walk together on deck. It is raining, but a little rain will not hurt us."

"My coat is on the chair over there."

"Then I will meet you on the top deck in a few minutes' time."

Graham was waiting at the head of the companionway when Moeller came up. They moved into the lee of one of the lifeboats.

Moeller came straight to the point.

"I gather that you have seen Kuvetli."

"I have," said Graham grimly.

"Well?"

"I have decided to take your advice."

"At Kuvetli's suggestion?"

This, Graham reflected, was not going to be as easy as he had thought. He answered: "At my own. I was not impressed by him. Frankly, I was amazed. That the Turkish Government should have put such a fool of a man on the job seems to me incredible."

"What makes you think he is a fool?"

"He seems to think that you are making some attempt to bribe me and that I am inclined to accept the money. He threatened to expose me to the British Government. When I suggested that I might be in some personal danger he seemed to think that I was trying to trick him in some stupid way. If that's your idea of a clever man, I'm sorry for you."

"Perhaps he is not used to dealing with the English brand of self-esteem," Moeller retorted acidly. "When did this meeting take place?"

"Last night, soon after I saw you."

"And did he mention me by name?"

"Yes. He warned me against you."

"And how did you treat the warning?"

"I said that I would report his behaviour to Colonel Haki. He did not, I must say, seem to care. But if I had any idea of securing his protection, I gave it up. I don't trust him. Besides, I don't see why I should risk my life for people who treat me as if I were some sort of criminal."

He paused. He could not see Moeller's face in the darkness but he felt that the man was satisfied.

"And so you've decided to accept my suggestion?"

"Yes, I have. But," Graham went on, "before we go any further, there are one or two thinks I want to get clear."

"Well?"

"In the first place, there is this man Kuvetli. He's a fool, as I've said, but he'll have to be put off the scent somehow."

"You need have no fears." Graham thought he detected a note of contempt in the smooth heavy voice. "Kuvetli will cause no trouble. It will be easy to give him the slip at Genoa. The next thing he will hear of you is that you are suffering from typhus. He will be unable to prove anything to the contrary."

Graham was relieved. Obviously, Moeller thought him a fool. He said doubtfully: "Yes, I see. That's all right, but what about this typhus? If I'm going to be taken ill I've got to be taken ill properly. If I were really taken ill I should probably be on the train when it happened."

Moeller sighed. "I see that you've been thinking very seriously, Mr. Graham. Let me explain. If you were really infected with typhus you would already be feeling unwell. There is an incubation period of a week or ten days. You would not, of course, know what was the matter with you. By to-morrow you would be feeling worse. It would be logical for you to shrink from spending the night in a train. You would probably go to a hotel for the night. Then, in the morning, when your temperature began to rise and the characteristics of the disease became apparent, you would be removed to a clinic."

"Then we shall go to a hotel to-morrow?"

"Exactly. There will be a car waiting for us. But I advise you to leave the arrangements to me, Mr. Graham. Remember, I am just as interested as you are in seeing that nobody's suspicions are aroused."

Graham affected to ponder this. "All right then," he said at last. "I'll leave it to you. I don't want to be fussy, but you can understand that I don't want to have any trouble when I get home."

There was a silence and for a moment he thought that he had overacted. Then Moeller said slowly: "You have no reason to worry. We shall be waiting for you outside the Customs shed. As long as you do not attempt to do anything foolish—you might, for example, decide to change your mind about your holiday—everything will go smoothly. I can assure you that you will have no trouble when you get home."

"As long as that's understood."

"Is there anything else you want to say?"

"No. Good night."

"Good night, Mr. Graham. Until to-morrow."

Graham waited until Moeller had reached the deck below. Then he drew a deep breath. It was over. He was safe. All he had to do now was to go to his cabin, get a good night's sleep and wait for Mr. Kuvetli in cabin number four. He felt suddenly very tired. His body was aching as if he had been working too hard. He made his way down to his cabin. It was as he passed the landing door of the saloon that he saw Josette.

She was sitting on one of the *banquettes* watching José and Banat playing cards. Her hands were on the edge of the seat and she was leaning forward, her lips parted slightly, her hair falling across her cheeks. There was something about the pose that reminded him of the moment, years ago it seemed, when he had followed Kopeikin into her dressing-room at Le

Jockey Cabaret. He half expected her to raise her head and turn towards him, smiling.

He realized suddenly that he was seeing her for the last time, that before another day had passed he would be for her merely a disagreeable memory, someone who had treated her badly. The realisation was sharp and strangely painful. He told himself that he was being absurd, that it had always been impossible for him to stay with her in Paris and that he had known it all along. Why should the leave-taking trouble him now? And yet it did trouble him. A phrase came into his head: "to part is to die a little." He knew suddenly that it was not Josette of whom he was taking his leave, but of something of himself. In the back streets of his mind a door was slowly closing for the last time. She had complained that for him she was just a part of the journey from Istanbul to London. There was more to it than that. She was part of the world beyond the door: the world into which he had stepped when Banat had fired those three shots at him in the Adler-Palace: the world in which you recognised the ape beneath the velvet. Now he was on his way back to his own world; to his house and his car and the friendly, agreeable woman he called his wife. It would be exactly the same as when he had left it. Nothing would be changed in that world; nothing, except himself.

He went on down to his cabin.

He slept fitfully. Once he awoke with a start, believing that someone was opening the door of his cabin. Then he remembered that the door was bolted and concluded that he had been dreaming. When next he awoke, the engines had stopped and the ship was no longer rolling. He switched on the light and saw that the time was a quarter past four. They had arrived at the entrance to Genoa harbour. After a while he heard the chugging of a small boat and a fainter clatter from the deck above. There were voices too. He tried to distinguish Mr. Kuvetli's among them, but there were too muffled. He dozed.

He had told the steward to bring coffee at seven. Towards six, however, he decided that it was useless to try to sleep any more. He was already dressed when the steward arrived.

He drank his coffee, put the remainder of his things in his case and sat down to wait. Mr. Kuvetli had told him to go into the empty cabin at eight o'clock. He had promised himself that he would obey Mr. Kuvetli's instructions to the letter. He listened to the Mathises arguing over their packing.

At about a quarter to eight the ship began to move in. Another five minutes and he rang for the steward. By five to eight the steward had been, received with barely concealed surprise fifty lire, and gone, taking the suitcase with him. Graham waited another minute and then opened the door.

The alleyway was empty. He walked along slowly to number four, stopped as if he had forgotten something, and half turned. The coast was still clear. He opened the door, stepped quickly into the cabin, shut the door, and turned round.

The next moment he almost fainted.

Lying across the floor with his legs under the lower berth and his head covered with blood, was Mr. Kuvetli.

CHAPTER XI

Most of the bleeding seemed to have
been caused by a scalp wound on the back of the
head; but there was another wound, which had bled
comparatively little and which looked as if it had
been made with a knife, low on the left side of
the neck. The movements of the ship had sent the
slowly congealing blood trickling to and fro in a mad-
man's scrawl across the linoleum. The face was the
colour of dirty clay. Mr. Kuvetli was clearly dead.

Graham clenched his teeth to prevent himself
retching and held on to the washing cabinet for support. His first thought was that he must not be sick,
that he must pull himself together before he called
for help. He did not realise immediately the implications of what had happened. So that he should not
look down again he had kept his eyes fixed on the
porthole and it was the sight of the funnel of a ship
lying beyond a long concrete jetty that reminded him
that they were going into harbour. In less than an
hour the gangways would be down. And Mr. Kuvetli
had not reached the Turkish Consulate.

The shock of the realisation brought him to his
senses. He looked down.

It was Banat's work without a doubt. The little Turk had probably been stunned in his own cabin or in the alleyway outside it, dragged out of sight into this, the nearest empty cabin, and butchered while he was still insensible. Moeller had decided to dispose of a possible threat to the smooth working of his arrangements for dealing with the principal victim. Graham remembered the noise which had awakened him in the night. It might have come from the next cabin. "Do not leave your cabin under any circumstances until eight o'clock the following morning. It might be dangerous." Mr. Kuvetli had failed to take his own advice and it *had* been dangerous. He had declared himself ready to die for his country and he had so died. There he was, his chubby fists clenched pitifully, his fringe of grey hair matted with his blood and the mouth which had smiled so much half open and inanimate.

Someone walked along the alleyway outside and Graham jerked his head up. The sound and the movement seemed to clear his brain. He began to think quickly and coolly.

The way the blood had congealed showed that Mr. Kuvetli must have been killed before the ship had stopped. Long before! Before he had made his request for permission to leave by the pilot boat. If he had made the request, a thorough search for him would have been made when the boat came alongside and he would have been found. He had not yet been found. He was not travelling with an ordinary passport but with a diplomatic *laisser passer* and so had not had to surrender his papers to the Purser. That meant that unless the Purser checked off the passenger list with the passport control officer at Genoa—and Graham knew from past experience that they did not always bother to do that at Italian ports—the fact that Mr. Kuvetli did not land would not be noticed. Moeller and Banat had probably counted on the fact. And if the dead man's baggage had been packed, the steward would put it in the Customs shed with the rest and assume that its owner was lying low to avoid having to give a tip. It might be hours, days even, before the body were discovered if he, Graham, did not call anyone.

His lips tightened. He became conscious of a slow cold rage mounting in his brain, stifling his sense of self-preservation. If he did call someone he could accuse Moeller and Banat; but would he be able to bring the crime home to them? His accusation by itself would carry no weight. It might well be suggested that the accusation was a ruse to conceal his own guilt. The Purser, for one, would be glad to support that theory. The fact that the two accused were travelling with false passports could, no doubt, be proved, but that alone would take time. In any case, the Italian police would be amply justified in refusing him permission to leave for England. Mr. Kuvetli had died in trying to make it possible for him to reach England safely and in time to fulfil a contract. That Mr. Kuvetli's dead body should become the very means of preventing the fulfilment of that contract was stupid and grotesque; but if he, Graham, wanted to be sure of saving his own skin, that was what must happen. It was strangely unthinkable. For him, standing there above the dead body of the man whom Moeller had described as a patriot, there seemed to be only one thing of importance in the world—that Mr. Kuvetli's death should be neither stupid nor grotesque, that it should be useless only to the men who had murdered him.

But if he were not going to raise the alarm and wait for the police, what was he going to do?

Supposing Moeller had planned this. Supposing he or Banat had overheard Mr. Kuvetli's instructions to him and, believing that he was sufficiently intimidated to do anything to save himself, had thought of this way of delaying his return. Or they might be preparing to "discover" him with the body and so incriminate him. But no: both those suppositions were absurd. If they had known of Mr. Kuvetli's plan they would have let the Turk go ashore by the pilot boat. It would have been his, Graham's, body that would have been found and the finder would have been Mr. Kuvetli. Obviously, then, Moeller could neither know of the plan nor suspect that the murder would be discovered. An hour from now he would be standing with Banat and the gunmen who were to meet him, waiting for the victim to walk unsuspectingly . . .

But the victim would not be unsuspecting. There was a very slender chance . . .

He turned and, grasping the handle of the door, began to turn it gently. He knew that if he thought twice about what he had decided to do he would change his mind. He must commit himself before he had time to think.

He opened the door a fraction of an inch. There was no one in the alleyway. A moment later, he was out of the cabin and the door of it was shut behind him. He hesitated barely a second. He knew that he must keep moving. Five steps brought him to cabin number three. He went in.

Mr. Kuvetli's luggage consisted of one old-fashioned valise. It was standing strapped up in the middle of the floor, and perched on one of the straps was a twenty lire piece. Graham picked up the coin and held it to his nose. The smell of attar of roses was quite distinct. He looked in the wardrobe and behind the door for Mr. Kuvetli's overcoat and hat, failed to find them, and concluded that they had been disposed of through the porthole. Banat had thought of everything.

He put the valise up on the berth and opened it. Most of the things on top had obviously been stuffed in anyhow by Banat, but lower down the packing had been done very neatly. The only thing of any interest to Graham, however, was a box of pistol ammunition. Of the pistol which fired them there was no sign.

Graham put the ammunition in his pocket and shut the valise again. He was undecided as to what he should do with it. Banat had obviously counted on its being taken to the Customs shed by the steward, who would pocket the twenty lire and forget about Mr. Kuvetli. That would be all right from Banat's point of view. By the time the people in the Customs shed started asking questions about an unclaimed valise, Monsieur Mavrodopoulos would be non-existent. Graham, however, had every intention of remaining in existence if he could possibly do so. Moreover, he intended—with the same proviso—to use his passport to cross the Italian frontier into France. The moment Mr. Kuvetli's body was found the rest of the passengers would be sought for questioning by the police. There was only one thing for it: Mr. Kuvetli's valise would have to be hidden.

He opened the washing cabinet, put the twenty lire piece on the corner by the bowl, and went to the door. The coast was still clear. He opened the door, picked up the valise, and lugged it along the alleyway to cabin number four. Another second or two and he was inside with the door shut again.

He was sweating now. He wiped his hands and forehead on his handkerchief and then remembered that his fingerprints would be on the hard leather handle of the valise as well as on the door handle and washing cabinet. He went over these objects with his handkerchief and then turned his attention to the body.

Obviously the gun was not in the hip pocket. He

went down on one knee beside the body. He felt himself beginning to retch again and took a deep breath. Then he leaned across, gripped the right shoulder with one hand and the right side of the trousers with the other and pulled. The body rolled on to its side. One foot slid over the other and kicked the floor. Graham stood up quickly. In a moment or two, however, he had himself in hand sufficiently to bend down and pull the jacket open. There was a leather holster under the left arm but the gun was not in it.

He was not unduly disappointed. The possession of the gun would have made him feel better but he had not been counting on finding it. A gun was valuable. Banat would naturally take it. Graham felt in the jacket pocket. It was empty. Banat had evidently taken Mr. Kuvetli's money and *laisser passer* as well.

He got up. There was nothing more to be done there. He put on a glove, cautiously let himself out and walked along to cabin number six. He knocked. There was a quick movement from within and Madame Mathis opened the door.

The frown with which she had prepared to meet the steward faded when she saw Graham. She gave him a startled "good morning."

"Good morning, Madame. May I speak to your husband for a moment?"

Mathis poked his head over her shoulder. "Hullo! Good morning! Are you ready so soon?"

"Can I speak to you for a moment?"

"Of course!" He came out in his shirt sleeves and grinning cheerfully. "I am important only to myself. I am easy to approach."

"Would you mind coming into my cabin for a moment?"

Mathis glanced at him curiously. "You look very serious, my friend. Yes, of course I will come." He

217

turned to his wife. "I will be back in a minute, *chérie*."

Inside the cabin, Graham shut the door, bolted it and turned to meet Mathis' puzzled frown.

"I need your help," he said in a low voice. "No, I don't want to borrow money. I want you to take a message for me."

"If it is possible, of course."

"It will be necessary to talk very quietly," Graham went on. "I do not want to alarm your wife unnecessarily and the partitions are very thin."

Fortunately, Mathis missed the full implications of this statement. He nodded. "I am listening."

"I told you that I was employed by an armaments manufacturer. It is true. But in a sense I am also, at the moment, in the joint services of the British and Turkish governments. When I get off this ship this morning, an attempt is going to be made by German agents to kill me."

"This is true?" He was incredulous and suspicious.

"I am afraid it is. It would not amuse me to invent it."

"Excuse me, I ..."

"That's all right. What I want you to do is to go to the Turkish Consulate in Genoa, ask for the Consul and give him a message from me. Will you do that?"

Mathis stared hard at him for a moment. Then he nodded. "Very well. I will do it. What is the message?"

"I should like to impress upon you first that this is a highly confidential message. Is that understood?"

"I can keep my mouth shut when I choose."

"I know I can rely on you. Will you write the message down? Here is a pencil and some paper. You would not be able to read my writing. Are you ready?"

"Yes."

"This is it: 'Inform Colonel Haki, Istanbul, that agent I.K. is dead, but do not inform the police. I am forced to accompany German agents, Moeller and Banat, travelling with passports of Fritz Haller and Mavrodopoulos. I ...' "

Mathis' jaw dropped and he let out an exclamation. "Is it possible!"

"Unfortunately, it is."

"Then it was not seasickness that you had!"

"No. Shall I go on with the message?"

Mathis swallowed. "Yes. Yes. I did not realise. . . . Please."

" 'I shall attempt to escape and reach you, but in the event of my death please inform British Consul that these men are responsible.' " It was, he felt, melodramatic; but it was no more than he wished to say. He felt sorry for Mathis.

The Frenchman was staring at him with horror in his eyes. "Is it not possible," he whispered. "Why . . . ?"

"I should like to explain but I am afraid that I can't. The point is, will you deliver the message for me?"

"Of course. But is there nothing else that I can do? These German agents—why can you not have them arrested?"

"For various reasons. The best way you can help me is to take this message for me."

The Frenchman stuck out his jaw aggressively. "It is ridiculous!" he burst out and then lowered his voice to a fierce whisper. "Discretion is necessary. I understand that. You are of the British secret service. One does not confide these things but I am not a fool. Very well! Why do we not together shoot down these filthy Bosches and escape? I have my revolver and together. . . ."

Graham jumped. "Did you say that you had a revolver—here?"

Mathis looked defiant. "Certainly I have a revolver. Why not? In Turkey ..."

Graham seized his arm. "Then you can do something more to help me."

Mathis scowled impatiently. "What is that?"

"Let me buy your revolver from you."

"You mean you are unarmed?"

"My own revolver was stolen. How much will you take for yours?"

"But...."

"It will be more use to me than to you."

Mathis drew himself up. "I will not sell it to you."

"But...."

"I will give it to you. Here...." He pulled a small nickel-plated revolver out of his hip pocket and thrust it in Graham's hand. "No, please It is nothing. I would like to do more."

Graham thanked his stars for the impulse which had led him to apologise to the Mathises the previous day. "You have done more than enough."

"Nothing! It is loaded, see? Here is the safety catch. There is a light pull on the trigger. You do not have to be a Hercules. Keep your arm straight when you fire ... but I do not have to tell you."

"I am grateful, Mathis. And you will go to the Turkish Consul as soon as you land."

"It is understood." He held out his hand. "I wish you luck, my friend," he said with emotion. "If you are sure that there is nothing else that I can do. . . ."

"I am sure."

A moment later Mathis had gone. Graham waited. He heard the Frenchman go into the next cabin and Madame Mathis' sharp voice.

"Well?"

"So you cannot mind your own business, eh? He is

broke and I have lent him two hundred francs."

"Imbecile! You will not touch it again."

"You think not? Let me tell you he has given me a cheque."

"I detest cheques."

"I am not drunk. It is on an Istanbul bank. As soon as we arrive I shall go to the Turkish Consulate and see that the cheque is a good one."

"A lot they will know—or care!"

"Enough! I know what I am doing. Are you ready? No! Then ..."

Graham breathed a sigh of relief and examined the revolver. It was smaller than Kopeikin's and of Belgian manufacture. He worked the safety catch and fingered the trigger. It was a handy little weapon and looked as if it had been carefully used. He looked about him for a place to put it. It must not be visible from the outside yet he must be able to get at it quickly. He decided eventually on his top left hand waistcoat pocket. The barrel, breech and half the trigger guard just fitted in. When he buttoned his jacket the butt was hidden while the lapels set in a way that concealed the bulge. What was more, he could, by touching his tie, bring his fingers within two inches of the butt. He was ready.

He dropped Mr. Kuvetli's box of ammunition through the porthole and went up on deck.

They were in the harbour now and moving across to the west side. Towards the sea the sky was clear but a mist hung over the heights above the town, obscuring the sun and making the white amphitheatrical mass of buildings seem cold and desolate.

The only other person on deck was Banat. He was standing gazing out at the shipping with the absorbed interest of a small boy. It was difficult to realise that, at some moment in the last ten hours, this pale creature had come out of cabin number four with a knife which he had just driven into Mr. Kuvetli's neck; that in his pocket at that moment were Mr. Kuvetli's papers, Mr. Kuvetli's money and Mr. Kuvetli's pistol; that he intended to commit within the next few hours yet another murder. His very insignificance was horrible. It lent a false air of normality to the situation. Had Graham not been so acutely alive to the danger he was in, he would have been tempted to believe that the memory of what he had seen in cabin number four was the memory not of a real experience, but of something conceived in a dream.

He was no longer conscious of any fear. His body was tingling in a curious way; he was short of breath, and every now and again a wave of nausea would rise up from the pit of his stomach; but his brain seemed to have lost touch with his body. His thoughts arranged themselves with a quick efficiency that surprised him. He knew that short of abandoning all hope of reaching England in time to fulfil the Turkish contract by the specified date, his only chance of getting out of Italy alive lay in his beating Moeller at Moeller's own game. Mr. Kuvetli had made it clear that Moeller's "alternative" was a trick devised with the sole object of transferring the scene of the killing to a less public place than a main street of Genoa. In other words, he was to be "taken for a ride." In a very short time now, Moeller, Banat and some others would be waiting with a car outside the Customs shed ready, if necessary, to shoot him down there and then. If, however, he were considerate enough to step into the car they would take him away to some quiet place on the Santa Margherita road and shoot him there. There was just one weak spot in their plan. They thought that if he were to get into the car he would do so believing that he was to be driven to a hotel in order to make an elaborate show of falling ill. They were mistaken; and in their being mistaken they presented him with the beginnings of a way out. If he acted quickly and boldly he might be able to get through.

They would not, he reasoned, be likely to tell him as soon as he got in the car what they were going to do. The fiction about the hotel and the clinic near Santa Margherita would be maintained until the last moment. From their point of view, it would be much easier to drive through the narrow streets of Genoa with a man who thought he was going to have six weeks' holiday than with a man who had to be forcibly prevented from attracting the attention of passers-by. They would be inclined to humour him. They might even let him register at a hotel. In any case, it was unlikely that the car would go right through the city without being held up once by the traffic. His chances of escape lay in his being able to take them by surprise. Let him once get free in a crowded street, and they would have great difficulty in catching him. His objective, then, would be the Turkish Consulate. He had chosen the Turkish Consulate rather than his own, for the simple reason that with the Turks he would have to do less explaining. A reference to Colonel Haki would simplify matters considerably.

The ship was approaching the berth now, and men were standing on the quay ready to catch the lines. Banat had not seen him, but now Josette and José came out on deck. He moved quickly round to the other side. Josette was the last person he wanted to talk to at that moment. She might suggest that they share a taxi to the centre of the city. He would have to explain why he was leaving the quay in a private car with Moeller and Banat. There might be all sorts of other difficulties. At that moment he came face to face with Moeller.

The old man nodded affably. "Good morning, Mr. Graham. I was hoping to see you. It will be pleasant to get ashore again, won't it?"

"I hope so."

Moeller's expression changed slightly. "Are you ready?"

"Quite." He looked concerned. "I haven't seen Kuvetli this morning. I hope everything is going to be all right."

Moeller's eyes did not flicker. "You need not worry, Mr. Graham." Then he smiled tolerantly. "As I told you last night, you can safely leave everything to me. Kuvetli will not worry us. If necessary," he went on blandly, "I shall use force."

"I hope that won't be necessary."

"And so do I, Mr. Graham! So do I!" He lowered his voice confidentially. "But while we are on the subject of the use of force, may I suggest that you are not in too much of a hurry to land? You see, should you happen to land before Banat and I have time to explain the new situation to those who are waiting, an accident might happen. You are so obviously an Englishman. They would have no difficulty in identifying you."

"I had already thought of that."

"Splendid! I am so glad that you are entering into the spirit of the arrangements." He turned his head. "Ah, we are alongside. I shall see you again in a few minutes, then." His eyes narrowed. "You won't make me feel that my confidence has been misplaced, will you, Mr. Graham?"

"I shall be there."

"I am sure that I can count on you."

Graham went into the deserted saloon. Through

one of the portholes he could see that a section of the deck had been roped off. The Mathises and the Beronellis had already joined Josette, José and Banat and, as he watched, Moeller came up with his "wife." Josette was looking round as if she were expecting someone, and Graham guessed that his absence was puzzling her. It was going to be difficult to avoid an encounter with her. She might even wait for him in the Customs shed. He would have to forestall that.

He waited until the gangway had been hoisted into position and the passengers, headed by the Mathises, were beginning to troop down it, then went out and brought up the rear of the procession immediately behind Josette. She half turned her head and saw him.

"Ah! I have been wondering where you were. What have you been doing?"

"Packing."

"So long! But you are here now. I thought that perhaps we could drive together and leave our luggage in the *consigne* at the station. It will save a taxi."

"I'm afraid I shall keep you waiting. I have some things to declare. Besides, I must go to the Consulate first. I think that we had better keep to our arrangement to meet at the train."

She sighed. "You are so difficult. Very well, we will meet at the train. But do not be late."

"I won't."

"And be careful of the little *salop* with the perfume."

"The police will take care of him."

They had reached the passport control at the entrance to the Customs shed and José, who had walked on ahead, was waiting as if the seconds were costing him money. She pressed Graham's hand hurriedly. "*Alors, chéri! A tout àl'heure.*"

Graham got his passport and slowly followed them through to the Customs shed. There was only one Customs officer. As Graham approached he disposed of Josette and José, and turned to the Beronellis' mountainous bundles. To his relief, Graham had to wait. While he was waiting he opened his case and transferred some papers that he needed to his pocket; but several more minutes passed before he was able to show his transit *visa*, have his suitcase chalked and give it to a porter. By the time he had made his way through the group of mourning relatives which had surrounded the Beronellis, Josette and José had gone.

Then he saw Moeller and Banat.

They were standing beside a big American sedan drawn up beyond the taxis. There were two other men on the far side of the car: one was tall and thin and wore a mackintosh and a workman's cap, the other was a very dark heavy-jowled man with a grey belted ulster and a soft hat which he wore without a dent in it. A fifth and younger man sat at the wheel of the car.

His heart thumping, Graham beckoned to the porter, who was making for the taxis, and walked towards them.

Moeller nodded as he came up. "Good! Your luggage? Ah, yes." He nodded to the tall man, who came round, took the case from the porter, and put it in the luggage boot at the back.

Graham tipped the porter and got in the car. Moeller followed him and sat beside him. The tall man got in beside the driver. Banat and the man in the ulster sat on the pull-down seats facing Graham and Moeller. Banat's face was expressionless. The man in the ulster avoided Graham's eyes and looked out of the window.

The car started. Almost immediately, Banat took out his pistol and snapped the safety catch.

Graham turned to Moeller. "Is that necessary?" he demanded. "I'm not going to escape."

Moeller shrugged. "As you please." He said something to Banat who grinned, snapped the safety catch again and put the gun back in his pocket.

The car swung into the cobbled road leading to the dock gates.

"Which hotel are we going to?" Graham inquired.

Moeller turned his head slightly. "I have not yet made up my mind. We can leave that question until later. We shall drive out to Santa Margherita first."

"But ..."

"There are no 'buts.' I am making the arrangements." He did not bother to turn his head this time.

"What about Kuvetli?"

"He left by the pilot boat early this morning."

"Then what's happened to him?"

"He is probably writing a report to Colonel Haki. I advise you to forget about him."

Graham was silent. He had asked about Mr. Kuvetli with the sole object of concealing the fact that he was badly frightened. He had been in the car less than two minutes, and already the odds against him had lengthened considerably.

The car bumped over the cobbles to the dock gates, and Graham braced himself for the sharp right turn that would take them towards the town and the Santa Margherita road. The next moment he lurched sideways in his seat as the car swerved to the left. Banat whipped out his gun.

Graham slowly regained his position. "I'm sorry," he said. "I thought we turned right for Santa Margherita."

There was no reply. He sat back in his corner trying to keep his face expressionless. He had assumed quite unwarrantably that it would be through Genoa itself, and on to the Santa Margherita road that he would be taken for his "ride." All his hopes had been based on the assumption. He had taken too much for granted.

He glanced at Moeller. The German agent was sitting back with his eyes closed: an old man whose work for the day was done. The rest of the day was Banat's. Graham knew that the small deep-set eyes were feeling for his, and that the long-suffering mouth was grinning. Banat was going to enjoy his work. The other man was still looking out of the window. He had not uttered a sound.

They reached a fork and turned to the right along a secondary road with a direction sign for Novi-Torimo. They were going north. The road was straight and lined with dusty plane trees. Beyond the trees there were rows of grim-looking houses and a factory or two. Soon, however, the road began to rise and twist, and the houses and factories were left behind. They were getting into the country.

Graham knew that unless some wholly unexpected way of escape presented itself, his chances of surviving the next hour were now practically non-existent. Presently the car would stop. Then he would be taken out and shot as methodically and efficiently as if he had been condemned by a court-martial. The blood was thundering in his head, and his breathing was quick and shallow. He tried to breathe slowly and deeply, but the muscles in his chest seemed incapable of making the effort. He went on trying. He knew that if he surrendered himself to fear now, if he let himself go, he would be lost, whatever happened. He must not be frightened. Death, he told himself, would not be so bad. A moment of astonishment, and it would be over. He had to die sooner or later, and a bullet through the base of the skull now would be better than months of illness when he was old. Forty years was not a bad lifetime to have lived. There were many young men in Europe at that moment who would regard the attainment of such an age as an enviable achievement. To suppose that the lopping off of thirty years or so from a normal span of life was a disaster was to pretend to an importance which no man possessed. Living wasn't even so very pleasant. Mostly it was a matter of getting from the cradle to the grave with the least possible discomfort; of satisfying the body's needs, and of slowing down the process of its decay. Why make such a fuss about abandoning so dreary a business? Why, indeed! And yet you did make a fuss . . .

He became conscious of the revolver pressing against his chest. Supposing they decided to search him! But no, they wouldn't do that. They'd taken one revolver from him, and another from Mr. Kuvetli. They would scarcely suspect that there was a third. There were five other men in the car, and four of them at least were armed. He had six rounds in the revolver. He might be able to fire two of them before he himself were hit. If he waited until Banat's attention had wandered he might get off three or even four of them. If he were going to be killed, he'd see that the killing was as expensive as possible. He got a cigarette out of his pocket and then, putting his hand inside his jacket as if he were looking for a match, snicked off the safety catch. For a moment he considered drawing the revolver there and then, and trusting to luck and the driver's swerving to survive Banat's first shot; but the gun in Banat's hand was steady. Besides, there was always a chance that something unexpected might happen to create a better opportunity. For instance, the driver might take a corner too fast and wreck the car.

But the car purred steadily on. The windows were tightly shut, and Banat's attar of roses began to scent the air inside. The man in the ulster was becoming drowsy. Once or twice he yawned. Then, obviously to give himself something to do, he brought out a heavy German pistol and examined the magazine. As he replaced it, his dull pouched eyes rested for a moment on Graham. He looked away again indifferently, like a passenger in a train with the stranger opposite to him.

They had been driving for about twenty-five minutes. They passed through a small straggling village with a single fly-blown-looking café with a petrol pump outside it, and two or three shops, and began to climb. Graham was vaguely aware that the fields and farmlands which had flanked the road till then were giving way to clumps of trees and uncultivable slopes, and guessed that they were getting into the hills to the north of Genoa and west of the railway pass above Pontedecimo. Suddenly the car swung left down a small side road between trees, and began to crawl in low gear up a long twisting hill cut in the side of a wooded slope.

There was a movement by his side. He turned quickly, the blood rushing up into his head, and met Moeller's eyes.

Moeller nodded. "Yes, Mr. Graham, this is just about as far as you are going."

"But the hotel . . . ?" Graham began to stammer.

The pale eyes did not flicker. "I am afraid, Mr. Graham, that you must be very simple. Or can it be that you think that I am simple?" He shrugged. "No doubt it is unimportant. But I have a request to make. As you have already caused me so much trouble, discomfort and expense, would it be asking too much of you to suggest that you do not cause me any

230

more? When we stop and you are asked to get out, please do so without argument or physical protest. If you cannot consider your own dignity at such a time, please think of the cushions of the car."

He turned abruptly and nodded to the man in the ulster who tapped on the window behind him. The car jerked to a standstill, and the man in the ulster half rose and put his hand down on the latch which opened the door beside him. At the same moment Moeller said something to Banat. Banat grinned.

In that second Graham acted. His last wretched little bluff had been called. They were going to kill him, and did not care whether he knew it or not. They were anxious only that his blood should not soil the cushions he was sitting on. A sudden blind fury seized him. His self-control, racked out until every nerve in his body was quivering, suddenly went. Before he knew what he was doing, he had pulled out Mathis' revolver and fired it full in Banat's face.

Even as the din of the shot thudded through his head, he saw something horrible happen to the face. Then he flung himself forward.

The man in the ulster had the door open about an inch when Graham's weight hit him. He lost his balance, and hurtled backwards through the door. A fraction of a second later he hit the road with Graham on top of him.

Half stunned by the impact, Graham rolled clear and scrambled for cover behind the car. It could, he knew, last only a second or two now. The man in the ulster was knocked out; but the other two, shouting at the tops of their voices, had their doors open, and Moeller would not be long in picking up Banat's gun. He might be able to get in one more shot. Moeller, perhaps . . .

At that moment chance took a hand. Graham real-

231

ised that he was crouching only a foot or so away from the car's tank, and with some wild notion of hindering the pursuit should he succeed in getting clear, he raised the revolver and fired again.

The muzzle of the revolver had been practically touching the tank when he pulled the trigger, and the sheet of flame which roared up sent him staggering back out of cover. Shots crashed out, and a bullet whipped by his head. Panic seized him. He turned and dashed for the trees, and the slope shelving away from the edge of the road. He heard two more shots, then something struck him violently in the back, and a sheet of light flashed between his eyes and his brain.

He could not have been unconscious for more than a minute. When he came to he was lying face downwards on the surface of dead pine needles on the slope below the level of the road.

Dagger-like pains were shooting through his head. For a moment or two he did not try to move. Then he opened his eyes again and his gaze, wandering inch by inch away from him, encountered Mathis' revolver. Instinctively he stretched out his hand to take it. His body throbbed angonisingly, but his fingers gripped the revolver. He waited for a second or two. Then, very slowly, he drew his knees up under him, raised himself on his hands and began to crawl back to the road.

The blast of the exploding tank had scattered fragments of ripped panelling and smouldering leather all over the road. Lying on his side amid this wreckage was the man in the workman's cap. The mackintosh down his left side hung in charred shreds. What was left of the car itself was a mass of shimmering incandescence, and the steel skeleton buckling like paper in the terrific heat was only just visible. Farther up the road the driver was standing with his hands to his face, swaying as if he were drunk. The sickening stench of burning flesh hung in the air. There was no sign of Moeller.

Graham crawled back down the slope for a few yards, got painfully to his feet and stumbled away, down through the trees towards the lower road.

CHAPTER XII

IT WAS after midday before he reached the café in the village and a telephone. By the time a car from the Turkish Consulate arrived, he had had a wash and fortified himself with brandy.

The Consul was a lean, business-like man, who spoke English as if he had been to England. He listened intently to what Graham had to say before he said much himself. When Graham had finished, however, the Consul squirted some more soda water into his vermouth, leaned back in his chair and whistled through his teeth.

"Is that all?" he inquired.

"Isn't it enough?"

"More than enough." The Consul grinned apologetically. "I will tell you, Mr. Graham, that when I received your message this morning, I telegraphed immediately to Colonel Haki, reporting that you were very likely dead. Allow me to congratulate you."

"Thank you. I was lucky." He spoke automatically. There seemed to be something strangely fatuous about congratulations on being alive. He said: "Kuvetli told me the other night that he had fought for the

Gazi and that he was ready to give his life for Turkey. You don't, somehow, expect people who say that sort of thing to be taken up on it so quickly."

"That is true. It is very sad," said the Consul. He was obviously itching to get to business. "Meanwhile," he continued adroitly, "we must see that no time is lost. Every minute increases the danger of his body being found before you are out of the country. The authorities are not very well disposed towards us at the moment, and if he were found before you had left, I doubt if we could prevent your being detained for at least some days."

"What about the car?"

"We can leave the driver to explain that. If, as you say, your suitcase was destroyed in the fire, there is nothing to connect you with the accident. Are you feeling well enough to travel?"

"Yes. I'm bruised a bit and I still feel damnably shaky, but I'll get over that."

"Good. Then, all things considered, it will be as well if you travel immediately."

"Kuvetli said something about a 'plane."

"A 'plane? Ah! May I see your passport, please?"

Graham handed it over. The Consul flicked over the pages, shut the passport with a snap and returned it. "Your transit visa," he said, "specifies that you are entering Italy at Genoa and leaving it at Bardonecchia. If you are particularly anxious to go by air we can get the visa amended, but that will take an hour or so. Also you will have to return to Genoa. Also, in case Kuvetli is found within the next few hours, it is better not to bring yourself to the notice of the police with a change of arrangements." He glanced at his watch. "There is a train to Paris which leaves Genoa at two o'clock. It stops at Asti soon after three. I recommend that you get on it there. I can drive you to Asti in my car."

"I think some food would do me good."

"My dear Mr. Graham! How stupid of me! Some food. Of course! We can stop at Novi. You will be my guest. And if there is any champagne to be had we shall have it. There is nothing like champagne when one is depressed."

Graham felt suddenly a little light-headed. He laughed.

The Consul raised his eyebrows.

"I'm sorry," Graham apologised. "You must excuse me. You see, it is rather funny. I had an appointment to meet someone on the two o'clock train. She'll be rather surprised to see me."

He became conscious of someone shaking his arm and opened his eyes.

"Bardonecchia, signore. Your passport, please."

He looked up at the wagon-lit attendant bending over him and realised that he had been asleep since the train had left Asti. In the doorway, partly silhouetted against the gathering darkness outside, were two men in the uniform of the Italian railway police.

He sat up with a jerk, fumbling in his pocket. "My passport? Yes, of course."

One of the men looked at the passport, nodded and dabbed at it with a rubber stamp.

"*Grazie, signore.* Have you any Italian bank-notes?"

"No."

Graham put his passport back in his pocket, the attendant switched the light off again, and the door closed. That was that.

He yawned miserably. He was stiff and shivering. He stood up to put his overcoat on and saw that the station was deep in snow. He had been a fool to go to sleep like that. It would be unpleasant to arrive home with pneumonia. But he was past the Italian passport control. He turned the heating on and sat down to smoke a cigarette. It must have been that heavy lunch and the wine. It ... And then he remembered suddenly that he had done nothing about Josette. Mathis would be on the train, too.

The train started with a jerk and began to rumble on towards Modane.

He rang the bell and the attendant came.

"Signore?"

"Is there going to be a restaurant car when we get over the frontier?"

"No, signore." He shrugged. "The war."

Graham gave him some money. "I want a bottle of beer and some sandwiches. Can you get them at Modane?"

The attendant looked at the money. "Easily, signore."

"Where are the third-class coaches?"

"In the front of the train, signore."

The attendant went. Graham smoked his cigarette and decided to wait until the train had left Modane before he went in search of Josette.

The stop at Modane seemed interminable. At last, however, the French passport officials finished their work and the train began to move again.

Graham went out into the corridor.

Except for the dim blue safety lights, the train was in darkness now. He made his way slowly towards the third-class coaches. There were only two of them, and he had no difficulty in finding Josette and José. They were in a compartment by themselves.

She turned her head as he slid the door open and peered at him uncertainly. Then, as he moved forward into the blue glow from the ceiling of the compartment, she started up with a cry.

"But what has happened?" she demanded. "Where have you been? We waited, José and I, until the last moment, but you did not come as you had promised.

We waited. José will tell you how we waited. Tell me what happened."

"I missed the train at Genoa. I had a long drive to catch it up."

"You drove to Bardonecchia! It is not possible!"

"No. To Asti."

There was a silence. They had been speaking in French. Now José gave a short laugh and, sitting back in his corner, began to pick his teeth with his thumbnail.

Josette dropped the cigarette she had been smoking on to the floor and trod on it. "You got on the train at Asti," she remarked lightly, "and you wait until now before you come to see me? It is very polite." She paused and then added slowly: "But you will not keep me waiting like that in Paris, will you, *chéri?*"

He hesitated.

"Will you, *chéri?*" There was an edge to her voice now.

He said: "I'd like to talk to you alone, Josette."

She stared at him. Her face in that dim, ghastly light was expressionless. Then she moved towards the door. "I think," she said, "that it will be better if you have a little talk with José."

"José? What's José got to do with it? You're the person I want to talk to."

"No, *chéri.* You have a little talk with José. I am not very good at business. I do not like it. You understand?"

"Not in the least." He was speaking the truth.

"No? José will explain. I will come back in a minute. You talk to José now, *chéri.*"

"But ..."

She stepped into the corridor and slid the door to behind her. He went to open it again.

"She will come back," said José; "why don't you sit down and wait?"

Graham sat down slowly. He was puzzled. Still picking his teeth, José glanced across the compartment. "You don't understand, eh?"

"I don't even know what I'm supposed to understand."

José peered at his thumbnail, licked it, and went to work again on an eye tooth. "You like Josette, eh?"

"Of course. But . . ."

"She is very pretty, but she has no sense. She is a woman. She does not understand business. That is why I, her husband, always look after the business. We are partners. Do you understand that?"

"It's simple enough. What about it?"

"I have an interest in Josette. That is all."

Graham considered him for a moment. He was beginning to understand only too well. He said: "Say exactly what you mean, will you?"

With the air of making a decision, José abandoned his teeth and twisted on his seat so that he was facing Graham. "You are a business man, eh?" he said briskly. "You do not expect something for nothing. Very well. I am her manager and I do not give anything for nothing. You want to amuse yourself in Paris, eh? Josette is a very nice girl and very amusing for a gentleman. She is a nice dancer, too. Together we earn at least two thousand francs a week in a nice place. Two thousand francs a week. That is something, eh?"

Memories were flooding into Graham's mind: of the Arab girl, Maria, saying, "She has many lovers"; of Kopeikin saying, "José? He does well for himself"; of Josette herself saying of José that he was jealous of her only when she neglected business for pleasure; of innumerable little phrases and attitudes. "Well?" he said coldly.

José shrugged. "If you are amusing yourself, we cannot earn our two thousand francs a week by dancing. So, you see, we must get it from somewhere else." In the semi-darkness, Graham could see a small smile twist the black line of José's mouth. "Two thousand francs a week. It is reasonable, eh?"

It was the voice of the philosopher of the apes in velvet. *"Mon cher caïd"* was justifying his existence. Graham nodded. "Quite reasonable."

"Then we can settle it now, eh?" José went on briskly. "You are experienced, eh? You know that it is the custom." He grinned and then quoted: *"Chéri, avant que je t'aime t'oublieras pas mon petit cadeau.'"*

"I see. And who do I pay? You or Josette?"

"You can pay it to Josette if you like, but that would not be very *chic*, eh? I will see you once a week." He leaned forward and patted Graham's knee. "It is serious, eh? You will be a good boy? If you were, for example, to begin now. . . ."

Graham stood up. He was surprised at his own calmness. "I think," he said, "that I should like to give the money to Josette herself."

"You don't trust me, eh?"

"Of course I trust you. Will you find Josette?"

José hesitated, then, with a shrug, got up and went out into the corridor. A moment later he returned with Josette. She was smiling a little nervously.

"You have finished talking to José, *chéri?*"

Graham nodded pleasantly. "Yes. But, as I told you, it was you I really wanted to talk to. I wanted to explain that I shall have to go straight back to England after all."

She stared at him blankly for a moment; then he saw her lips drawing in viciously over her teeth. She turned suddenly on José.

"You dirty Spanish fool!" She almost spat the words at him. "What do you think I keep you for? Your dancing?"

José's eyes glittered dangerously. He slid the door to

behind him. "Now," he said, "we will see. You shall not speak to me so or I shall break your teeth."

"*Salaud!* I shall speak to you as I like." She was standing quite still, but her right hand moved an inch or two. Something glittered faintly. She had slipped the diamanté bracelet she was wearing over her knuckles.

Graham had seen enough violence for one day. He said quickly: "Just a moment. José is not to blame. He explained matters very tactfully and politely. I came, as I said, to tell you that I have to go straight back to England. I was also going to ask you to accept a small present. It was this." He drew out his wallet, produced a ten-pound note, and held it near the light.

She glanced at the note and then stared at him sullenly. "Well?"

"José made it clear that two thousand francs was the amount I owed. This note is only worth just over seventeen hundred and fifty. So, I am adding another two hundred and fifty francs." He took the French notes out of his wallet, folded them up in the larger note and held them out.

She snatched them from him. "And what do you expect to get for this?" she demanded spitefully.

"Nothing. It's been pleasant being able to talk to you." He slid the door open. "Good-bye, Josette."

She shrugged her shoulders, stuffed the money into the pocket of her fur coat and sat down again in her corner. "Good-bye. It is not my fault if you are stupid."

José laughed. "If you should think of changing your mind, Monsieur," he began mincingly, "we . . ."

Graham shut the door and walked away along the corridor. His one desire was to get back to his own compartment. He did not notice Mathis until he had almost bumped into him.

241

The Frenchman drew back to let him pass. Then, with a gasp, he leaned forward.

"Monsieur Graham! Is it possible?"

"I was looking for you," said Graham.

"My dear friend. I am so glad. I was wondering.... I was afraid...."

"I caught the train at Asti." He pulled the revolver from his pocket. "I wanted to return this to you with my thanks. I'm afraid that I haven't had time to clean it. It has been fired twice."

"Twice!" Mathis' eyes widened. "You killed them both?"

"One of them. The other died in a road accident."

"A road accident!" Mathis chuckled. "That is a new way to kill them!" He looked at the revolver affectionately. "Perhaps I will not clean it. Perhaps I will keep it as it is as a souvenir." He glanced up. "It was all right, that message I delivered?"

"Quite all right, and thank you again." He hesitated. "There's no resturant car on the train. I have some sandwiches in my compartment. If you and your wife would like to join me...."

"You are kind, but no thank you. We get off at Aix. It will not be long now. My family lives there. It will be strange to see them after so long. They ..."

The door of the compartment behind him opened and Madame Mathis peered into the corridor. "Ah, there you are!" She recognized Graham and nodded disapprovingly.

"What is it, chérie?"

"The window. You open it, and go out to smoke. I am left to freeze."

"Then you may shut it, chérie."

"Imbecile! It is too stiff."

Mathis sighed wearily and held out his hand. "Good-bye, my friend. I shall be discreet. You may depend upon it."

"Discreet?" demanded Madame Mathis suspiciously. "What is there to be discreet about?"

"Ah, you may ask!" He winked at Graham. "Monsieur and I have made a plot to blow up the Bank of France, seize the Chamber of Deputies, shoot the two hundred families and set up a Communist government."

She looked round apprehensively. "You should not say such things, even for a joke."

"A joke!" he scowled at her malevolently. "You will see if it is a joke or not when we drag these capitalist reptiles from their great houses and cut them to pieces with machine-guns."

"Robert! If someone should hear you say such things ..."

"Let them hear!"

"I only asked you to shut the window, Robert. If it had not been so stiff I would have done it myself. I ..."

The door closed behind them.

Graham stood for a moment looking out of the window at the distant searchlights: grey smudges moving restlessly among the clouds low down on the horizon. It was not, he reflected, unlike the skyline that he could see from his bedroom window when there were German planes about over the North Sea.

He turned and made his way back to his beer and sandwiches.

ABOUT THE AUTHOR

Born in London in 1909, ERIC AMBLER was grad-
uated from London University and served an
apprenticeship in engineering. He established himself as a writer with the five classic novels of
intrigue published between 1937 and 1940: *Background to Danger, Epitaph for a Spy, Cause for
Alarm, A Coffin for Dimitrios* and *Journey into
Fear*. During World War II he served in the British Army and was discharged a lieutenant colonel.
He then wrote and produced a number of motion
pictures and was nominated for an Academy
Award for his screenplay of Nicholas Monsarrat's
The Cruel Sea. He returned to novel-writing with
Judgment on Deltchev, which was published in
1951. He has since written ten more novels and,
with translations of his books appearing in over
fifteen other languages, his reputation has become
worldwide. He lives in Switzerland.

Bestsellers you've been hearing about—and want to read